# FINDING TRUE NORTH

*a Novel*

## Dianne Beck

FROM THE TINY ACORN...
GROWS THE MIGHTY OAK

www.AcornPublishingLLC.com

For information, address:
Acorn Publishing, LLC
3943 Irvine Blvd. Ste. 218
Irvine, CA 92602

*Finding True North*



Edited by Molly Lewis
Cover design by Damonza
Interior design and formatting by Debra Cranfield Kennedy



Printed in the United States of America

ISBN-13: 979-8-88528-027-3 (hardcover)
ISBN-13: 979-8-88528-026-6 (paperback)
LCCN #: 2022916203

*To all the seekers.*

*May you find your heart's desire.*

# North Carolina Simon

May 1974

# Chapter 1

After the three-mile trek home from Sage Hill Middle School in the near ninety-degree heat, I stood at the edge of our walkway and wished I felt relieved to be home. The house looked like nearly every other one in the West Valley suburbs of Los Angeles. The mowed lawn, a couple rose bushes, and a white picket fence with a creaky gate made it appear so nice and normal, but I knew the inside told a very different story.

I took a deep breath, hoping the scent of the roses would stick with me when I entered the house. I could hear the television blasting, and above that my older sister Aria cawing. Yes, cawing, like a crow, one of her new favorite birds. When a baby crow recently fell from its nest into our yard, she kept a watchful eye on it, worried it wouldn't survive. Her fears ended when she saw the tender care its mother gave it. On the day that baby crow flew away, she stared out the window and said, "I used to think crows were sort of noisy and annoying, but they're actually pretty amazing. That mama crow never gave up on her baby."

That was a great reason to like a crow, but I wished she'd found a different bird to mimic, one with a sweeter sound. Once she had a favorite, it usually stayed in her rotation of sounds for a while.

I opened the door as far as it would go, blocked by a stack of newspapers, magazines and books in the way. Squeezing through, the rose scent quickly disappeared in the pungent odor of our living room. Today it was a mix of paint and mustiness. Making a conscious effort not to breathe in too deeply, I waited to see how long it might take my mother, Belinda Simon, to notice me. Surrounded by bottles of oil paint, she was deeply focused on a large canvas, a paintbrush in her hand.

Aria noticed me first. "North! You're home!" She ran over to me, her arms outstretched, flapping them like wings. "Caw!" She cried one last time as she jumped in front of me and closed her arms around me in a tight hug. "How was your day?" she said without loosening her hold.

No matter how bad my day was, this welcome from my big sister always made me smile. As I hugged her, I heard the television blast another unpleasant headline. "A shootout at a home in South Los Angeles. We'll take you live to the scene after the commercial break." I thought about how much happier people would be with an Aria in their lives. All their anger might melt away long enough to stop all their useless violence.

"My day was okay, Aria," I lied. "How about you?" I pulled away to look at her since eye contact was something we were working on. Her bangs hadn't been trimmed in months and with her head down they hung over her eyes like little orange curtains in front of two beautiful bright blue windows. I brushed them aside with my fingers.

"Mmmm," she mumbled as she glanced at me, then looked down again. "Hard," she said.

I could usually count on her to be honest, even if I didn't always get a lot of clear details. "Oh, I'm sorry. Do you want to talk about it?"

She kept her gaze downward and shook her head.

"Okay, well maybe later you will." I looked at Mom, still fixed on her painting. "Hello, Mother," I said, "I'm home."

She snapped out of her focus, her eyes wide open as if I startled her. "Oh, yes honey, I saw you. I was letting you talk to Aria first. Everything okay? How'd you get home early?"

How did she not know what time it was? I was home nearly an hour after school let out, long past when she was supposed to pick me up. Every Wednesday Aria's high school had a shortened day so teachers could have meetings, and almost every time, Mom somehow missed getting me when my school day was done. With only three days left of the school year, it didn't seem unreasonable to have this figured out.

"Mom, it's almost four o'clock. I'm not home early. I walked because you never showed up." Her expression of surprise changed to shock. She dropped her paintbrush as she put her hand over her mouth. "Oh no, North. I'm so sorry. I can't believe I did it again." She stepped forward and hugged me, careful to keep a bit of distance between me and her paint-splashed shirt. Her bleached blonde hair smelled slightly of paint thinner on top of her familiar coconut-scented shampoo. I could tell she was genuinely sorry for screwing up, but I was really tired of this.

"Can we go to the woods now, Mama? You said we could go with North. Can we go now? She's here!" Aria exclaimed.

I was definitely not in the mood to go to the woods, which weren't actually woods anyway. The large open space, named Crescent Ridge Park, with hiking trails and patches of oak trees, was as close to woods as we got in Southern California. Conveniently located at the end of our street, Aria and I first called this place the woods when we were little, when our minds transformed the terrain into the settings of some of our favorite imaginary places. We spent hours pretending to be in Sherwood Forest from the legend of Robin Hood or the magical land of Narnia.

While we no longer pretended to be in these imaginary forest settings, we still called this escape from reality our woods.

Today all I wanted was to grab one of the sixty-five cans of soda stacked against the wall in the hallway, head to my room, and blast some music. But I knew that wasn't happening. Turning down Aria would most likely result in a night in which she'd cry a lot, yell about her terrible day, stomp and pace, ask Mom over and over why she'd made her a promise she couldn't keep, bring up all the other times this had happened.

"Yes, Aria, we can go," Mom said.

She jumped up and down, flapped her arms, spun in circles. "Yes! Thank you, Mama! Thank you, North! Let me go get my bag." She dashed away toward her room, bumped into a tall stack of Kleenex, napkins, and paper towels that had served as a dividing wall between the family room and the dining room. Mom shook her head and put her hands over her eyes to keep from seeing the wall tumble down.

"Oh Aria," she said as she looked at the pile of paper goods all over the floor.

Mom knew it wasn't Aria's fault. She wasn't the only one to bump into the paper wall.

"You might not want to go to the woods. I can take her on my own if you have other things to do," Mom said.

I really wanted to take her up on that offer, but I didn't want to let Aria down, and I didn't want to be inside with this mess either.

"No, Mom. I'll go. I'm just tired, that's all."

She placed her hand on my cheek, looked in my eyes. "I really am sorry about today. Can I make it up to you one day this week? Take you for a Slurpee at 7-Eleven? Get ice cream? Browse at the record store?"

That last one got me. I really wanted the new Carole King album, especially since I planned to sing her song "Nightingale" for the end-of-year talent show in two days. If I had the album, I wouldn't have to wait for it to come on the radio all the time. I could sing along over and over until I felt less terrified to perform for a crowd, something I've wanted the courage to do since I was nine. That was the year my dad took me to a concert at the park, where I learned that live music was one of the best sounds on earth. I heard every instrument clear and sharp and listened to a tall blonde woman sing about one of her friends who was ridiculed for being different. I knew at that moment that I had a lot of songs to sing.

"The record store would be great," I said.

"Okay, you got it. You let me know when," she said as she returned her attention to her painting.

"Any time is good for me for that trip, Mom. How about tomorrow?"

"Okay, tomorrow it is. Maybe I'll paint that on my arm or something so I remember." I laughed at that idea, but she earnestly examined her left arm, looking for a space of bare skin somewhere near the decorated yellow sunflower tattoo just above her upper wrist. I loved that tattoo, even though other moms looked at it with disgust when they saw it. I wished they'd take a good look at the painted parts of themselves more and see that her arm looked better than an overly made-up fake face.

Unlike those moms, mine knew what to do with color. She was an artist, even though she made barely any money from her work and had to clean houses to earn a living. Aside from the tattoo, she also dressed a lot different than all the moms I'd met. She would find cheap, plain clothes at garage sales or on discount racks and turn them into bright tie-dyed shirts, jeans with embroidered flowers, and scarves painted in bold patterns and shapes. Then she'd accessorize with colorful beaded bracelets and dangling earrings, my favorites being ones she made out of feathers. One day last year when she was running late from picking Aria and me up from school, I heard another mom say to the two women next to her, "Those poor girls, it's no wonder the older one acts so strange and the younger one looks so gaunt and sickly. Their mother is too busy creating all her weird outfits that make her look like the town clown. I hear their house is a mess, filled to the rim with junk the husband collects." If this woman really felt bad for us, she wasn't making things better. Her words were much more hurtful than anything my parents had done.

"I'm ready! Let's go!" Aria yelled, snapping me back to reality. She trotted into the living room with the items she took everywhere: the ceramic bird she had named Adagio, sculpted by Mom, her canvas tote bag filled with sunflower seeds, a notepad, two books on bird identification, and far too many leaves and sticks that we'd gathered on our last walk, plus a small Bible someone had handed out to students at her high school earlier this year. Her head was bent over the open Bible and she read out loud, "*This is the day that the Lord has made. Let us rejoice and be glad in it*! Psalm 118:24."

As a bunch of leaves spilled from her bag, her eyes opened wide. "Oops, I forgot to empty these into our yard. I hope the birds haven't needed them for their nests! I'll be right back!" She ran to our sliding glass door, leaping over two paper towel rolls, kicking one out of the way, and barely missing another in uncharacteristic coordination. When she returned, she carefully put Adagio into her bag and said, "I'll take you out when we get to the woods."

We walked down our suburban street without saying much. Aria had trained us to listen more than talk. When we heard a bird, Aria was the first to acknowledge it with a call back as she searched the air or the trees for the source of the sound. Most of the time she didn't need to see it to know what it was. I watched her skip ahead of Mom and me, one arm securing her bag, the other lifting and falling in bird-flight motion.

All the energy she'd held in all day at school was finally set free. A few children stopped kicking a ball in the street, stood watching this flying girl, then giggled. This wasn't the first time they'd seen her, and unlike older kids, they weren't mean. One of the younger ones was waiting for Aria with a big smile. When Aria reached her, she leaped and flapped her arms alongside her, tweeting and chirping, trying to sync up with Aria as much as possible.

"That girl gets it," I whispered to Mom.

Mom nodded and smiled, "Yes, she does. She's not afraid to be herself and have some fun."

"It must be nice to not care at all what people think about you," I said. Mom stopped walking. I turned around, and she stared at me like she was either upset, confused, or both.

"Are people still giving you a hard time, North?" Mom asked.

I had to think about how honest I should be with her. "I don't know, Mom. Sometimes. It's okay. I've got Matthew and Ronnie. They think I'm cool." I tried to sound like I meant that, like I actually didn't need any more than two friends. I hoped she couldn't see through my act. She kept her eyes on me like I was one of her paintings. "Mom, I'm okay. Don't worry."

Mom knew I struggled with how people treated Aria, and how they treated me when I was with her. Since Aria started high school this year, at least we weren't at school together, but I wasn't the most popular person anyway. There seemed to be plenty of things for people to criticize, my parents being one of them. I never told her that. It would crush her. I also didn't tell her how often people criticized my name.

My father, Frank Simon, being really into sports at the time, thought it would be cool to name me after his favorite basketball team, the North

Carolina Tar Heels. Mom agreed to name me North, and thought Carolina was actually a great middle name as well. She told me North reminded her of the expression "finding your true north," which is a person's internal compass, guiding them successfully through life. I did like that idea, and supposed I should be glad neither of them chose to name me Tar Heel.

But no matter what my name was supposed to mean, I grew up hearing a lot of teasing about it. When I was in third grade, Billy Hitch ran up to me at recess and said, "Hey, North! Are the other people in your family South, East, and West?" He and the group of boys behind him laughed and left me in a cloud of sand that they kicked up as they ran away.

Then in seventh grade, I walked into the bathroom to hear Susan Carbonne telling all the popular girls that I was absurdly tall and skinny because I was named after a pole. I stared at them as they giggled and scampered out of the bathroom. I looked in the mirror, my eyes blurred with tears, and wished I didn't have a name that was as weird as my lanky shape, my bright red hair, and my freckled face.

Mom might have tried to pry more out of my unhappy attitude if it weren't for the fact that Aria was calling to us, "Mom? North? Why'd you stop? Did you hear something?"

"No, we're coming!" Mom shouted and picked up her pace to a jog. I looked up and saw Dahlia Kline standing in front of her perfect house with her perfect hair and her perfect clothes, arms crossed as she looked at me and laughed. I turned away and tried to pretend I didn't seem completely crazy as I hustled down the street after my chirping sister and paint-splashed mom.

# Chapter 2

Once we arrived at Crescent Ridge Park, I was especially thankful for the freedom of our woods, where Aria could be herself without stares and comments from anyone. We walked through the grassy park to the trailhead, where I could see the golden hillsides ahead, dotted with the large oak trees we would soon pass under. The heat of the day had worn off and a cool breeze rustled the tall mustard plants that framed the trail. I wished this peace and quiet were something I could simply toss into Aria's bag and take back home with us. As we approached a patch of trees, I heard the clear hoot of an owl, echoed by a softer, higher-pitched one. Above the trees, a red-tailed hawk circled.

"Girls, did you hear that?" Mom stopped in her tracks, put her arms out to block us from moving forward. Aria nodded and donned a huge smile as the owls hooted again. They continued long enough for Mom to spot them, and she pulled out her binoculars to get a closer look at a tree several yards away.

Aria stood on her tiptoes and tapped Mom's shoulders, "I wanna see, I wanna see," she whispered, followed by, "hoot, hoot." She mimicked the owls almost perfectly. The owls had stopped calling, maybe because they sensed our presence, but they didn't fly away.

Mom handed the binoculars to Aria. "Look, they're beautiful."

Aria grabbed the binoculars and peered through, slowly moving them upward to spot the owls. Mom watched her carefully, and as Aria smiled wide with amazement at what she saw, she whispered, "It's unusual to hear or see an owl before dark, but not impossible." She shifted her eyes upward. "That hawk is probably the reason. Looks like mama owl is protecting her baby."

When I finally got my turn to look, I could see why Aria was so excited. The mama owl, the same color as the tree bark, stood several inches taller than her baby which was mostly a ball of white fuzz with brown speckles. Mama owl spread her wings, puffed her feathers, and hovered over baby owl. Her eyes blinked quickly as she stared in the direction of the hawk.

When the hawk turned away from the owls, Aria said, "Oh, I bet mama owl scared the hawk away with its eyes. Owls can do that really well. I wish I could do that when something frightens me."

"Me too," I said.

"God protects us when we're afraid, you know. He says in Isaiah 41:10, '*Do not fear for I am with you; do not be dismayed, for I am your God.*' He says to not fear a lot."

With Aria around I was never short on bird or Bible facts, her two favorite topics. I wished her thoughts on God would have distracted her from the owls so I could watch them longer, but it was maybe two seconds more before she tugged gently on the binoculars. I handed them back to her and sat next to Mom on a large rock. I was glad we went to the woods. I needed it more than I thought.

"You didn't bring your sketch pad today," I said to Mom.

"No, not today. I figured I'd soak everything in and draw it later." She patted my knee. "Maybe you can join me. I have a lot of extra clay for you to sculpt another bird for Aria. I don't know how that one I made her has lasted this long. It's kind of a miracle it hasn't broken yet with the way she carries it around everywhere."

I laughed. "Ha, funny. I don't think I could sculpt a good bird. I clearly didn't get your artistic talent."

"Well that's absolutely not true. That voice of yours is one of the most talented works of art I've ever known."

I was glad she thought that. "Thanks, Mom. Maybe someday I'll actually get others to believe that."

"Practice for us. Sing us a song," Mom replied.

Aria kept her eyes in the binoculars and chimed in. "Yeah North, sing."

"Uh, wouldn't you rather listen to the owls?" I said, stalling. "You know it might scare them away, right?"

"I like hearing the owls, but I like your voice more." Aria had taken her eyes off the owls and turned her attention to me now. "Come on, please?" She smiled.

She could get me to do almost anything. "Okay, fine."

I took a deep breath, sat up taller, and began to sing "Nightingale." I closed my eyes while I sang loud and bold, unhindered with Mom and Aria as my audience. I wished I could always sing that way. It would make my dream of being a famous singer much easier if I weren't so afraid of people thinking I was terrible. I stopped after the first stanza and chorus to see Aria smiling, Adagio clutched close to her chest. That was the way I wanted everyone to hear me.

"I like that song," Aria said. "I think it's my favorite because of how you sing it and because the nightingale is Mom's favorite bird."

"Really?" I turned to Mom who nodded her head.

"Yep, sure is," Mom said, "and now that's my favorite song. That was truly beautiful. You really should do that in front of more people."

I agreed with her, but that didn't mean I felt great about the performance that was frighteningly close to reality. That would either prove I had a shot at this singing thing or show me I needed to stay quiet. "I'm working on it, Mom," I said. "You do remember I'm singing in front of the entire school for the talent show on Thursday, right?"

She responded quickly even though she looked a little surprised. "Oh, yes, of course I remember. I can't wait. You're going to be a superstar. Look out, Carole King. Here comes North Carolina!"

That got me to laugh at my name in a good way for once, the idea of sounding like a huge state somehow making me feel like I might be able to reach my favorite singer's greatness.

We stayed until the sun began to set, turning the sky a brilliant blend of orange and purple. The hawk had abandoned its predatory circling of the owls who had remained silent since we spotted them. Aria was her same carefree self on the walk home, but now belted out "Nightingale" every few skips in a key I was pretty sure did not match the way I sang it.

Mom's laugh confirmed that truth. "You don't want to sing like that, North, but you definitely want her boldness."

"Yeah," I said. "I definitely could use some of that." I thought back to that singer at the park, how she lifted up her sister in a song just for her. I closed my eyes and pictured myself doing the same thing. If I wanted to make that vision real, I had to risk being heard.

# Chapter 3

We managed to get home without anyone staring at us. The kids at play had probably gone inside to eat dinner or finish homework. Dahlia was probably on the phone gossiping, or painting her nails, or planning how to be the meanest yet most popular girl alive. Mom and Aria went inside, but I stayed out front a bit longer, not quite ready to enter the confining walls of our home. I peered down the street past a few houses to see if Matthew was out. He usually played basketball in his driveway or rode around on his skateboard in the evening before it got completely dark. I didn't see him, so he was probably eating dinner. Glancing around at the neighborhood, I imagined most of the people sitting around their neat dining room tables, near their clean kitchens and nicely decorated living rooms, everything in its place.

I used to think every house was like ours, filled with extra supplies, random collections, and stacks of grocery items. I realized that wasn't true in fourth grade when I went to Dahlia's house to play. There was room to run down the hall, to dance in the living room, to set out toys, and to eat at the kitchen table that was only covered with placemats and a single vase of fresh flowers. Her house felt a little more like the woods, where there was space and air to breathe, but I still thought most people had houses similar to mine.

When I invited Dahlia over to my house, I was so excited about it. Mom wasn't. She spent two days moving stuff into her bedroom and bathroom. Then she moved things into one corner of the living room and put a sheet over it. There was still a lot of stuff, but Mom had managed to create a small circle of space in the family room. She laid a patchwork quilt down on the floor, set some art supplies out for us, put one of our many boxes of Twinkies on the small coffee table she had cleared, and said, "What do you think, North? Is this okay?"

I didn't know why she would think it wasn't okay. It looked great to me. "Yes, this is perfect. I'm excited you're letting us have all those Twinkies!"

"Well, I'm not talking about the Twinkies. I'm wondering if the house is okay for you and your friend to play."

I was still confused by her question. "Yes, the house is fine," I said.

When I heard Dahlia's knock on the door, I jumped up to open it. Dahlia stood with her mom, a bright smile on her face and a plate of homemade cookies in her hands. "Hi, North! These are for our snack," Dahlia said.

"Wow, thank you!" Mom took the plate from Dahlia and I grabbed Dahlia's hand, excited to lead her into the best playdate ever.

A few steps in, I felt a tug on my hand. I looked back to see Dahlia, frozen, eyes wide as she stared around at the room. "Why do you have so much stuff?" She asked.

I followed her shocked eyes to the wall that still looked the same today and had looked the same for as long as I could remember. Books were piled high next to newspapers and magazines, beside boxes filled with old mail and receipts, laundry baskets with clothes piled high, stuffed animals, hats, unused garbage bags. Thing, upon thing, upon thing—all lined up against a wall you could barely see. She immediately said she felt sick and needed to go home, then ran out the door.

The next day at school, I walked up to Dahlia on the playground where she stood in line to jump rope. Her sleek mahogany hair was neatly clipped on the sides with little pink barrettes and even then, with no mascara, she flashed long thick eyelashes above her piercing black eyes. "Hi, Dahlia!" I said, expecting a hello and a smiling face in return.

She looked at me, narrowed her eyes, turned her head away and grabbed the arm of the girl next to her. "Ewww, come on Sophie, let's get away from here. It suddenly smells." They both giggled as they darted away, and two other girls in line backed away from me like I was deadly poison or something.

The rest of the day went pretty much that way, with my questions about why everyone was avoiding me answered when I approached the lunch tables and heard Dahlia telling the girls surrounding her that my house was disgusting. I stood there, humiliated, not sure where to sit, as they looked up at me. A few of them quickly turned their glances away. Pamela Quinn quickly set her sweater on the empty space next to her and announced, "This place is saved." I knew she was lying. Everyone had a seat except for me. I looked around and saw Matthew Jones and Rhonda Patinski. Rhonda, who preferred to be called Ronnie, caught my eye, smiled through a mouth full of food, and waved me over to their table. The three of us soon became the best of friends. Visiting their homes confirmed the fact that mine really was weird, but I also learned that they didn't care.

When the bright light of the porch came on, I snapped out of my terrible memory. The sky was now dark, with little chance of Matthew coming outside. Time to face my cluttered reality and go in. I didn't know why each day seemed harder to enter. Instead of getting more used to the mess, I'd become more disgusted with it. By the time I went to bed each night it often felt harder to breathe or I had a terrible headache. My best escape was my bedroom, with the door shut and the window open to let in fresh air.

I could tell at least one other light was on through the front window. When Dad came home, he'd probably turn the porch light off, and possibly the light inside if no one really needed it. He usually liked the house to be sort of dark to save electricity.

Once inside, I saw Aria on the floor in front of a stack of encyclopedias, reading owl facts aloud. "Many birds, like doves, can make sounds that people mistake as owls. You'll recognize a great-horned owl by its deep, soft hoots with a stuttering rhythm: hoo-h'hoo-hoo-hoo."

I heard Mom clanging around in the kitchen, probably finding something for dinner, so I went to my room, shut the door, and flipped on the light switch. Lucky for me, Mom had demanded that my room be my room—not a place to store things, so Dad hardly ever had a reason to go in it. I made sure to keep it as different from the rest of the house as possible, which meant it was clean and bright. In addition to the dome-shaped ceiling light, a sky blue desk lamp lit up my desk, and a yellow lamp on the nightstand glowed next to my bed. Last summer I decorated my room the colors of sun and sky. I painted my walls a pale blue, hung three of Mom's bird paintings, and sewed yellow curtains that stayed open all day and matched my bed that was covered in a quilt Mom had sewn from swatches of yellow T-shirts and faded jeans she no longer wore. I painted the knobs on my white dresser and desk the same blue as my wall and used a toothpick dipped in yellow paint to dot tiny flowers on each one.

My favorite spot in the room was the corner between my desk and bed, right near the window, where I had a cozy blue bean bag chair, a large floppy cat stuffed animal Dad had brought home from his store one day for me, my record player, and a small shelf that held my growing record collection, books, and journals where I'd usually write lyrics of my favorite songs or ones I tried to make up myself.

I headed straight to my record stack to find an album to play. I thumbed through the stack—The Eagles, Fleetwood Mac, Carly Simon, James Taylor, Stevie Wonder, and finally went to my turntable to play the album that was already there—Carole King. It wasn't her new album, but it was still a favorite. I remembered getting it with Dad at a garage sale three years ago when I was eleven. He was surprised to see it there, and told me it would be a good one to put on the old record player he had just given me. I couldn't wait to get home to play it. Once I heard it, I was in love, and I played it enough to know every single word of every single song.

I lifted the needle and placed it gently on the song I wanted to hear and plopped onto my beanbag as the tune swept me away to my own imaginary rooftop, far away from the real world.

As the song came to an end, I heard Mom yell, "North, come get some dinner!"

Even though my stomach rumbled, I didn't feel like eating. I wiggled my toes into my green shag carpet, stretched, and forced myself up from my cushy spot. Before the next song began, I lifted the needle from the album and let the turntable slow to a stop. My perfect excuse to delay leaving my room came when the phone rang. I jogged to my desk to get the call before Mom picked up the phone in the kitchen, which I knew wouldn't be too hard since she had to scamper around things to find it. "I got it!" I yelled, and picked up the bright yellow receiver, hoping it was for me. "Hello?" I said.

"Hey, North, thank God you answered." It was Matthew.

"Hi, what's up?" I asked, concerned about the desperation in his voice.

"Did you see the news today?" he asked.

"No, I was out with Aria and my mom. Why? What happened?"

"There was a shooting in Los Angeles, the same neighborhood where my aunt and cousins live." I could hear him crying. He never cried.

"Oh no, Matthew, are they okay?" My heart beat fast. I wished he was in front of me so I could see his face. Finally he spoke.

"They're okay, as far as I know. When they were talking, my aunt said she was going with my cousins to another house for safety, then hung up real quick. My mom said she could hear shouting and screaming in the background. I hate this stuff, North. Why is this world so crazy?"

I had the same question. "I hate it too, Matthew. Do you want to come over? Or I can come to you?"

"You want to just meet outside? I want to be near my house when my mom hears from my aunt. She told me I could use the phone for a minute, but she wants the line available for her sister to call back."

"No problem, I'll see you outside."

"Okay. Thanks, North."

I hung up the phone and hustled to the living room. I hopped over the encyclopedias still in front of Aria while she continued to read out loud between nibbles of a cheese sandwich. Mom sat on the couch with her plate on her lap, but she didn't seem to be listening to Aria or eating. She was staring at the television news, her hand over her mouth like she couldn't believe what she saw. The screen showed a news reporter hunkered behind a car, police with rifles running before a house in flames, gunshots exploding from the house, one after the other like the grand finale of a fireworks display.

"I'll be right back, Mom. I'm meeting Matthew outside. His aunt lives where all that's happening."

Mom unlocked her stare from the screen and looked up at me. "Oh no, is she okay?"

"I think so. He just needs to talk."

"Are you going out to see the owls again?" Aria shouted. "I'll come too!" She stood up.

"No, Aria, I'm just saying hi to Matthew for a sec. You stay here. Keep reading those facts."

Her expression lit up. "Matthew? I like him. He's cool. He'd want to see the owls."

"Yes, he would." I smiled and wished the sight of an owl would be enough to make him feel better. "He can come with us next time we go to the woods."

"Cool," Aria said as she sat back down and hunched over her books.

Mom lifted her sandwich from her plate and stood quickly. "Do you want to take this with you to eat? I haven't eaten any of it."

"No, that's okay, I'll eat when I come back in. Thanks though."

She nodded her head. "Tell Matthew I hope everything's okay."

"I will."

I stepped outside into the cool air, the images from the television fresh in my mind, wondering, *How is it possible that so many people think my family is crazy when truly insane people are lighting fires and shooting guns?*

# Chapter 4

The thump of my feet on the ground echoed the gunshot sounds I'd heard on the television. I slowed my jog to a walk when I saw Matthew step out of his house and head towards me. I was glad he lived only a few houses away, especially at times like this. The street lamp lit up his brown cheeks, wet from tears.

"Hey," was the only word I could say. I reached out and touched his shoulder, and he pulled me into a hug. I felt his chest heave up and down as he cried with barely a sound. I knew he didn't like people to see him upset, and I'd never seen him cry like this. An occasional teary eye during a sad movie, which he'd blame on something being in his eye, was the most I'd noticed from him.

When he pulled away, he wiped his face on the sleeve of his red sweatshirt. "Man, I'm sorry. I don't mean to be such a baby."

"Matthew, are you kidding me? I know you're usually the happy one, but that's some scary stuff going on. I'd be a wreck if my family was in that mess."

He sniffled, nodded his head, and looked down at me. Since the end of seventh grade I'd become increasingly short next to him, and I was considered a tall girl at 5' 8". Ronnie always said she felt like a toddler around the two of us. I wished I had that problem. Instead I felt like a giant weirdo.

"Yeah, this is pretty messed up. I mean, I'm glad my aunt and cousins are alive. It's not like they were shot. It's just that every time something like this happens it reminds me that my family isn't really safe, you know?"

I knew what he was saying, but I couldn't entirely relate. Even though I felt like a complete oddball with my giant skinny frame, uncontrollable reddish hair, eyes that seemed too wide, and a nose that seemed too short, I never thought my life was really in danger. No matter how understanding I tried to be, I could never truly know what it was like for him being Black. I only knew I hated to see him so upset. I nodded as we stared at each other. Aside from getting taller in the past year, he'd also gotten a lot cuter. I snapped out of my gaze at that thought. "Well, you're totally safe with me," I joked in an attempt to lighten the mood, "If anyone messes with your family, I will immediately get Ronnie to make their life miserable."

That did get a laugh from him. "Okay, that's good to know. No one messes with Ronnie."

He took a seat on a low brick wall in front of his neighbor's house. I sat next to him. "So what happened, anyway? What was the cause of the shooting and the fire?"

"Oh, well. You know that crazy group of people who kidnapped Patty Hearst?"

"Yeah, is that who started this?" I remembered Patty Hearst's pretty face from the newspaper and television reports when she was kidnapped, and then later, a picture of her robbing a bank with a machine gun in her arms.

"I guess they'd been hiding out in the home that caught on fire in the middle of the shootout when police shot tear gas into the home. My mom was talking to my aunt again after I hung up the phone with you, and I guess they're fine, but they aren't going back to their house tonight. It's only a block away from all this chaos. My mom might go get them tomorrow to stay with us. We'll see."

"I'm glad they're okay, but I'm sure they're going to be pretty shaken up for a while."

"Yeah, for sure. It's a good thing I like my cousins. If all three of them and my aunt stay with us this weekend, our house is going to be a bit crowded."

"You can always stay at my house," I offered, but then I realized that might not be ideal.

Matthew's right lip curled up into a slight smile as he gave me a side glance. "Right, because you've got a lot of extra room."

I gave him an eye roll and a glare back, even though I actually thought his comment was funny. He and Ronnie were the only ones who could joke about my jam-packed house without getting me upset.

He nudged me with his elbow. "I'm just kidding. I'd stay in your house anytime, even if I had to sleep in a box or a laundry basket, but I don't think your dad would want a boy to spend the night."

"My dad is going to have to get used to you being around, Matthew," I said.

His eyes widened as he looked at me. "Oh, really?"

"Yep, 'cause you and me are going to be . . ." I held up my fist and waited for him to tap it back like he always did as we said in unison "to—" (we fist pumped) "geth" (we high fived) "er" (we fist pumped) "forever!" (we tapped our fingers together). "Together forever," I repeated as we kept our palms together longer than usual. I stared into his eyes again, knowing that chant we'd been doing since fifth grade might mean a bit more now than it did back then.

With our hands still together, a pair of bright headlights shifted my gaze from Matthew to my dad's car as it labored up the street and into our driveway.

"Looks like my dad decided to come home for his lunch break," I slowly pulled my hand away from Matthew's. I wanted to keep my hand on his, stay on that brick wall next to him, but I stood up, knowing I probably needed to go inside since my dad wouldn't be home for long.

"Lunch break?" Matthew laughed as he stood up.

"Yeah, I know it sounds weird, but I guess that's what the store calls it even for those working the night shift."

My dad got out of the car, his long legs appearing first, then his lanky body, and finally his normal armfuls of grocery bags.

"Looks like he brought some more supplies to keep us alive if we need to go into hiding for a few years," I joked.

"Hello, Matthew! How are you this evening?" Dad yelled.

"I'm good, Mr. Simon. How are you?

"Oh, I'm fine as well, just coming home from the job of my dreams for a little break."

I wasn't sure who would win the most phony person award at that moment. Matthew was not good, and there was no way Dad thought working at the store was his dream job. Most days it was a miracle he made it to work. He usually got distracted sorting through all his stuff, and then he'd rush around saying stuff like, "I'm going to get in so much trouble. I'm almost an hour late for my shift."

He'd told me about his dream jobs before. He wanted to be a musician, to play his guitar and sing in front of crowds. He also wanted to be a professional basketball player when he was in high school, but gave up on that when he realized his star days on a small high school team in North Carolina didn't prepare him for the pros. As he ambled toward our front door, I wondered if he'd possibly given up on all of his big dreams, or if he was still searching for one somewhere in the stuff he collected and saved. If anything, his life of unfulfilled dreams made my urgency to make it as a singer even bigger. I knew I didn't want to end up unhappy like him.

"I should probably go in now," I said.

"Yeah, me too. Thanks for coming out and talking to me."

"Not a problem." I looked in his eyes, trying to determine if he was feeling any better. The street light no longer showed any tears, but I still saw sadness and worry in his expression, understandably. I thought about giving him a hug, but wasn't sure if that would be too much after that long hand hold.

"See you tomorrow morning," Matthew said as he turned slightly in the direction of his home.

"Yeah, see you tomorrow," I said. "Call me later if you need to talk, though."

He nodded and smiled. "I will, thanks."

I headed back to my house, the porch light off as I predicted. When I entered, the only lights in the living room were from the television and the flashlight Aria held over her opened Bible. Dad and Mom sat on the couch staring at the news, sharing Mom's grilled cheese sandwich. I maneuvered my way past and grabbed my sandwich from the kitchen table, then found a small open space to sit on the floor by Aria.

As the screen switched from a news reporter to an ad for Rice-A-Roni, Dad said, "Hey, I brought a few boxes of that home today. Maybe we can eat some of it this week." He wiped crumbs from his newly grown beard. It was a switch from his normal clean-shaven look and quite a contrast to his short, dark hair that he slicked back to perfection and sealed with hairspray every morning.

I tried to think of something to say back to match his Rice-A-Roni enthusiasm, but I really wasn't thrilled about adding a few more boxes to the ever growing stack on the kitchen counter. Dad had a proud smile on his face as he watched the two women on the screen talk about the delicious new savory rice flavors. They smiled and chewed in their bright clean kitchens like it was the best thing ever. When the screen switched back to the news of the shootout in Los Angeles, the jolt from overly cheerful to terrible made me want to cook some Rice-A-Roni, or do anything other than watch the sadness play out in front of me. I bit into my grilled cheese sandwich, which was now cold, and turned to Aria, the only person in the room with a smile on her face. She read her Bible in a loud whisper, completely focused on the words in front of her.

*"Because you are my helper, I sing for joy in the shadow of your wings."* She paused and looked up at me. "That's from Psalm 63. It reminds me of you, North. When you sing, you're so happy. You must know God is helping you."

I smiled back at her. I hadn't actually thought much about God helping me, but as blaring sirens and shouting people blasted from the television, I hoped she was right.

# Chapter 5

The next day at school was the same as nearly every day with Matthew, Ronnie, and me managing to stand out in every way possible. The news of the shootout didn't help. Our homeroom teacher, Mrs. Holt, brought up the story during our morning current events time. "The shooting occurred in South Los Angeles," she said.

At least five people turned and looked at Matthew, knowing he had family there. Up until a few months ago, his aunt lived nearby and his cousins went to our school.

Later at break, as we walked to Mr. Creighton's class for English, Ricky Bandt said, "Dude, did your family get a front row seat for that circus yesterday? That was insane!" His chin-length blond hair swung side to side in rhythm to his bobbing head. He reminded me of the parrots I'd seen in the pet store. Aria told me baby parrots bobbed their heads when they were hungry for food, and adult parrots sometimes did this when they were hungry for attention. I figured that last one applied to Ricky. He was always doing something to get attention.

Matthew didn't answer him, but as usual, Ricky didn't give up. "Do you know whose house that was all up in flames? Totally radical!" He exclaimed like he was talking about some fun movie he watched. Matthew halted abruptly. Two people behind him weren't expecting that and bumped into him. Everyone else nearby, including me, slowed down or stopped and turned back to hear Matthew's response.

Matthew looked at me and took a deep breath, then at Ronnie, and then at everyone nearby with narrowed eyes that finally stopped on Ricky. "No, I don't know whose house that was, Ricky, and yep, my aunt got a front row seat and totally described it like you just did—a circus—full of laughter and acrobats and best of all, clowns like you, who somehow think it's funny and cool to watch their neighborhood go up in flames while gunshots fly all around their heads."

Everyone fell quiet except for Ricky. "Woah, really?" he asked, clearly showing his inability to understand sarcasm.

Matthew shook his head in disgust. "You're an idiot, Ricky."

Matthew stepped forward, but fell back as Ricky shoved him and shouted, "Hey, who are you calling an idiot? You're the one with family in the hood!" He glared at Matthew.

Matthew looked angrier than I'd ever seen. He barged toward Ricky, towering over his tiny build, and pushed him back. Even my stick-thin, unmuscular self could probably knock Ricky to the ground. Matthew, whether he meant to or not, sent him flying. Ricky's binder and all its loose papers sprung into the air, and everyone around him scurried aside as they watched him fall. Ricky remained still for a moment, and then lifted his head. He finally seemed speechless and scared.

"You don't know anything about my family's neighborhood, and the location of a person's family doesn't make them an idiot. You should know from personal experience that idiots can live anywhere," Matthew said.

Shouts of "Ohhhhh, good one!" and "I think he gotcha there, Ricky!" preceded a chorus of laughs as Matthew stepped over Ricky. I caught up to him right before our principal, Mr. Z., politely called Mr. Zimmerman, appeared in front of us.

"What's happening down the hall, Mr. Jones and Ms. Simon? Looks like there's some commotion." He pulled a small notepad out of the front pocket of his suit jacket, then clicked the top of his ballpoint pen and waited for our response.

Matthew looked more scared than angry now. He rubbed the back of his head, his eyes on the notepad, and then looked up at Mr. Z. "Yes, Mr. Zimmerman, there is a bit of commotion. Ricky and—"

"Ricky fell down, Mr. Zimmerman," I interrupted. "That's all. But he's fine." I knew Matthew would have given a more truthful version of the events, but I didn't think Mr. Z. needed to know all those details.

Mr. Z. wrote in his notepad, looked up at me, then at Matthew as if he expected him to say more. I decided distraction was a good idea. "Since you're here, Mr. Zimmerman, I've been meaning to ask you something. Your talk at the assembly the other day about how to be successful in high school was really inspiring. We have to write our final essay for English about our goals for the future. Could I get a quote from you for mine? It would be really helpful."

Mr. Z.'s stern, suspicious demeanor magically transformed—from glary-eyed to bright-eyed, turned-down lips to delighted smile, gruff tone to friendly conversation. "Ah, well yes, Ms. Simon. I would love to give you a quote."

The bell to be in class rang before he could continue. He waved his hand at the sound, "Ah, you two don't worry about that. Who's your next teacher? I'll write you each an excused tardy note." He flipped a page in his notepad and waited for my response.

"Oh, we have English next with Mr. Creighton," I said.

"Well now, that's perfect," he laughed. "I guess this talk can count as part of your English time, then. Mr. Creighton won't mind."

I looked at Matthew who was finally smiling and looked like he might actually burst out in laughter. Mr. Z. then proceeded to repeat nearly his entire assembly speech while Matthew and I tried to look interested. Then he gave us the tardy slip that excused us from more than half the class period.

"Thanks, North," Matthew said while we walked to class. "I don't know why you don't talk that convincingly to everyone all the time. You're really good at it."

I looked up at him and smiled. It was usually easier for me to talk to adults than kids my own age, who seemed to be constantly judging me. "The thought of you getting in trouble over Ricky's stupidity seemed worse than Mr. Z. getting mad at me. You've had my back plenty of times." I probably couldn't count how often he'd stopped people from making fun of my name, my height, my wimpy arms, my parents, my sister. It was a long list.

The rest of the school day was easy compared to the way it started, maybe even better than normal. Matthew gained a bit of respect for his ability to silence Ricky, and for once Ricky actually seemed sort of afraid. He was quiet in class, kept to himself in the halls, and didn't yell and shout or try to flirt with the girls at lunch. When the final school bell rang, Ricky quietly went to his locker, then walked out the school gate alone, his head down as if to avoid any possible interaction with anyone.

"I'm not sure I've ever seen Ricky so quiet," Ronnie remarked as we waited by our locker for Matthew. She pulled out the hair clip that had been holding back her side swept bangs, the only part of her short brown hair that was more than a couple inches long.

"No kidding. I almost feel sorry for him," I said.

Ronnie swung her bangs out of her eyes to give me an icy blue glare. "No, you do not. He deserves to be knocked down a peg or twenty. It's about time he realized people don't appreciate his obnoxious comments. He's a mean person."

I agreed with that for the most part. "Yeah, he definitely needs to be nicer, but sometimes I don't think he realizes what he's saying is as bad as it is, you know?"

She looked at me and shook her head. "No, I don't know that. I do know you're insane if you have any sympathy for him, though."

"Hey, you both want to hang out today?" Matthew's voice boomed from behind us. "I have hardly any homework." I turned around, amazed that this large presence had the remarkable ability to appear out of nowhere sometimes.

Ronnie raised her hand up. "I'm in," she said.

"Me too," I said, "but I might need to help with Aria, so can we go to my house? We can go to the woods or hang outside." I remembered Mom's promise to take me to the record store, and realized she might not remember or be up for it anyway. At least I had friends to distract me.

"I sort of figured that would be the case," Matthew said. "Sounds good to me. I could use some time in the woods, and actually, hanging out with Aria always makes my day better."

"No kidding, me too," Ronnie said. "If everyone was as cool as her, life would be much better. I'm glad we get to see her at school next year."

"Yeah, thanks," I said as I watched a couple of Ricky's friends wad up torn pieces of paper, put them in their mouths, and peer around a row of lockers to shoot through straws at people who walked by. "I wish there were more people like you who would get to know her before they ridiculed her. You remember how it was for her at school here. It doesn't seem like high school is much better." Unlike Ronnie, I dreaded being at school with Aria again. It was kind of a nice break this past year to be at separate schools, to not witness first-hand the way people laughed and made fun of her, or the way they avoided me when I was with her.

"Well, if I have anything to do with it, things will be better for her next year," Ronnie said. "I'm going to have such a strong arm from working on my softball pitch over the summer. People will look at me next to Aria and be afraid to say anything mean." She held up her right arm and flexed her bicep. Matthew and I both stood speechless, not sure whether she was serious or kidding. She dropped her arm and put her hand on her hip. "Okay, guys. I know it's not much now, but you wait and see." She looked away, and crossed her arms over her notebook.

"Hey, I believe it." Matthew tapped Ronnie's upper arm with his closed fist. "Looks strong to me already. I wouldn't fight you."

"Uh, nobody would," I chimed in. "Well, maybe Ricky would, but we know how that would end."

We all laughed at that, and headed towards the front gate. The golden brown Plymouth Duster in the parking lot let me know Mom remembered to pick me up this time.

"Do either of you need a ride to my house?" I asked.

"Let me go talk to my mom," Ronnie said. "I'll be quick."

"I think I definitely need a ride. My mom is not going to drive me all the way to your house," he said sarcastically.

"Very funny," I laughed. "I'll see you soon, then?"

"For sure," he said before he quickly jogged away toward the loud honking car in the parking lot. Matthew's mom waved her arm out the window of her blue Oldsmobile. She usually had to hurry to get back to work, so Matthew's chatting was not tolerated for long. We tried carpooling for a bit, but my mom's unreliability didn't make Matthew's mom a fan of the idea.

Ronnie was already running back towards me. She bounded up the school steps, one arm carrying her binder and books, the other pumping up and down. If anyone was destined for the Olympics, it had to be her. "Okay, I'll take that ride home with you," she said between short breaths.

Before we even got down the steps, Aria was shouting out the window, "Ronnie! Hi! You coming home with us?"

I didn't have to look around to know that every eye in the parking lot was on Aria, and I didn't need to listen hard to hear the laughs.

Ronnie looked at me, then at our car. "You bet I am, Aria!" Ronnie cupped her hands to her mouth as she shouted as loud as ever and then glanced around at everyone who stared at her. "Hear that everyone? I'm going over to Aria's house!" She ran to the car, yelling as she went, "Because she is the coooooooolest!"

Aria laughed loud enough to match Ronnie's enthusiasm, rocking back and forth in the back seat. Ronnie looked back and smiled at me when she reached the car. She didn't need bigger biceps to stand up for my sister. Being herself was enough.

# Chapter 6

Matthew sat under the large jacaranda tree on our front lawn when we pulled into our driveway. With its purple flowers in bloom, the tree proudly claimed its place as the most beautiful thing on our property. Aria had not stopped talking since we left the parking lot. After reciting two Bible verses, she began spewing out fact after fact about the owls we recently saw in the woods, telling Ronnie she couldn't wait to show them to her. Ronnie responded with "wow," and "cool," whenever Aria paused, which wasn't often.

When Aria saw Matthew, she interrupted her sentence about how baby owls begin to fly with, "Oh! Matthew's here! Look! There on the lawn!" Before we could respond, Aria had climbed over the front seat, scooted herself over me, reached for the door handle and was out the door. Ronnie, Mom, and I stayed put, laughing as she bolted over to Matthew.

"Hey! Aria! What's up?" Matthew shouted and held up his hand to give her a high five as she bounded in front of him and met his hand with a loud smack.

Ronnie and I took our time getting out of the car while Mom went ahead inside, knowing Aria was in good hands, and likely seeking a bit of peace and quiet after cleaning houses all day.

After about ten more minutes of Aria repeating the same owl facts to Matthew that she had told Ronnie, we decided a walk to the woods might be a good idea. Mom was asleep on the couch when I went inside to tell her where we were going, so I left her a note, and told Aria to let her sleep when she opened the door and began to invite Mom to go with us.

"She needs to rest, Aria. You can tell her all about it when we get back," I whispered. She was so excited to be with Matthew and Ronnie that I knew she'd be fine with letting Mom stay back.

"Okay!" Aria responded with a smile, clueless that her shout might interrupt Mom's nap, "but can we bring her binoculars?"

"Yes, I'll get them," I whispered.

Mom lifted her head and squinted at me, "Everything okay?" she asked.

"Yes Mom, we're fine. We're going for a walk. We'll be back in a bit." I grabbed the binoculars from the pile of mail, books, and plastic containers on the table.

"Okay, have fun," she said and plopped her head back down. She was so tired lately, working more than ever. She said it was only temporary, until Dad got a raise at the grocery store, but we'd been waiting for that raise for at least two years. The only perk the store provided so far was his grocery discount, and that only contributed to my dad's hoarding, a problem that increased significantly every year. Dad said his plan to make it better was to build an additional room for his stuff. That did not sound like a solution to me.

Aria was still gabbing when I returned outside. Matthew and

Ronnie sat on the lawn and listened intently as she paced around them.

"You guys ready, or do you prefer to stay here? I don't want to ruin this party," I asked.

Aria stopped mid-sentence and said, "We're ready! We've been waiting for you!"

Matthew agreed, "Yes, we are absolutely ready."

Ronnie stood and brushed purple blossoms off her pants, "Thanks for all the info, Aria. I'm excited to see those owls."

"Me too!" Aria said. She was already ahead of us, gazing up at the trees as she took one big determined stride after another to the woods.

The closer we got to Crescent Ridge, the faster Aria walked, then skipped, then flapped her arms. Once the entrance to the park was in view, I noticed a large group of Boy Scouts in khaki shirts and shorts crowded in front of the main entrance. Two adults chatted near them, pointing at the trail map posted on the park information board while three boys ran around annoying others by grabbing their snacks or pulling hats off their heads. But what mostly caught my attention was a huddle of about ten teens who were clearly not part of the Boy Scout crowd. A few of them sat on the low wooden fence facing us, two stood arm in arm, one appeared to be smoking a cigarette, and a few talked and laughed animatedly. I felt panic rise up in me and picked up my casual walk to a slow jog to get ahead of Aria. Matthew and Ronnie saw my change of pace and knew exactly what to do. They caught up to Aria, one on each side of her, and did their best to engage her in conversation.

"So Aria, does your bird guide book actually have every bird listed in it?" Matthew asked. "I think I need you to look up something for me."

That was the perfect question to get her focused on her book instead of all the excitement around her. She stopped skipping and flapping her arms, slowed to an easy walk, and grabbed the book out of her bag. "Sure, Matthew. What do you want to know?" Aria asked.

"Oh, uh, I'm not sure what it would be called. I saw it in my yard. It was black with a little bit of yellow on its head and tail. Do you know what that might be?"

"Hmm, black with a yellow head would most likely be a Yellow-headed Blackbird, but they're usually found in wetlands, so that doesn't make sense. Are you sure it wasn't mostly yellow with some black on its face, wings, and tail? That would be a Hooded Oriole. They aren't very common, but they're here. They like to nest in palm trees, and they love sugar water. Do you have a bird feeder at your house? It might be attracted to that. Hooded Orioles are really cool. Here, let me show you a picture."

This could go on for a while, and hopefully long enough for us to get through the crowd with Aria simply looking like a studious girl with her head in a book instead of someone who pretended to fly and make bird sounds. But as we approached, I realized some of the kids looked familiar, and with a closer look, I spotted Ricky. And right next to him was Dahlia. It didn't matter what Aria did now. We were heading right into a storm.

I turned around to warn Matthew and Ronnie. "Ricky and Dahlia are over there," I said. Matthew and Ronnie both looked up from Aria's book.

"Oh, great," Matthew said. "This is not going to be good."

"Just keep walking," Ronnie said. "You know they're going to be rude. Let's ignore them and keep our heads up."

I knew we didn't really have a choice at this point.

"Hey, look. It's our favorite people from school. Wanna push me again, Mattie boy?" Ricky said, obviously feeling like a king next to queen Dahlia and a sturdy, tall blond boy I didn't recognize. I really didn't understand how anyone would want to be near Ricky, or how they didn't see how stupid he sounded.

"Oh, so it is," Dahlia said, "And they brought the North Pole with them. Hi, North Pole! Hi, Aria!" Dahlia waved as she flashed her fake smile, answering my question of what type of person would want to hang with Ricky.

Aria looked up from her book at the sound of her name. "Oh, hi! Who's that?" she yelled, squinting her eyes at Dahlia.

Dahlia giggled and ducked behind Ricky, "Oh my gosh, hide me. I don't want her to come over here and talk to me."

Aria looked confused, "Hey, why are you hiding? I heard you yell my name." Aria started to walk toward them, and I stepped in front of her.

"Aria, let's go. We don't have time for them. Let's see how those owls are doing, okay?" I grabbed her arm and pulled her the other direction.

"Oh, okay, yeah, let's go find the owls! Hoot! Hoot!" Aria trotted ahead toward the gate.

"Ha! Enjoy the owls!" Ricky yelled, and a moment later added, "Weirdo!"

I jogged to catch up with Aria, but looked over my shoulder to see that Matthew and Ronnie hadn't followed.

"Matthew, Ronnie, come on!" I said.

They both stood still, staring at each other, and shook their heads. Then they took off full speed at Ricky. I froze, stunned at their boldness, or possible stupidity. Ronnie reached Ricky first, grabbed him by his yellow T-shirt and yelled in his face, "Why are you such a jerk? Do you really feel good about picking on a girl? Well maybe you should pick on me instead if that's your thing!"

Ricky's pack of friends closed in, and as he broke loose from Ronnie's hold and fell to the ground, one of the adults with the Scouts, the taller male one, ran over to them. "Hey! What are you kids doing? Knock it off!"

Ricky's friends scattered, running towards the street. Ronnie and Matthew ran back in my direction, while Ricky picked himself up from the ground and proceeded to be yelled at by Mr. Scout Leader. Dahlia stood by dumbfounded, mouth open wide, like a little girl in big trouble.

"Come on, North, let's go!" Matthew yelled while he and Ronnie sprinted past me, as if I had been the one to delay them.

I stood for a moment watching Dahlia's face before I followed them. Within seconds we had caught up to Aria, who was back to skipping and hooting, unaware of all the chaos that had occurred. While we followed her, I kept thinking of Dahlia's troubled expression, and remembered when she didn't used to be so mean. One hot summer day in fourth grade, we were playing outside with a bunch of kids in the neighborhood. Dahlia sat on the sidewalk while several of us watched a small pill bug she'd found as it crawled around in the palm of her hand.

"Dahlia, why are you out here on the ground? I'll bet your clothes are a mess now." It was Dahlia's mom, Mrs. Kline. She stood next to another woman, a tall blonde in a narrow pink skirt, a white flowy blouse, shiny black high-heeled pumps and a disgusted expression on her face. "You see what I mean? She really needs to learn to act like a lady and choose friends who do the same." She pulled Dahlia up by the elbow. "Come on, let's go, and leave that filthy bug behind. This is my model friend I told you about, and she's going to give you some tips on how to act like a lady." She gave me a cold stare, like I was the bug.

Dahlia looked humiliated as she stood up and stretched her hand out for me to take the bug, but before I had a chance, Mrs. Kline swiped the bug off her hand. I watched it fly, then land on the ground, unroll itself, and crawl away while Mrs. Kline told Dahlia to stand up straighter and stop crying. That was the last time I saw Dahlia cry.

Aria finally slowed down as we reached the large oak tree where we'd stood the other day.

"We have to be really quiet," Aria turned and put her index finger to her lips while she stepped ever so softly toward the tree. She reached into her bag and pulled out the binoculars.

"Hoot, hoot!" she piped as she looked across at the opposite tree a couple hundred yards away.

"Are they there?" Matthew whispered.

Aria stared a bit longer, then lowered the binoculars and shook her head. "I don't see them. They're not there." Her lips turned down, her shoulders slumped.

"Maybe they're sleeping, or looking for food," Ronnie chimed in. "Can I take a look?" She reached out her hand and Aria reluctantly handed her the binoculars before creeping quietly toward the owl's tree. She circled the entire tree twice, searching every possible spot for the owls.

"They're not here!" she shouted. "I bet they've moved on to a new spot!" She turned around, surveying possibilities, then rested one hand on her hip and pointed the other to the cliffs beyond. "Over there! That's probably where they went! I read the other night that they like to hide in trees and crevices of cliffs. Hopefully they're safe from that hawk. We should see if we can find them there!"

Ronnie took her eyes off the binoculars and looked at me as if asking permission to do that.

"Uh, no. It'll be dark before we make it that far, and have you seen those cliffs? They're really high. I doubt we'd be able to spot an owl from down below."

Aria responded quickly with, "Obviously we wouldn't see them from below, but we could climb and see them, and if it's dark, that's better. That's when we're most likely to see them."

Matthew and Ronnie both laughed while I gave Aria a stern face and said, "No, Aria. We can't climb those cliffs, especially in the dark."

I knew that once Aria set her mind on something there wasn't an easy way to stop her. If I didn't clearly rebuke her idea, we'd be chasing her away from the cliffs in an hour.

Aria stared at me and cocked her head like she didn't understand me. "Why not? We haven't even tried yet. I'll bet it's not that hard," she said.

"They're actually really tough to climb, Aria," Matthew said.

Matthew's opinion carried a lot of weight with Aria, but she still looked skeptical.

"Really? How do you know? Have you tried it?" she challenged.

Matthew and Ronnie both looked at me, as if asking how important the truth was at that moment. I shook my head slightly at Matthew, hoping Aria wouldn't notice. This was one time when I hoped Matthew could convincingly lie. I held my breath as he turned from me to Aria.

"No," he said. I let out my breath, relieved he didn't share the truth about our cliff disaster.

"Well then, we need to try it!" Aria exclaimed.

I rolled my eyes and gave Matthew my best "you've gotta be kidding me" look.

Matthew put his hands on his hips, surveyed the cliffs ahead of us and said, "I haven't tried it myself, Aria, but everyone knows those cliffs are dangerous. Why do you think we never see anyone climbing them? Also, it's probably one of the few places the animals here can go to be safe from people."

Aria's slumped shoulders returned, and her wide, excited eyes lowered. "Hmm, yeah, I suppose that's true." She looked back at the cliff. "But I really want to see those owls again."

"Hey, I'll bet we see them again," Ronnie said. "Don't lose heart, Aria."

Aria turned to Ronnie, "Well, of course I won't lose my heart. It's always right here in my chest, Ronnie."

"Well yes, of course," Ronnie agreed.

"Do you want to sit here for a while and see what other birds we see, Aria?" I asked, not ready to go back to civilization quite yet.

"Sure, that would be great," she said, "and speaking of hearts, did you know that Jesus can live in our hearts? I read that in my Bible. I didn't know that before."

"Yep, true," Matthew said, as he took a seat next to me under the tree.

Matthew and his mom went to church nearly every Sunday. I'd been with him one time a few years ago, and the one thing I did remember, aside from the beautiful voices in the choir, was the pastor saying Jesus was always with us. I'd never thought of him being in my heart.

"You've read that too, Matthew?" Aria asked before she sat down, pulled Adagio out and set it on the dirt next to her, and then grabbed her Bible.

"Yeah, I don't remember exactly which verse that is, but I know it's in there," Matthew said.

Aria flipped through the Bible's pages. "I can tell you where it is. I marked it. It's right here." She placed a finger on the page and read, "Ephesians 3:16-17—*I pray that out of his glorious riches he may strengthen you with power through his Spirit in your inner being, so that Christ may dwell in your hearts through faith.*" She continued to stare at the Bible, then looked upward, clearly thinking about what she'd read. "I guess that means we need to have faith for him to live there. I probably need to work on that."

"Yeah, me too, Aria." Matthew drew in the dirt with a twig he'd found. "It's not easy sometimes, but I do believe Jesus is with me."

I believed that too, at least in Matthew's case. Why wouldn't Jesus live in a heart like his? It was a good one.

"It's like the owls. I can't see them, but I know they're here some-where," Aria said.

She tilted her head back and closed her eyes, gave a soft "hoot," and though no owl called back, I pictured them in the crevice of the cliff, looking back toward us.

# Chapter 7

On our walk home, with Aria leaping and skipping ahead of us as she often did, I had a chance to thank Matthew for keeping our climb on the cliffs a secret.

"Yeah, that was the scariest day ever," Matthew said. "That verse Aria read reminded me that we definitely didn't make it through on our own."

I thought back about that day last summer, when we thought a climb up the cliffs would simply be a fun adventure with the reward of a great view. Instead, we got a lesson on the value of obeying warning signs that are posted on trailheads.

Matthew led the way, letting us know when there was a slippery spot or something on the trail we might stumble on. Ronnie and I walked side by side until we were about halfway up the hill. That's when the trail became increasingly narrow and Ronnie slowed down to keep a few feet behind me. I kept my eyes focused on the trail, careful to take steady, short steps, refusing to look to my left for more than a brief moment at the deep ravine below. If any of us lost our balance, or if someone came down the trail toward us, there was no room to move aside.

As my heart beat fast and sweat dripped into my eyes, I suddenly heard Matthew shout, "Aahhh!" I lifted my eyes from the trail to see Matthew slip and fall to the ground. "Oh God, oh God, oh God!" he yelled in between panicky heaves of breath.

"Matthew! Are you okay?" Ronnie shouted behind me while I inched toward him.

"Don't come this way! Stay where you're at! The cliff just drops off here!" With his head and shoulders off the ground, he'd raised himself up on his elbows and began to scoot slowly backwards.

My body felt tingly, like I might fall over. I could barely get a breath in, the fresh air no help at that moment.

When Matthew finally reached me, I knelt down and touched his shoulders. "Are you able to stand up?"

"Yeah, I just need a second," he said. He sat up and pulled his knees toward his chest, taking big, deep breaths.

"I can't believe that just happened," he said. "I almost went over that cliff."

As I held his shoulders, I could feel his body shaking. "It's okay, Matthew. You're okay." I said even though I still felt terrified.

When he finally stood up, we all turned around and went back down the trail. Once we made it all the way down, we looked at each other and gave the biggest group hug ever. Then we promised to never go up that trail again, to make sure no one else we knew did either, and to obey trail warning signs.

Thinking back on the terror of that day should have made singing in front of a crowd seem like nothing, but I still felt a heavy thump in my chest as I imagined myself standing on that school stage tomorrow. Matthew and Ronnie made sure I had plenty of practice singing once we returned from the woods to my house.

"Come on, North, sing it again, but this time imagine that I'm Dahlia." Matthew said after my third time through Carole King's "Nightingale." He sat with his arms folded in front of his chest and his right leg crossed over his left like girls often sit. "Aren't I pretty and perfect? Look at me and sing it, North." He spoke in a higher-pitched, sassy tone, and of course, trying to sing while looking at him that way was nearly impossible.

"Okay, Matthew, I can't do it. Singing while laughing does not work."

"Hey, if you can sing now, tomorrow will be a breeze," Ronnie said through her laughs.

I managed to do it with my eyes closed, and realized that might be the way to get through the real performance as well. If I didn't look at everyone, didn't see how they looked at me with their expressions of disgust, shock, pity or humiliating amusement at my voice, I could do it.

"I don't understand why you're so nervous, North," Ronnie said. "Every teacher since fourth grade has heard you sing and asked you to perform a solo for one of our musicals. You should have taken them up on it."

"I never sang a solo because I didn't want to compete against Dahlia. Can you imagine how miserable she would have made my life if I got a part over her?"

Ronnie rolled her eyes. "Someone like her doesn't deserve all the power she gets. Her voice is sort of awful. She only got the solos because she was the only one who volunteered. Why do you think the teachers always put strong background singers with her?"

That was true. Her voice was drowned out most of the time. But how did I know I wouldn't sound bad in front of an audience too? When I was nervous, my voice cracked and squeaked. If I couldn't calm down,

I'd be a disaster. At least Dahlia had her looks too. Everyone thought she was pretty. When I looked in the mirror and compared myself to her, I felt like an ugly monster.

I barely slept all night, my mind swirling with all the worst possible scenarios. While it was still dark, the glow from my alarm clock showing 4:30 a.m., I gave up on any rest and searched for something semi-acceptable to wear. That didn't take long. A recent growth spurt had left me with only one pair of jeans that fit. They weren't the cool bell bottoms everyone was wearing, but at least they reached to my ankles. Skimming my hands across my shirts, I stopped at one I hadn't worn yet, a white gauze peasant shirt with embroidered red and yellow flowers at the round neck. It was donated to Mom by a woman whose house she cleaned. There was a slight stain at the bottom left side, but if I tucked it into the jeans, no one would see it. I laid the pants out on my bed, and placed the shirt on top. Then I looked down at myself, disappointed with the flat chest, straight hips, big feet, and far too many freckles on my chalk white skin. With my head down, my hair fell into view as it framed my face. It reminded me of a slightly better version of Bozo the clown, with orangey red steaks that poofed out on the sides. I pulled it back with the hair tie I'd left on my wrist from yesterday, knowing a stubby ponytail on top of my head was still better than trying to wet it down and style it. I didn't want to look like I'd tried too hard. That would give Dahlia way too much to criticize.

After I dressed, I turned on my radio in the slight hope Carole King might come on and inspire me or remind me how the song should be sung.

"K-Rock 101!" the radio theme tune blasted. I quickly adjusted the volume so I wouldn't wake Aria and my parents. After one ad for toothpaste, another for Lucky Charms, and a final one for Budweiser beer, I turned it off. Those were not theme songs I needed right now. I stood several feet away from my mirror, closed my eyes like I knew I'd have to do today, and began to sing. I did it perfectly, at least in my opinion, and when I opened my eyes, my mom confirmed it.

She stood in the doorway, nightgown on, hair disheveled from sleep, but a glow on her face that outshined any bit of morning weariness.

"That was perfect," she said, "absolutely beautiful, and that top is adorable on you."

I hoped I could tell myself that all day long. "Thanks, Mom."

Getting Aria up and out the door on time didn't always go well, but today she was motivated by Mom's reminder of going to my performance after school. Upon hearing that, she belted out her rendition of "Nightingale" while she spent a half hour in her room finding the most comfortable outfit to wear. She continued singing it in the kitchen through mouthfuls of cornflakes, and kept going in the car all the way to school.

As Mom drove into the high school parking lot, Aria's pitchy singing seemed perfect for the scene. Cars and teens converged into one huge ball of chaos and stress.

"See you this afternoon, North!" Aria yelled as she got out of the car. It may have been the first time I felt relieved for that song to end.

While inside the car seemed peaceful, outside was chaos. Drivers honked, sped up abruptly to try and pass others who followed the rules, and parked in red zones. Students either laughed and strutted happily or kept their heads down and inched along like they were entering the most torturous place ever. I felt like a mix of both groups.

I spent the first part of the day wishing my performance time would hurry up and arrive, and the last half dreading it. In spite of my mixed feelings, two-thirty arrived promptly along with hundreds of chatty middle schoolers who were more interested in school ending than in watching their classmates perform. I prepared to walk the plank and either fall fast into this pit of hungry, critical crocodiles or be saved by their standing ovation and thunderous praise.

The two performers before me were a blur in my mind. I plugged my ears and softly hummed "Nightingale" during the last part of Shari Cauldwell's violin solo. She was really talented and played beautifully. I sort of wished she had messed up so that my act would sound better.

"Thank you Shari for that outstanding performance," Mr. Z. said as he clapped enthusiastically above the crowd's weak applause. Shari beamed a big grin at him and exited the stage.

My heart thumped through my chest. My mouth felt dry, like my tongue might stick to the top of my mouth and keep it from opening. The air felt stuffy, the smell of fresh-baked cookies to be served when this was over now making me feel sick. I breathed deep. "Okay God, help me out here," I whispered while picturing Matthew, Ronnie, Mom, and Aria in the audience waiting for me. I pictured my dad for a moment, even though I doubted he could get off work to attend. Since he started working several late shifts at the store, I hardly ever saw him.

"And now, singing Carole King's 'Nightingale,' let's welcome 8th Grade student North Carolina Simon," Mr. Z. announced. Applause followed, but above that was a sound that was all too familiar, and for a time like this, all too unwanted—the sound of a bird.

"Caw! Caw! Nightingale!" I heard from the crowd as I entered the stage, and the clapping quieted as heads turned in the direction of my sister and mom. My eyes followed. Aria stood in the middle of the seated audience, waving her arms at me, and I froze. She was so happy to see me, and at that moment I couldn't love her more for how much she loved me. But at the same time, I guiltily wished she weren't there. As much as she was my motivation to sing, her actions had the potential to steal my spotlight. Mom stood and whispered something to her. Aria looked around, saw everyone staring at her, and started a small but noticeable flapping of her arms. I knew she was trying to calm herself so I could sing. I knew she needed a moment to get there. But of course, others weren't so understanding.

"You need to sit down! This is an important occasion!" A disheveled woman fanning herself with the program two rows over yelled.

And that comment was all it took to steal my shining moment at Sage Hill Middle School and turn it instead to an entirely different show starring my very own mom.

"Excuse me?" Mom yelled as she stood next to my sister. "This is my daughter, not yours. I will tell her what to do. Have a little patience please."

Aria continued to stand and move her arms, then turned from side to side, side to side. She was getting more anxious, not less, as people giggled and whispered to each other.

"How much patience do we need? Maybe she should leave if she can't be respectful," the same woman shouted to my mom.

I knew that comment wasn't going to go over well.

"My daughter has every right to be here, and if you can't understand that, maybe YOU need to be the one to leave."

Aria's arms beat faster and she began to sing, "Nightingale! She sails away upon a sea of song! Nightingale!"

The only eyes I could see on me now were Matthew's. While everyone else looked at my mom, and then at that other woman who stood and shouted back, Matthew stayed focused on me. Tears welled up in my eyes. My face felt hot. Matthew nodded his head, mouthed "Go" and touched his lips, then gave a thumbs up. He was telling me to go ahead and sing, but all I processed was the word "Go," leave, sail away like the words Aria kept singing. As a sob burst from my mouth instead of a melody, I ran off the stage, past the staring crowd, out the side door to the fresh air where I kept walking and crying with no clue where I was heading other than away. Birds chirped in trees above me, an annoying noise to me now as I realized all my practice and excitement for this day had been a complete waste of time. How could they be so cheerful? I looked through my tears at them as they fluttered from one tree to another. Must be nice to sing with such carefree ease.

"North! Wait! Hold up!" I turned around to see Matthew running toward me. "Hey, you planning to walk home?" He stood in front of me, out of breath, his hands on my shoulders, his eyes telling me how sorry he was about what happened.

"I don't know. I just had to get out of there, and I don't want to stick around to see what's about to happen with my mom and that horrible lady and my poor sister who no one understands. How does that lady say that? Isn't she supposed to act like a grown-up and be a little bit nice? And couldn't my mother try a little harder to quiet Aria instead of fighting with someone so I could actually sing?"

"Yeah, they were both being pretty stupid." He wiped a tear from under my eye. "Come here," he said, and pulled me into a hug. I felt his heartbeat, steady like him. "What do you say I walk home with you? I've got nothing else to do." He pulled back and looked down at me. "Other than listen to you sing. You know I'm not letting you give up just because some lady and your mom decided to steal your show."

"Yeah, I don't think I'm up for singing right now."

"Okay, then. I guess you'll have to listen to me. Here we go. When you're down and troubled, and you need a helping hand . . ." Matthew sang loud and shamelessly the song we often sang together—"You've got a Friend," and even though he wasn't Carole King, and claimed wrongly that he had a terrible voice, he sang right to my heart. Several more lines in, I joined him. With each line, I sang louder and louder, pouring out all my frustration. When we finished, he looked at me and said, "Man, that was good, North. That's the way you need to sing all the time."

He was right. That was how I needed to sing. I needed to stop being silent. I needed to make a change.

# Chapter 8

Normally the chaos inside my home wasn't obvious until I opened the front door. This evening was different. Mom had obviously sped home, her car parked askew in the driveway with her front wheels on the lawn. Her screechy shouts combined with booming yells from my father bellowed out to the sidewalk.

"Doesn't sound good in there," Matthew said. "You can come over to my house if you want."

As much as I wanted an escape plan, the thought of Aria alone with my parents yelling made me stay. "Thanks, I might need to if things don't calm down, but I think I'd better check on Aria. She doesn't do well when people fight."

"Yeah, me neither. I really think Aria and me are one in the same. What is it my mom always says? Birds of a feather flock together? We must have the same feathers," he said.

I hadn't thought about that until now. As different as they were, Matthew and Aria had a lot of similarities. They definitely understood when wrongs should be right, and they absolutely knew how to bust me out of a bad mood on most days.

"Good job with the bird metaphor. Mr. Creighton and Aria would both be proud."

He laughed, but then put his hand to his mouth and widened his eyes. "Oh, shoot. Mr. Creighton won't care how many metaphors I come up with if my essay isn't finished. Isn't that due tomorrow?"

This day kept getting better. I had completely forgotten about school work.

"Ahhh, yes, it's due tomorrow. I need to finish mine too."

He reached his hand in the air for a high-five. "Good job, North. Welcome to the procrastinator's club."

My hand met his, but instead of the typical smack, he grabbed my hand in a tight grip. I looked up at him, a closed-lip grin on his face. "Thanks, Matthew. It's really nice of you to allow me into your club, but I'll need to cancel my membership after this. Unlike you, I'm not able to whip out a polished English paper in one night. Hopefully, Creighton will be kind since it's our last paper."

"Yeah, like you have to worry. You've probably got the highest grade in the class. You'll be fine."

I was pretty sure I had the second highest, according to Mr. Creighton, but considering it might be my only A, it wasn't much to brag about. "Well, I guess we'd better start writing. Don't expect me to be in my usual happy mood tomorrow. It's going to be a long night."

After one final hand squeeze, he let go of his grip. "See you tomorrow, North Carolina," he said. He was probably the only one who could say my full name without offending me.

The yelling had stopped when I approached the door, but the aftermath of the storm appeared on the other side. I tiptoed around spilled paint bottles, the fallen paper towel wall, clothes, a spilled box of screwdrivers, nails, hammers, and another box tipped on its side to start a trail of Dad's collection of microphones, record albums, music sheets, tambourines, maracas, guitar strings, and posters of rock stars. I hadn't seen that last box in a while. Dad had sealed it tight a few years ago when he gave up his own dreams of being a musician. He'd labeled it "Don't Open" and placed it high on a shelf in the garage. I didn't understand why he wrote that, or why he placed it so far out of reach. I especially wanted the maracas, which I remembered getting at a garage sale when I was five. I was the one who found them, their bright red, yellow, and green tips peeking out of a box of stuffed animals and Barbie dolls. I pulled them out of the box that day, held them in front of me and shook. Minutes later they had inspired me to dance and sing a very upbeat version of the alphabet song I had recently mastered, and continued to entertain me after Dad bought them for me and carried me home on his shoulders.

Since then the only music in the house came from my room or my voice. Whenever dad heard me sing, he'd stop what he was doing and listen, often closing his eyes, but he never said anything. As soon as I stopped, he'd go back to whatever task was at hand, usually sorting through all his stuff or looking for something he claimed he needed at that moment.

So the fact that the banished music box had reappeared on the day of my performance and likely caused a big fight was unsettling. As I approached the kitchen, I saw Aria. She was pacing back and forth, Adagio in her hand.

"Aria? Are you okay?" I asked, knowing she wasn't.

She looked at me briefly, and stopped for a second, then went back to pacing. "Mom and Dad are mad," she said. "Really mad."

"Okay, well, that happens sometimes. It's okay. Do you want to go to my room? We can listen to music."

She kept moving, four steps in my direction, then four steps away, four steps forward, four away.

"Come on, Aria. Let's go."

She looked up at me, nodded her head, but tears began to roll down her face. I could tell a meltdown was on the way, so I did what always seemed to work. I sang. "You've Got a Friend" was fresh in my mind, so I sang it like I did with Matthew and watched Aria's tears disappear as she joined me in singing.

Unfortunately, when we stopped singing, we heard Mom yelling again. This time it felt like as much of an attack on me as Dad.

"Did you really have to waste your time searching for the perfect microphone for North instead of actually coming to the performance? Do you really think she would have used it instead of the one provided by the school? What she really needed was her father to be there, or for him to take care of Aria so she could actually sing, or better yet, for him to tell her to give up that dream of singing so she doesn't turn out like you."

That hurt. I thought she believed in my voice. She obviously didn't think I had what it takes to succeed. And why would she yell at Dad for trying to do something special for me? I wanted to run in and thank him, tell him how much that meant to me.

Aria cupped Adagio in her hands and held it close to her face, seeming calmer. "E.O. Wilson is a really smart man. He's a biologist who went to school at Harvard, and do you know what he says?" she asked.

I gave her my attention even though I wasn't that interested in what anyone had to say at the moment.

"He says that when you've seen one bird, you have not seen them all." Her eyes met mine. "Dad might not be much of a songbird, but you are, North."

# Chapter 9

Normally I would have jumped out of bed easily on the last day of school, but not this year. Aside from staying up way too late to finish my English paper, the idea of facing everyone at school made lifting my head from the pillow in the morning nearly impossible. I tried to think of some good excuses to stay home, but I knew that wouldn't make me feel better. Dad would be at work, and Mom probably wouldn't be working until later, which meant I'd have to spend most of my time home with her. After what she said last night, that seemed unbearable.

So with only ten minutes left before we had to leave, I hauled myself out of bed, and unlike yesterday, looked in my closet for whatever felt comfortable to wear instead of what might brand me as a brilliant singer. A loose navy blue T-shirt and faded denim overalls were my pick even though they made me resemble a skinny scarecrow. With a few minutes to spare, I grabbed my binder and books and headed to the living room, thankful that my last-minute appearance would mean little time to talk with Mom or Aria.

"Are you ready?" Mom said as she grabbed her purse. Her hair was messy and she didn't lift her eyes to look at me, but I knew they were probably bloodshot from tears and restless sleep. When I finished my paper at 2 a.m., I crept out of my room to get a glass of water in the kitchen, and saw her on the couch, sniffling, wads of Kleenex piled like a small mountain on the floor next to her. I turned back and drank from the bathroom sink instead, not knowing what to say to her. Hearing her say my singing was a worthless dream made me think she'd been lying to me all those times she'd told me to keep singing. Maybe if I would have belted out my song loud and clear, all eyes would have turned to me, and Mom would have stopped yelling along with that other lady. Maybe I would have given her reason to be proud and happy instead of ashamed, and the whole fight between her and Dad wouldn't have even happened.

Aria stood by the door, tote bag over her shoulder, wearing white culottes topped with the same shirt she'd worn yesterday—a bright orange polo shirt with a penguin logo on the upper right side that Dad had only worn once. Like me, she had clearly chosen comfort over fashion.

"Last day of school, North. Are you excited?" She flashed a bright smile.

"More excited than ever," I said, wishing I could skip the school part of this day and go straight to being done.

"Me too!" she said as she jutted her head forward and strode with her usual deliberate quick steps out the door to the car. As always, her enthusiasm lightened my mood, and even got a slight smile from Mom. But the day had only begun, and unfortunately, Aria's smile wasn't enough to keep my sky from falling.

Dahlia managed to be as unkind as ever all day at school, glaring at me while whispering and laughing to anyone near her as I walked into her view. Sometimes when she was mean like that I realized how much she looked like her mom did that day she sent the pill bug flying, disgusted with anyone who didn't fit into her idea of perfection, like our flaws might be contagious or something.

As soon as the day was over, I went straight to the parking lot, thankful I didn't need to get anything out of my locker since we had cleaned them out and given all our books back earlier in the day. Mom had told me to be out front as soon as possible because she had to get to a house cleaning job where the owner threatened to find someone new if she was late again.

In spite of my rush to leave, I still managed somehow to be slower than Dahlia. As I approached the front steps, I saw her at the bottom, standing in front of a shiny green bike occupied by a boy I didn't recognize, likely one of her friends from our town's other middle school, Eagle Ridge. Dahlia liked to brag about how she had a bunch of friends there, like that somehow made her so much cooler than anyone at our school. The boy flashed a wide smile, his teeth bright white against a very cute, tanned face. Dahlia had her hands on the handlebars and stood smiling and laughing loudly while he talked to her and Susan Carbonne. I assumed Dahlia was simply being her normal loud and flirty self, but when I saw her turn her head and point toward the parking lot, I realized she was being her normal mean self.

"Oh my gosh, hilarious!" Dahlia shouted as she pointed to Aria.

Aria marched under the trees that edged the sidewalk, as she usually did when waiting with Mom for me to get out of school. She was gathering handfuls of leaves and stuffing them in her bag while educating anyone with even the worst hearing about the intricate design of bird nests.

I refused to look at Dahlia as I passed her, kept my eyes on Aria as I crossed the parking lot. I heard music coming from our car and saw Mom through the closed window with her eyes closed, her fingertips rubbing her forehead, likely a sign that her patience was in short supply.

"Hey, Aria, I see you're finding a lot of good leaves here," I said.

"Oh, yes! I am! Hi, North!" She stopped for a moment to greet me and then returned to her leaf hunt.

"I think Mom wants to go. Why don't you show me those in the car?" I asked.

"Oh, sure! These are going to be great for all the birds in our yard," she said. "And they'll also be good to bring with us to the woods if it's cold. Did you know you can survive in cold temperatures by covering yourself in leaves? And look! I found a little white bird feather too, probably from a dove." She held the tiny feather up to show me.

"Okay, great," I said. "Tell me more about that in the car." I didn't really want more information about how to use leaves in place of a perfectly good jacket, or to hear more about what beautiful thing she was creating with the feathers she'd been collecting, but I needed to get her in the car.

"Gathering more junk for your house, Aria?" Dahlia shouted.

Aria looked at Dahlia, "Junk? No! I'm gathering leaves! They're for the birds in our yard, and to keep us warm in the woods!"

How I wished Aria knew when to ignore someone, but she would never turn down an opportunity to tell someone what she knew about birds. Dahlia had given her the perfect opening, "Wow! Okay, I guess you need to stay warm when you live with the North Pole!" She burst into laughter at her stupid joke. Susan joined in. The boy stood with a slight grin, but he didn't seem to think it was that funny. He'd never met me, so he probably didn't know my name was North, or that my house was full of junk, or that we were the chosen target for Dahlia's piercing jokes all the time.

Aria tilted her head and furrowed her brows, "Huh? We don't live at the North Pole. We live a few miles away. It doesn't get that cold, but it still gets chilly enough for leaves to be helpful. If you're ever lost and cold, remember that. "

"Aria, I think she's already lost and cold." As soon as that came out of my mouth, I realized that was the wrong thing to say. Aria took that seriously and responded in the sweetest yet most horrible way possible.

"Well, if she's cold and lost, she needs these more than I do right now!" Aria stomped away toward Dahlia before I could explain what I actually meant. I went after her, but when a car drove up I had to wait for it to pass, allowing Aria to reach Dahlia before I could stop her. She extended her hands full of leaves and said, "Here! You can have these to stay warm. Go on, take them."

Dahlia gave the most disgusted look and said, "Eww, no, get away. I don't want your dirty leaves." Then she smacked the bottom of Aria's hands as the leaves went flying all over her and the boy on the bike.

Aria stood with wide, fearful eyes, then began flapping her arms, clearly stressed by Dahlia's aggression. I had to get her away from there. Dahlia would only humiliate her. I jogged over to Aria and put my hands on her shoulders. Other than her arms, her body was stiff and wouldn't budge. I knew I couldn't force her to turn around, and I knew there was one sure way to calm her. I had to sing. I moved between her and Dahlia so she could see me, then leaned in close so I could sing loud enough for only her to hear.

While I sang the beginning lyrics of Carole King's "You've Got a Friend," Aria looked in my eyes, and calmed her arms.

"Oh wow, lucky us. We finally get to hear North sing! Listen carefully everyone. The meek little mouse is trying to sing!"

Aria's attention moved to Dahlia again, so I sang one last line, a little louder this time, and gently grabbed Aria's elbow to turn her toward the car.

Seconds later, Dahlia said, "I guess the show is over folks. Once again, another failed performance from our dear North Carolina."

I wanted to tell her she was the failure, but instead said, "Keep going, Aria. I don't want to sing in front of her. I'll sing when we get to the car, okay? Keep walking."

"Dahlia, knock it off! What's your problem? Did you even hear her voice?"

I turned around and saw the boy on the bike move away from Aria. He pedaled toward us, flipped his blond hair out of his eyes, and stopped behind our car. "Hey, don't listen to her. You've got a nice voice."

I wanted to speak back, but every possible response stuck like a wad of gum in my throat. This cute boy who knew nothing about me actually said something nice to me. I couldn't remember that ever happening. So I said nothing, like a dummy, nodded, and looked up at Dahlia, who stood with a scowl and arms crossed. If flames and smoke shot out of an angry person's head like they did sometimes in cartoons, her head would have been on fire. That made me brave enough to respond.

"Thanks," was all I said as I sat down and closed the car door, basking in the glow of my first strong performance.

# Chapter 10

In spite of how bad the last week of middle school had been, I went home happier than I'd been in a long time. I couldn't stop thinking about that boy. Other than Matthew and Ronnie, I'd been brushed aside or criticized by everyone at school for years. But this time someone I didn't even know, someone who hung out with Dahlia of all people, noticed my voice—not my weird name, my terrible outfit, my ugly hair, or my sister. He heard me sing, and he said I was good.

After Mom dropped us off, I dashed as quickly as possible to the phone and dialed Ronnie's number.

"You're never going to believe what happened to me after school," I said when she answered.

"I'm surprised anything happened," Ronnie said. "You left before I even saw you, and I thought I was rushing to get out of that place."

I proceeded to tell her about the cute boy who put Dahlia in her place by complimenting me.

"Oh my gosh, I wish I could have seen the look on Dahlia's face when he did that."

"Yeah, it was a great look. She was really mad. Would have made a great yearbook picture." I twirled the phone cord around my finger and remembered angry, jealous Dahlia.

"Yes! Just keep that picture in your head, and what that boy said too. I'd say that means you win the Dahlia versus North competition, finally," Ronnie said.

"It does sort of feel that way, even though I never wanted there to be a competition."

"I know you didn't, but she definitely did. I'm glad that boy stood up for you. Did you get his name? Is he going to Sage High?"

"I have no idea," I said, "but I sure hope so."

"Me too," Ronnie said. "How early do we need to be back at the fun zone for our graduation ceremony?"

"We're supposed to be there at five-thirty, so hopefully my parents both get home from work on time."

Ronnie laughed and said, "I doubt they'd be late for your graduation, but if you get stuck, I'll give you a ride. I'm not getting promoted without you and Matthew."

"Okay, you got it, thanks!"

When we hung up, I went back to my room, opened my closet, and eyed the graduation dress Mom had miraculously found on sale. It was a long white gauze dress that reminded me of so many magazine photos I'd seen recently. Being tall, most dresses ended up too short, but this one reached a few inches above my ankles.

"A lot of girls would have to wear uncomfortably high heels with that or take the hem up. It's perfect on you." Mom had said when I tried it on and eyed myself in the mirror.

Luckily, I actually liked it, which wasn't common with things I tried on. I hated to disappoint Mom when she surprised me with something she bought, knowing we probably could use the money for something else. When that happened, I'd fake a smile and act like I loved whatever it was. This time I didn't have to pretend. It had flowy, elbow length sleeves and an attached belt that I could tie in the back just enough to give me some shape. I especially liked the brown embroidery on the chest in the shape of a flower, reminding me a little of the flower tattooed on Mom's arm, only not as bright and obvious.

"I could make you a necklace to spice it up a bit if you want, add some color," Mom had added. But I told her I liked it as it was.

That was a couple months back, when the idea of wearing anything that would bring more attention to myself sounded horrible. While I still didn't want any bad attention, I wondered if I should have taken her up on that offer of a necklace. Plain, simple and shy had been me all this time, but that hadn't kept me from standing out and being noticed. Maybe I needed to be seen differently, as more bold.

I put a Carole King album on my record player, turned the volume up loud, and grabbed my journal. Then I plopped onto my bed to jot out my plan of attack for high school:

Get new clothes: no more boring shirts and uncool pants. Pick up the latest edition of *Seventeen* magazine to see what's in style and then LOOK COOL for a change!

Change hair: Maybe cut it short, or do anything that will keep it from looking like a mop.

Accessorize: scarves, bracelets, earrings.

Practice singing every day to try out for a band.

CHANGE NAME! No more being called North Pole, a direction on a compass, one of the 52 states, or anything else humiliating. People can call me by my middle name, Carolina, or even better, Carol!

I felt ready for eighth grade graduation now. The sooner I could put middle school behind me, the sooner I could embrace the new me. With an hour left before I had to leave, I closed my journal and got ready for one last middle school appearance. I put on the dress, ran a brush through my hair and clipped the sides back into a single barrette at the back of my head. I put a pink tinted lip gloss on, and blended a little on my cheeks just to give a little color since I didn't own any blush. I decided that buying some makeup should be another item on my list.

As excited as I was to get to the ceremony, once it started I couldn't wait for it to be over. It dragged on and on with three student speeches from people who hadn't been particularly nice talking about the importance of being kind and then rambling about their fond memories of middle school. I glanced at Ronnie and Matthew several times as we each in turn rolled our eyes, or shook our heads, or concealed a slight laugh at some of the remarks.

When my name was called to receive my diploma, Aria let out a loud, "Yay, North!" followed by a familiar bird cry, "Coo-coo!" Since others had gotten shout-outs, this didn't seem so out of place, so I looked at her with a quick smile before I shook hands with Mr. Z. Back at my seat, I stared at the crisp, off-white paper with Sage Hill Middle School printed at the top, and North Carolina Simon typed just below it. I breathed a deep sigh of relief. I didn't feel particularly proud and accomplished for graduating eighth grade, but I was grateful to not have to stay. Other than some of the teachers I liked, I wouldn't miss this place.

While names continued to be announced, I remembered an article I'd read about Carole King that described how she was so much smaller than everyone in her grade because she started kindergarten at age four and was promoted to second grade the next year because she was so smart. When she started high school, she had hopes of being popular.

Boys called her cute, but not in a dating sort of way. She found a place in music, where she rose above her small stature. Even though I was tall, I definitely could relate to that desire to find my place. As the last graduate was named, everyone stood and cheered, and I let out the loudest cheer ever, ready for my new name and new look to raise me above my lowly existence too.

The hard part of graduation night was saying goodbye to Ronnie and Matthew. Ronnie was leaving the next day for Minnesota to visit her grandparents all summer, and Matthew was leaving to be with his dad in Northern California. It was going to be tough without them around. We embraced in one big group hug in the middle school parking lot with the promise to talk on the phone as much as we could. With long distance calls so pricey, we all knew the conversations wouldn't be nearly long or often enough.

When we pulled away from each other, Matthew and I clutched our hands like we had the other night.

"Have a good summer, North," he said. "Stay cool."

I wanted to tell him I needed to get cool first, but instead just said, "You too, Matthew."

Mom and Dad stood impatiently by the car waiting for me while Aria stared up at the same tree she'd gathered leaves under the other day, likely hoping to find some sort of bird or nest. My excitement over graduating had faded after my goodbyes to Ronnie and Matthew.

When we got home, I tried to act cheerful as Mom served cake Dad had picked up from his store.

"We're very proud of you," Dad said before opening up to a thickly frosted bite. I nodded and mumbled a thank you through my own mouthful. It was definitely more frosting than cake, just the way I liked it.

We finished the evening by watching *The Sonny and Cher Show*. I loved Cher's voice and her decorative, flashy clothes. When they sang their popular song "I Got You Babe," we all sang along. We sounded terrible, completely out of sync, but I imagined myself dressed like Cher, performing before an adoring crowd in awe of my beautiful voice.

# Chapter 11

I awoke the next morning to the warm summer sun streaming through the window onto my face. I squinted to look at my clock, shocked to see I'd slept until 11:30. With no school and no obligations for the day, I stayed up late flipping through magazines, singing along to my favorite music, and imagining the new me.

I usually hated to go through my clothes, but now I couldn't wait to scour my closet and eliminate anything that made me look stupid or boring to make room for items that would make me look hip and interesting. Even though we didn't have a lot of money, Mom always found me a few inexpensive new things before each school year. I also had money from babysitting and helping Mom with housekeeping a few times. I'd been waiting for the right opportunity to spend it, knowing I wanted it to go towards something to enhance my future—maybe voice lessons, or a car, or college. Creating a new look could definitely get me on track to make life better.

I turned on my radio, let the music blast, and opened my closet to begin the purge. With each old, plain, unflattering item I tossed onto my carpet, I imagined a new outfit to replace it. With only two pants, three T-shirts, one summer dress, a sweater, and a pair of shorts left in my closet, I looked at the pile of clothes, turned around, and plopped backwards into it. When I was little, Dad would rake the leaves from the yard into a mound at the bottom of my slide. I'd glide into them, laughing as they cushioned my landing, and I'd wiggle my way out to do it again and again and again. I felt that same carefree feeling as I sunk into those old clothes. I closed my eyes, imagined myself on the first day of high school with bell bottom jeans, a beaded leather belt, a fitted T-shirt, a scarf around my head, big hoop earrings. I'd see that boy and he'd be unable to take his eyes off me. He'd ask me to sing and I would sing like I did with Matthew. Everyone would stop and listen and clap when I was done. Dahlia would look like she did today, and then she'd toss her hands in the air and give up on bothering me anymore.

I opened my eyes when I heard a car pull into the driveway. Its distinct rattling sound, like rocks rolling around in the engine, told me it was Dad's mustard yellow Datsun sedan. In serious need of repair, it was usually good for announcing Dad's arrival and reminding me I was supposed to help get dinner ready, but it was nowhere near dinner time. A glance at my clock radio told me it was 12:15.

Thinking he'd come home for lunch, I pulled myself up and exited my room. The house was quiet and Mom's bedroom door was shut. In the living room, I stepped carefully over Dad's music collection that still lay scattered on the floor and weaved through stacks of papers, boxes, clothes, cleaning rags, and other miscellaneous junk. Aria sat on the couch in the living room next to a pile of unfolded towels, her bird book and Bible in front of her as usual.

"Dad's home, North!" she said. "It seems a little early. Mom isn't even up yet." Aria was clearly as confused as me.

"Yes, it is. Maybe he came home for lunch. Are you hungry? I'm going to see what we have to eat," I said as I made my way to the kitchen.

"Yeah, I guess I am kind of hungry," Aria said.

Whenever Aria was deep into doing something, she'd forget all about food. Once reminded, she often became ravenous and a little grumpy. I hoped I could get something ready before she got to that point.

Mom had claimed the kitchen as her domain, so it was more orderly than most of the house, even though it still had stockpiles of food items Dad brought home from work. He claimed it saved us money because he'd buy things in bulk when they went on sale. We had so many of some items there was no way they weren't going to expire before we could get to them. On the floor, leaning against the kitchen counter was a three-foot tall stack of peanut butter jars. I picked up a jar from the top and checked the expiration—July 1974, only a couple weeks away. Knowing Mom, she had organized them so the older ones were on top. The one next to it had the same expiration, and same with the one next to that. It looked like peanut butter needed to be a regular part of our diet if we planned on getting our money's worth. I set one of the jars on the sink. Then I opened the window above the kitchen sink to air out the musty smell that worsened when the house was closed up all day. As a breeze blew in, I noticed Dad sitting in the car, his head bent down, hands gripping the steering wheel. I kept watching, wondering why he hadn't moved yet. He finally lifted his head but stayed in his seat, staring blankly through the window, a grim expression on his face.

I hurried to start lunch, seeing that he wasn't in the best mood and would likely want to eat soon. I opened the fridge, grabbed the colorful polka-dotted package of Wonder Bread, a jar of near empty grape jelly, and looked in the fruit bin for something fresh. A bag of apples was it. I grabbed them and set everything on the counter, ready to prepare another meal that would probably only bring excitement to Aria. Aside from macaroni and cheese, peanut butter sandwiches were a favorite choice of hers any time. On days I had time to make both, you'd think she was dining at a fine restaurant. She would go on and on about how I was the best cook ever, and how I should think about being a professional chef. She really was good for my self-esteem.

The front door creaked open and I heard Aria say, "Woah! What's all that?"

I stepped out of the kitchen to see Dad carrying a stack of frozen dinners in one arm, so high it reached to the top of his forehead, and in his other hand, a grocery bag filled with more.

"Wow, that's a lot of frozen dinners. Need some help?" I asked him as I reached for the bag.

"Yeah, sure," he said. "You can just set them on the table. I know they won't all fit in the kitchen, so I'll put most of them in the garage freezer."

"Okay," I said, noticing his face was splotchy and his eyes watery, like he'd been crying, something I hadn't ever seen on him before. Confused and unable to look away, I asked, "Everything okay, Dad?"

He looked at me, and the tower of frozen dinners began to tilt sideways. I reached up to stop the fall, but I was too late. They fell in different directions into Dad's face, onto the floor behind him, in front of him, and one landed in my hands—a Hungry Man turkey and gravy dinner that reminded me of a really disappointing Thanksgiving meal.

"Oh, cool! Spaghetti and meatballs! I want this one, Dad!" Aria lifted up a box from the floor and held it above her head like she'd found a valuable treasure, then ran to the kitchen.

Dad said nothing. He stood over the pile of frozen cardboard, his arms limp at his sides, mouth turned down. Then he looked me in the eye and said, "I lost my job."

# Chapter 12

I felt a surge of panic. We already had hardly any money, and the thought of what would happen once Mom heard this news made me feel sick. She wasn't going to take this news calmly, which meant Aria was going to get anxious and upset, and soon the house would explode with shouting and tears. Dad disappeared into the garage before I thought of anything to say to his news. I set the kettle on the stove, hoping a cup of tea might help Mom's nerves a bit. If not, at least it gave me something to do. I felt too nervous to be still.

I opened the bag of bread, pulled out a handful of slices, and began to spread peanut butter. I pressed the knife onto the bread with rapid strokes and accidentally poked a hole through one slice at the sound of Mom's bedroom door opening. I dropped the knife, quickly grabbed a teabag and dropped it into a cup with some hot water. Aria still clung to the spaghetti frozen dinner and jumped up from her seat at the table to greet Mom with her excitement.

"Mom! Hi! This is the best day! North is making peanut butter sandwiches, and Dad brought me this spaghetti and meatball dinner!"

She held it up in front of Mom's face.

"Wow, Aria, that's great!" Mom said in as cheery tone as she could probably muster. Her eyes, no trace of concealer left to hide the dark circles, and her weak smile, showed that she was exhausted.

"Hi, Mom," I said, "Do you want some tea?"

Her face perked up a little. "Oh yes, thank you, honey." She took the cup, sipped, and offered a hint of a smile as she said, "Mmmm, this is perfect. Did Aria say your dad was home? I went back to sleep after Mrs. Weaver called at six this morning to cancel her house cleaning for the day. I didn't sleep through the whole day, did I?"

"Uh, no, you didn't. Dad came home early. He's in the garage," I said.

Seconds later, he came back in through the garage door, his red, watery eyes staring at Mom.

"Oh my, are you okay, Frank?" She stepped toward him and a tear rolled down his cheek. The fight they had the other night was bad, but this would undoubtedly be worse. I needed to distract Aria before the fireworks began.

"Hey, Aria, how about we go eat outside and watch for birds?"

"Oh, sure!" she said as she shoved the frozen dinner at me and headed to the door. I set it down so I could grab the partially made sandwiches, paper plates, and a blanket from the couch to sit on. I was thrilled to get out into the fresh air.

Out front, Aria stood at the edge of the lawn, staring up at the sky. I laid the blanket under our jacaranda tree and set the sandwiches down.

"The doves are up there," Aria said as she pointed to the telephone wire. "Listen."

I sat on the blanket and waited. Seconds later I heard a "coo-oo, coo-coo-coo." Since I always had my record player or radio on, I usually didn't hear them, but next to an owl's hoot, this was the music Aria loved most. I looked at her and smiled as she beamed back at me. "If you watch them, you see their beaks don't open when they sing. They puff up their throats and the sound radiates through their skin. It's so cool." She was truly in her happy place, and I only wished it could be that way for my parents too.

"Here, there's room on the blanket for you," I said.

The dove flew away, making a twittering sound as it rose up and away. "Did you hear that?" Aria said, beaming with her eyes wide. "That sound is from the wind moving through the dove's feathers when it flies. It's like it has a built-in musical instrument."

"Very cool," I said, always surprised with how many bird facts she knew.

Aria kept her eyes on the dove as it flew across the street, and then she came and sat next to me. Without the dove, all I heard were the leaves on the tree above us dancing in the breeze. The sky was a brilliant blue and a sliver of moon could already be seen, winking at us, waiting to appear brightly tonight with a host of stars. The sky often made me wonder about heaven, what it was like. I'd heard it was where everyone was happy. Everything was peaceful. I really wished earth was more like that, a place where I could sing without fear, no one made fun of me or Aria, my parents never fought, violence and shootings weren't a thing.

"Aria, what does that Bible you've been reading say about heaven? Does it really exist?"

"Well, yes it exists. I haven't read everything, but I've read that we get to see Jesus face to face in heaven. I'm excited about that. Jesus loves everyone, North, even the people others don't like. And the Bible says God will wipe every tear from our eyes, and there won't be any more death, sadness or pain in heaven. So, yeah, we definitely want to go there someday."

I remembered the paintings I'd seen of Jesus, with his long brown hair, gentle smile, and the kindest eyes. I imagined him looking at me, telling me he loves me, that he loves Aria, maybe even telling her to chirp louder and flap her arms bigger because that is part of what makes her so awesome. I thought about what it would be like to never see her cry after a long day of school, to never cry myself after being humiliated, to never be sad about how hard life seems sometimes.

"I'll bet heaven is a lot like this," Aria said. "With time to look at the sky and listen for birds, and for sure there's peanut butter in heaven. I love peanut butter. But no one would be allergic to it like my classmate Jordan is, and it wouldn't expire like our jars sometimes do."

I laughed, wondering if heaven would have jars of things like peanut butter, or if it would be more like the movie *Willie Wonka and the Chocolate Factory* with chocolate rivers and candied flowers. "Are you hungry?" I asked. This dreaming of heavenly food was making my stomach growl.

"I'm starving," Aria said. "Let's eat." She sat up, and I handed her a plate. I took a bite of my sandwich, realizing that even though I was never as excited about peanut butter as Aria, this tasted pretty good. The doves were back and continued their calming song, which meant I wouldn't have any problem keeping Aria outside for a while.

Once we finished eating, we stared at the sky a bit longer before Aria announced, "I'm really thirsty. I think I'll go grab a soda. Do you want one?" She stood up and started walking to the door.

"Oh, I can get it. Why don't you stay and listen to the doves?"

"Okay, thanks," she said.

It was oddly quiet when I went inside. No yelling. No talking at all. But I heard someone rummaging around in the garage, and then I heard the opening and closing of drawers from Mom and Dad's bedroom. I crept down the hall and peeked through their doorway. Mom had a suitcase on the bed and she was tossing clothes into it. My stomach felt like a tangled mess of knots.

"Mom? What are you doing?" I asked, fearful of the answer.

She tossed a shirt in the suitcase and looked at me. Her cheeks were wet from tears and she was breathing heavier than normal, like she did when she had to rush to get us out the door or hurry to move things out of our way to get through the crowded living room.

"Your father told you he lost his job, right?"

I couldn't tell if she was mad at me for knowing before her, even though that didn't make much sense. "Uh, yeah, he told me."

She turned to grab another handful of shirts from her dresser drawers and threw them into the suitcase. "Well, I can't do this anymore." She continued to move between the dresser and her luggage, which was now full enough to take a very long trip somewhere. "I need to get out of here, away from him for a bit and figure out how on earth we're going to make ends meet on my measly income if he doesn't find a job that pays at least the small amount he was making at the store."

"Mom, I'm sure he'll find something. Don't leave. That's not going to help him find a job faster." As soon as I said it, I knew I should have kept quiet.

She stopped packing, put her hands on her hips, and said, "North, you don't know that he's going to find anything. It's not that easy. If he can't step away from his junk to get to work on time, how is he going to step away from it and find a job? There are only so many grocery stores around, and if he can't keep a job at one, the store down the street is probably going to find out why. I can't stay and watch him go through this without completely losing my mind. I can't take one more thing. So, I'm out for now."

I felt my breathing match her frantic pace. I knew I was about to cry and that my thoughts about everything she just said wouldn't make things better, but I couldn't hold them in.

"What about me and Aria? Aren't we worth staying for? You can't just leave. It's not fair to any of us. Aria will be devastated." I was rambling and blubbering at the same time—a complete hysterical fool, but Mom at least looked as sad as me now instead of raving mad. Maybe she would change her mind.

She stepped toward me and pulled me into a hug. "North, I'm not leaving you. I'm just taking a break. It's like when you go on a sleepover, or when a parent goes out of town for business, or if they're rich, go on a vacation. I'm coming back, okay?" She continued to hold me close and rubbed my head, like she always did when I was little and couldn't sleep, or fell and got hurt. It made me stop crying in those moments, but this time it only made me cry more knowing this might be the last hug I'd get from her for a while.

"That's what Matthew's dad said when he left," I said.

She pulled away and wiped my tears with her hand. "What do you mean?" she asked.

"When Matthew's dad got angry and left the house a few years ago, he told Matthew he'd be back." I paused and looked into her eyes. "He's still gone."

She kept her eyes locked on mine. "North, I'm not Matthew's dad, okay? I'll come back."

I wanted to believe her. I looked hard into her eyes for any trace of a lie. "Promise?" I asked.

And then I saw it—the small trace of doubt as she lowered her eyes from my stare and pulled me into another hug, no promise spoken.

# Chapter 13

I no longer felt excited that it was summer. Instead of looking forward to days of sleeping in and almost no responsibilities other than my transformation to a new me, I felt sadness and dread. With Mom gone, I would be responsible for everything. Dad wasn't going to pay attention to Aria if he was looking for a job, and he didn't seem that concerned with Mom leaving. When she left to go to her friend Tanya's house, he stayed in the garage, didn't go after her, didn't try to stop her, just remained in his own world of junk.

I watched her say goodbye to Aria, who had no idea that when Mom said she'd be staying at Tanya's for a bit that it was a bad thing.

"Oh, that's fun, Mama! You're having a sleepover. Say hi to Katelyn for me!"

Katelyn was Tanya's daughter, who had been in the same mixed grade classroom as Aria in middle school. I hoped Katelyn would remind Mom of us enough to feel bad and come home soon.

I sat with Aria outside for a long time after Mom left. Then I walked around in a daze the rest of the day and into the evening, doing mindless tasks like organizing the peanut butter jars and cereal boxes. I did them by date, then by brand, then decided to arrange them in a cool structure, then put them back knowing they'd fall down. I folded the pile of towels even though there was no place to neatly put them, and then went back to my room where I plopped onto my pile of clothes on the floor. Without any task to distract me, all I could do was think of Mom and try to believe that she would be back soon. As my eyes began to tear up, Aria bounced into the room with her frozen dinner in hand.

"North, it's seven-thirty. Since Mom is at a slumber party, can we have one too and eat frozen dinners and make popcorn?" She said with a huge smile and wide eyes.

"Sure," I said, shocked at how late it was. I wasn't the slightest bit hungry. "I'll get the dinners started in a little bit. Maybe you can write down some fun bird facts to share with me while you wait."

"Oh, yes! That's a great idea!" she said and bounded out into the living room.

I stared at my pile of clothes, realizing my plan for getting new clothes had to be different now that Dad had lost his job. I picked up a baggy T-shirt, the jeans that were too short on me, the flower-print dress that looked like something a third grader might love. With each item, I tried to imagine how I could make it look better. I'd definitely need to summon up a lot of creativity and sewing skills if that was going to happen. Realizing I hadn't seen Dad since he stared teary-eyed at Mom in the kitchen, I decided to check on him.

"It's a good thing I saved all this stuff," Dad said when I found him in the garage. "We might really need it now." His eyes were still watery, and I remembered as I looked at them that they were the same green color as mine. Mom often said that if his hair were red instead of dark brown, we'd look even more alike with our matching eye color and high cheekbones. I didn't see it, but maybe that was because the idea of looking like my dad didn't sound as good as looking like my beautiful, cool mom.

He sat in the middle of at least ten emptied cardboard boxes and all their contents: baseball cards, tools, toilet paper, comic books and magazines, glass sculptures, unopened Christmas decorations, and enough unsharpened pencils, pink erasers, notebook paper and binders to keep Aria and myself in school through a Ph.D. program.

"What's your plan with all this, Dad?" I asked him.

"Well, I'm going to get it all sorted out by things we can use and things we can sell." He motioned to two piles on each side of him as he said this. "I figure these baseball cards are worth at least a couple months of my salary, and so are the sculptures and comic books, so they're in the 'sell' section. All these other things we can probably use."

A sea of blue North Carolina Tar Heels fan gear caught my eye— shirts, bags, cups, posters, flags, hats—all in the section he'd pointed to as "things we can probably use." This was my first clue that his plan wasn't going to work out. Then I looked around at all the unopened packages and boxes that filled the rest of the garage. There was an awful lot left, and he'd said many times he would sell his things, but it never happened. He only kept collecting more.

"Do you plan to go through all your things this way? Even the stuff in the house?" I asked.

He nodded his head, "Oh, uh, yes. That's my plan, as always."

The "as always" phrase was the final clue confirming his plan wasn't happening. I knew he would carefully admire every item, hold them in his hands, remember the memory or purpose behind them, and then, "as always," he would put every "treasure" back. Their job would be to collect dust and hold the weight of more things. They wouldn't be seen again for a very long time.

"Mom left," I said, hoping on the small chance that he hadn't heard that news and would go beg her to come back.

He didn't look at me, didn't switch gears. He set down a glass sculpture in the "sell" pile and picked up a package of unopened erasers for the "save" pile.

"Yes, she did," he said. "She'll be back."

I wanted to shake him, yell at him to get up and do something. How did he know she'd be back? She wasn't one of his collectibles that he could tuck away and ignore until he was in the mood to pay attention to it. I knew saying something wouldn't help, so I walked away, making sure to slam the door behind me hard enough to cause something leaning against the wall on his side to crash down.

"Darn it, North! Why'd you do that?" I heard him yell. I kept walking.

Aria had fallen asleep on the couch with the spaghetti dinner box in her arms. I didn't have the energy to wake her, so I put a blanket over her and went to bed.

When I woke up the next morning to the bright morning sun streaming through my curtains, I was greeted by a savory smell from the kitchen. Was Dad making breakfast? It didn't really smell like eggs or bacon or toast. It smelled more like pizza or Mom's weekly homemade lasagna, something I'd really miss if Mom stayed away a long time. When it began to smell smoky, it hit me—the spaghetti and meatball frozen dinner.

I jumped out of bed and followed the aroma to find Aria, staring at the oven, a kitchen timer in her hand.

"Aria, what are you doing?"

"Hi North! It's got twelve more minutes left, see?" She held up our old timer that never seemed to work correctly.

I looked at the oven where spaghetti sauce bubbled and splattered. The noodles were brown and crispy. Smoke had begun to waft out from the oven doors.

"Aria, I think it was done a while ago. It's burning."

She turned to the oven. "What? That can't be! I followed the directions exactly as they said!" She opened the oven, peered inside, and started to put her hand in to grab it.

I darted to pull her back. "Aria, you're going to burn yourself!"

But she bumped her fingers on the inside edge of the oven anyway.

"Ahhh! That's hot!" she yelled as she flapped her hand in the air and jumped up and down.

"Oh, Aria, here, put some cool water on it." I turned on the faucet and she hurried over to put her fingers underneath.

She looked at me with wide eyes. "Wow, that stings," she said.

"I know, I'm sorry. Keep them under there for a while, okay?"

She nodded her head and added, "My spaghetti, can you get it out? Is it ruined?"

I was relieved her fingers looked okay, a little pink, but they didn't seem to be burned terribly. The fact that she was more concerned about her food was a hopeful sign.

"I'll check it," I said. I didn't mention to her that there was no way it was going to taste like she'd imagined.

I grabbed the hot pads and pulled the spaghetti out, then set it on the stovetop.

Aria left the sink and stood behind me with the cardboard packaging in her hands. "It doesn't look like the picture," she said. Her pink lips curved down in a sad pout as she switched her gaze from the box to the meal, and then began to tap the box rhythmically on her opposite hand and sway side to side.

I tried to think of what Mom might do in this situation. "Aria, what if I make you a special breakfast instead? Pancakes maybe? Or your favorite cereal?"

Aria looked at me, but it didn't seem to excite her. "I really wanted that spaghetti," she said. "but it looks really gross. Why do they make it look so good on the box? The picture has a heap of noodles and a bunch of big meatballs. Mine only has three tiny meatballs on top of a measly handful of noodles."

The misleading picture with an enlarged version of the meal's contents wasn't something I could fix. I really needed Mom's help. Did she understand how unfair it was to leave me with all this? I tried to imagine that she was only away at work, that things wouldn't be this difficult for long, but the image of her overstuffed suitcase kept taking over.

While I tried to keep from crying or screaming, Aria miraculously stopped wiggling and looked up—her thinking look. "Dad brought more of these home, right?" she asked.

"Yes, there are plenty of them," I said.

"Okay, well, I'm too hungry to wait for another one to cook now, but maybe we can cook one for dinner?"

I breathed a sigh of relief. "Sure, so how about cereal? Cheerios? Frosted Flakes? Rice Krispies?" I motioned to the cereal wall, thankful to have a stack of options at this point.

"Rice Krispies," she responded.

I pulled the box from the collection and set it on the table for her with a bowl, spoon, and orange juice for each of us. We ate to the sound of our crunching and a bit of conversation about birds. I didn't bring up Mom and luckily, Aria didn't either. Once she grabbed her Bible and bird books, I knew I didn't have to worry about her for a while. She could read and draw birds for hours.

I needed to do something to keep my mind off Mom. That pile of clothes would be the perfect distraction. On the way to my room, I noticed the door to Mom and Dad's bedroom was slightly open. I pushed it open a couple more inches, as far as it would go before bumping into something. For a second I thought about how great it would be if Mom had quietly come home in the middle of the night and was asleep next to Dad. But I only saw Dad snoring quietly on the bed, an island in the middle of a wall of boxes, books, cleaning supplies, unopened food packages that hadn't made their way to the kitchen yet, blankets, sheets, towels, clothes, and more. He clearly wasn't claustrophobic, and while I didn't think I was either, their bedroom made me wonder. The lack of free space combined with the earthy smell of mildew from the attached bathroom made me feel breathless and nauseous. I inched my way back into the hallway and closed the door.

Back in my room, I grabbed my scissors, thread, a needle, and attempted to create something from my mess of old, outdated clothes. I was glad Mom had taught me something about sewing, even though I was nowhere near as skilled as she. My stitches were a bit sloppy and uneven, but no one was going to examine me that closely.

A couple hours later, I had transformed boring jeans into bell bottoms by cutting a V shape in the legs and inserting some flowery fabric from that third-grade style dress. I'd also cut another pair of jeans into shorts, cropped two T-shirts to waist level, and set aside the pile of other items with plans to redesign or embellish them throughout the summer. Aria had joined me in my room and began cutting square shapes from clothes I didn't want and couldn't figure how to alter. She planned to sew them into a picnic blanket for our birdwatching trips to the woods.

"I thought it was dumb you were getting rid of all these clothes,"

Aria said, "but now I'm glad. This is going to be awesome." She had started cutting quicker, clearly excited to get to the sewing part. Luckily I wasn't counting on her to sew any of my clothes. While she snipped and laid out her fabric pieces on the floor, I decided it was a good time to work on number two from my list—cutting my hair.

I stood before my mirror, fingering through the thick, wavy strands that fell below my shoulders. I turned my head to one side, then the other, and then brought all my hair forward on each side and clamped it together like I would if I were to make two ponytails.

"Are you thinking about wearing your hair like that, North?" Aria asked. "It reminds me of when you were little and Mom always put your hair in big floppy ponies. She would try to do mine but I always hated it. It hurt my head. You looked so cute, though."

I wished it were still that easy to be cute. Ponytails definitely wouldn't do that anymore. "I think I'm going to cut it pretty short, Aria."

She dropped her scissors, and said, "What?" She looked more scared than she did when she burned herself. "Why would you do that?" She put her hands on top of her head and smoothed them through her long auburn hair.

I looked back into the mirror. "I need something different, Aria. My hair isn't smooth and straight like yours. It's too frizzy and poofy." I went to my desk and opened the drawer where I had saved pictures of different hairstyles. I flipped through and found the one I had imagined for myself. The photo torn from a magazine showed a bright smiling girl with wavy curls like mine, but they were short, cut at chin level and pulled away from her face with a scarf tied up into a headband. She looked amazing.

"I like this." I held it up to show Aria.

She came and held the photo next to my face. I watched her eyes move from the photo to me several times until she finally nodded her head with approval. "Hmm, yeah, it might work. I think you're perfect as you are, North, but if you want a change, you should do it."

I really wished the entire world was as good for my ego as her. "Thanks, Aria." I taped the photograph to my mirror and began my transformation. I started snipping tiny centimeters at a time, and eventually became braver, cutting more with each snip. When my final strands were at chin level, I attempted to add some layers, and then cut more to even it out. It was shorter than I intended.

Aria's first response was, "Why'd you make it so short?"

I could always count on her honesty.

"Aria, I didn't mean to, but I was trying to make it more even."

"Maybe you shouldn't have cut it, like I said in the beginning."

I stared at myself, trying to figure out how to look less like a boy, or at least slightly prettier than before, but the more I looked at myself, the more I realized it was hopeless, and that's when I lost it.

I sat on my bed, put my head between my legs, and let it all out. I felt Aria's arm on my back, and heard her tell me it was no big deal. It was just hair that would grow back. But the tears I cried weren't only about my hair. Those clippings of hair on the carpet in front of me were one more thing I had hoped to make better and had failed. I thought of Mom. If she were home, maybe she would have cut my hair and made it look pretty. Maybe she would have helped me sew my clothes. Maybe she would tell me things were going to be okay. But instead, she was absent, and I was left trying to hold everything together while it all crumbled and fell apart.

"You could always wear a hat, North, and it really doesn't look bad. It's just different."

Different. The thing I was trying NOT to be. I wiped my tears and stared at my list on the floor in front of me. The words I'd written the largest shouted out to me—CHANGE NAME.

Looking at Aria, knowing she wouldn't understand but would still listen, I said, "I need you to call me Carol."

# Chapter 14

Mom didn't come home that evening, or the next, or the one after that. She called, told us she needed more time on her own, and picked us up one day a week to have lunch. Sometimes she made sandwiches and we'd sit at the park. Other times we'd go to McDonald's or the local deli, which felt like a treat since we hardly ever ate in restaurants. I think the last time we'd been out to eat was when it had been Mom's birthday back in February, and Dad had saved up money to surprise her. It was nice except Mom kept changing her mind on what to order based upon how much it cost.

Now that it was August, her birthday seemed like forever ago. Even though things weren't exactly great then, they were better than now. Each day Mom wasn't home, Aria and Dad became increasingly unsettled. As I predicted, Dad never got rid of anything, and since he hadn't found a new job yet, he had plenty of time to start building an extra room on the backend of the garage for more storage space. Aria would have some sort of meltdown late morning, then again in the evening, and even when she was in a pretty decent mood at night, she was often so wound up that she couldn't sleep. Dad and I had each caught her trying to sneak out the front door for the woods in the middle of the night. After the third time it happened, I no longer slept soundly. On her really bad nights, when I figured she'd try to sneak out, I slept on the couch where I could easily hear the front door unlatch. I really missed a good night's sleep.

I spent my days wishing Ronnie and Matthew were around. I'd only spoken with each of them for a couple short phone calls, in which I told them Mom had left and didn't seem to be coming back soon. Even though they couldn't do anything about it, they each assured me I wasn't crazy to feel so overwhelmed by everything, and that made me feel a little better. Since the calls weren't very long, my transformation to cool Carol hadn't been fully revealed yet either. I'd only mentioned my haircut.

"I wish I could see it," Ronnie said on the phone one day. "I'll bet it looks great."

Matthew was also encouraging. "I can't picture you with short hair, but I know I'll like it."

Dad kept telling me he couldn't get used to it, and Mom said it was cute but I couldn't tell if she was being honest. She also said that if I liked it, no one else's opinions really mattered. While I wanted to agree, I still felt unsure of myself. That was probably the part of me I wanted to change the most, and while I'd hoped the new look and name change would have accomplished that, I still cared too much what other people thought. Dahlia had been out in front of her house one day when Aria and I walked by, but I made sure to look away from her and positioned myself on the opposite side of Aria so Dahlia couldn't get a clear view of me. My only positive experience as Carol had been with people who didn't know me. They didn't say anything about my name or my hair or my clothes, and it didn't seem like they stared at me, so I hoped that meant I at least didn't look weird.

My best days of summer were when Aria and I went to the woods, even on the hottest days, when the temperature was near 100 degrees. The high temperatures usually meant most people weren't there, so we could be ourselves and not worry about anyone bothering us. I could sing as loud as I wanted with my favorite fan, Aria, there to make me feel like a superstar, and Aria could observe birds, mimic their sounds, and read every possible fact about them. We always brought a sheet to hang on the tree as a shade covering or a hammock, a blanket to sit on, along with snacks, drinks, and whatever items we needed to stay entertained all day. For me, that meant some paper to write songs and lyrics, and for Aria it was her usual bag of bird books, her Bible, bird seed, and anything else she gathered for attracting birds, like leaves and sticks for them to build nests even though the woods provided plenty of that naturally.

"You know there are plenty of items for the birds to build nests without your help, right Aria?" I said one day as she kept picking up the leaves that fell from her bag while we walked to the woods.

She shoved a leaf into her bag and gave me a look that exclaimed, *Yes, I know, I'm not stupid,* followed by "I'm bringing these leaves for us, North, like I told you before, in case we stay too long and need the leaves as covering to keep us warm in the cold."

"Aria, it hasn't dropped below eighty degrees in weeks. You do realize we're in the heat of summer, right?"

Again, the *I'm not dumb* look. "It's hot now, but if we climbed the cliffs and stayed to see the owls one night it could get cold. This is in case we need it then, North, okay?"

"Right, got it," I said, knowing I'd better agree or hear another very long explanation of the value of leaves for body temperature survival. I also ignored the fact that she called me North. Telling her to call me Carol every time she forgot hadn't helped her anxiety, which was amping up in her quest to control her leaf collection.

She shoved her hand into the bag to squish the leaves down further, but with the bag filled to its limits, this only caused several leaves to spill out the sides. She threw the bag to the ground. More leaves tumbled out. She grabbed them one at a time and shoved them into the bag in rhythm to her exclamations: "Why? Won't? These? Stupid? Leaves? Stay?" With each leaf in, another popped out. Her face turned red, she was out of breath, she started to cry.

"Aria," I said as I looked around in hopes that no one was around to see this. Glad to not see anyone, I said louder, "Aria."

She kept gathering and shoving and crying, completely ignoring my voice.

"Aria!" I finally shouted and leaned in closer so she could see me.

She looked at me, threw herself on the ground on top of her bag of leaves, and sobbed.

I didn't want to sing at that moment. I wanted to tell her to get over it, to stop her tantrum over something so ridiculous, but I knew that wouldn't work. So I sang. With each note, she became quieter, then eventually stood back up as I helped her pick up the rest of the leaves, and we continued walking.

With the late morning meltdown over, I could look forward to several more hours of relative calm, but I wished I had more energy to enjoy it. By the time we arrived at our big oak tree, I was drenched in sweat and glad Aria had that sheet to give us more shade than what the tree provided. She dropped her bag and sat on a nearby rock to catch her breath. "It's really hot," she said. "We're definitely going to need more shade."

I nodded my head, too breathless to respond aloud. After a few sips of water from our thermos, we held the sheet at opposite ends and began to tie it across the tree branches. When we were done, we had a shade spot big enough to cover the two of us. I laid out a blanket and sat down. Aria gazed around for a few moments, then stopped to peer through her binoculars at the tall cliffs, took a big sigh like she was disappointed she didn't see anything, and sat down beside me. The birds near us were quite active in spite of the heat, flitting from branch to branch and pecking at the dirt. One bird sat a few yards in front of us and flapped its wings excitedly, shaking up little plumes of dirt. Watching them actually helped me feel a lot better.

"That's funny. What is that bird doing?" I asked.

"Oh, it's taking a dust bath," Aria said. "Birds do that when they don't have water nearby to keep their feathers in good condition. The dirt absorbs excess oil so the feathers don't become greasy or matted."

"Huh, that's interesting. Too bad we can't do that with our hair. We'd save a lot of money on shampoo and conserve a lot of water."

"Well, you could probably do it if you wanted to," Aria said. "But yeah, it wouldn't work so well on hair." We continued to be entertained by the dust-bath bird as the birds in the tree sang louder and louder. "This doesn't make much sense, but sometimes I think the birds might be talking to God. They can't have that much to say to each other," Aria said while looking up at the bird choir above.

"Really?" I smiled. "What do you think they're telling him?"

Aria turned her head and closed her eyes for a moment to listen. "I'm not sure. Maybe they're asking for food and stuff to make their nests? Maybe protection? Whatever they say, it seems to work. They're never worried."

She pulled her Bible out of her bag, flipped through the pages and said, "Aha, here it is in Matthew 6:26—'*Look at the birds of the air; they do not sow or reap or store away in barns, and yet your heavenly Father feeds them. Are you not much more valuable than they?'"* She paused, looked at me. "So, they don't do what Dad does, saving a bunch of stuff in case they need it, and look how happy they are."

This was Aria's way of saying she knew Dad was miserable. I wished she would have thought of that verse when she was losing all her leaves, and I hoped I could remember it in the future. Sometimes that was the hard part about Bible verses for me, remembering them when needed.

"Maybe Dad will figure out how to be happy one day, Aria," I said, not totally sure I believed it myself.

"And Mom too," she said. "She seems really sad."

I looked at that peppy, dirt-bathed sparrow who had joined three others on a branch, beaks in the air, chirping loudly. I joined in with a song of my own while Aria bobbed and swayed along. Whether the birds were talking to God or not, they certainly had the right idea. Singing made these long hot days of worrying about Mom, Dad, and the start of school a lot more tolerable.

# Chapter 15

On the last day of summer I awoke at six to the horrible ringing of my alarm clock. I slammed my hand onto the metal button to turn it off and rolled back onto my pillow. I'd thought it would be a good idea to get up early and get things ready for the first day of school. What a terrible plan. In the two months since Mom left, Aria had been interrupting my sleep with all her late night energy. I kept hoping it would get better, but it only seemed to be getting worse. I closed my eyes to catch a little more sleep, but my mind was filled with everything I had to do—organize supplies, make lunches, and most importantly, try out my new look.

My room had turned into a sort of fashion design workshop all summer with clothes I had trimmed, stitched, or embellished to look new. I'd placed different outfits on the floor and now had to decide which new ensemble to choose for day one. I wanted to choose something that would keep me cool in the blistering heat, as well as something that didn't remind anyone of who I was in middle school—awkward, boring, insecure, uncool. The cutoff denim shorts, cut from jeans that had become embarrassingly short as I grew taller, caught my eye first, and then, the two cropped T-shirts that used to hang sloppily below my hips. One shirt was a bright yellow, and the other I had tie-dyed in pink and purple. I held up the yellow one, thinking the gold and turquoise paisley scarf I found in Mom's dresser drawer would be the perfect accessory as a wrap around my head. I put everything on and glanced in the mirror. I wasn't thrilled with the fact that my bare tummy showed more now than when I originally shortened the shirt. I pulled at the bottom in an effort to stretch it longer. If I didn't stand up too straight, the bare skin barely stayed covered. I fluffed my hair a little around the scarf, and decided I'd need to figure out what earrings would look cool.

My door opened wide and Aria came bounding in. "Oh, hey, that's one of your new outfits, isn't it?" She asked cheerfully. Apparently the late nights hadn't caught up with her yet.

"Yes, it is. I'm planning to wear this to school tomorrow. What do you think?" I turned to face her.

She eyed me up and down and said, "I think it looks good, even though the shorts show a lot of leg. Are you sure that's going to be comfortable? If I wore shorts like that, I'd hate the way my legs would feel against everything I sat in."

"Yes, I'm sure I'll be comfortable," I said, glad her comment about showing leg wasn't a judgment of how I looked in short shorts. "Do you know what you're wearing?"

"Uh, I haven't really thought about it, but I usually don't need to figure it out the day before. I just grab what's clean and comfortable in the morning."

"Well, maybe you should make sure you don't need anything washed. I don't want to run around looking for stuff in the morning." The minute that blurted out, I knew I sounded too much like Mom.

"I'm really hungry. How about we eat breakfast?" she asked.

"Okay, but first, check your closet. I'll make us something while you do that."

"Fine," she said with a pout and slumped shoulders, "but please don't give me cereal if we're going to have that again for dinner." She trudged back to her room and I realized we had been eating a lot of cereal for dinner. It was so easy, and I never felt like making anything by the time the evening rolled around.

I kept my outfit on, knowing Aria would be quick and expect food soon. In the kitchen, I searched for anything easy other than cereal. I put some bread in the toaster, grabbed peanut butter, poured orange juice, and put water on for tea.

"Okay, got my outfit." I heard Aria say as I stood waiting for the toast to pop up. She had changed out of her pajamas and into a pair of light blue, burgundy, and brown plaid culottes with an oversized lime green T-shirt with a large eagle on the front.

"Oh, cool," I said, even though "cool" wasn't what I truly thought about the outfit. I thought about explaining that the tie-dye and plaid didn't really go well together, that maybe she should choose one of those and match with something plain, but decided it wasn't worth it. She knew what she was wearing. That was good enough.

While we sat at the kitchen table eating our toast and peanut butter, I asked, "So, what do you want for lunch tomorrow? I'm going to pack our lunches today so we're not rushing around in the morning. I think it'll take us about ten minutes to walk to the high school, so we should leave here around seven. I want to be early on the first day."

"I hate lunch time at school," Aria said after swallowing a bite and gulping a sip of orange juice. "Everyone says it's supposed to be a break, but for me it feels like the hardest work of the day. Everyone is so loud, and people bump into me, and some people have food that smells really gross. Sometimes I can't find a place to sit. I'd rather be in class with my teachers who are usually really nice. At least this year, you'll be there. I can always sit with you at lunch."

I nodded to her, but to myself the thought brought a terrible sense of dread. As much as I loved her, I really wanted people to get to know me apart from my sister, and while I hated to admit it, I also needed a break from her.

"Should we plan a meeting place for lunch?" Aria continued. "That would be best. It gets so chaotic on the quad and in the cafeteria. Maybe we could meet in front of the library. Is that good for you? What class do you have before lunch? I could meet you there." Aria blurted out her thoughts with the same energy as the birds we saw yesterday hopping from branch to branch, chirping and chasing each other.

"Aria, I get to see you every day at home. Wouldn't you rather sit with some of your friends?"

She crossed her arms in front of her chest and peered at me with a pouty face. "No, I wouldn't. I don't really have any friends. You're like my best friend."

A weight of guilt landed in my stomach. Here I was asking for a break while she was looking forward to being with me. I didn't know what to say back to her so I said nothing. I stood up to clear our plates and was stopped from taking hers when she shoved my hand out of the way.

"I can get it," she said as she glared at me.

"Oh, okay," I said, hoping it would end with that. I kept my eyes on her for a moment, trying to decide if I should walk away or sit down and try to change the subject. My hesitation and continued silence only made things worse.

"Why don't you want to have lunch with me? Who are you going to eat lunch with? Matthew and Ronnie? I bet they would eat lunch with me."

I sat down. "Aria, of course they would. They really like you, and you're my sister, so you know I love you, but I just think we should have some things we do separately, and I really want high school to go well."

"Well, obviously you do. So do I, North!" She pushed herself back from the table and stood up, grabbed her plate and dropped it in the sink with a loud clash.

"Aria, calm down, okay? You're going to break something." I rose from my seat to make sure the dish hadn't chipped, but stopped when I saw Aria flapping her hands, then smacking her wrists together. "I didn't break anything, North. Or should I call you Carol? I hate that name. It's a stupid name. Why can't you still be North? When you were North you had lunch with me, but now that you're Carol, you don't. I hate how everything is different!"

This was not how I wanted this to go. "God, how do I fix this?" I whispered. I hadn't exactly meant that as a prayer, but I miraculously got an idea. A rosy-cheeked, freckled face popped into my mind.

"Aria, what about Katelyn? She starts high school this year. She's probably nervous about starting, and I'm sure she'd want to sit with you. Why don't you call her and arrange it?"

Aria relaxed her shoulders, slowed her hands, and said, "Oh, hmm, I forgot about her."

I breathed a slight sigh of relief. She was calming down, and she looked like she liked this idea.

"I don't have Katelyn's phone number," Aria said, disappointment back on her face.

"Mom is staying at Katelyn's mom's house, remember? We do have her number," I said.

"Oh, right!" she exclaimed. "I'm going to call her right now!" She headed to the shelf by the garage door where we kept the phone, and picked it up, but after putting the receiver to her ear, she pulled it away with a confused look. "There's no sound," she said. "Is it plugged in?"

I saw the cord plugged into the phone jack on the wall, and checked to make sure it was connected into the phone itself. "Yep, it's plugged in. Let me listen," I said. Hearing nothing, I unplugged the cord from the wall, pushed it firmly back in, hung up the phone and held it to my ear again. Still nothing. "Huh, it's not working, Aria. Maybe Dad has another phone laying around somewhere. I'll go ask him."

Dad was hammering away at the frame of his new room addition, which was attached to the back end of the garage facing the backyard.

I entered the stifling hot garage and peered out the side door. "Dad?" I shouted. "Our phone isn't working. Do we have another one?" I wondered for a second if that was something most people would even bother to ask. I was guessing most people would assume they needed to go buy a new one, but at our house, there seemed to always be a chance that more than one of everything existed.

He climbed down from a ladder, wiped sweat from his forehead and said, "No, that phone is the only one we've got. Is it plugged in?"

After telling him it was, he came in and checked it himself. Then he stormed into the living room to grab a box filled with mail, rummaged through it, and finally pulled out two envelopes with glaring red "Past due" stamps on them. Apparently, the bill hadn't been paid.

"I don't have the money to pay this until I get my unemployment check next week," he said. "You'll have to live without a phone for a bit." He threw the envelopes back in the box along with all the other papers he'd scattered on the floor, then walked past Aria and me with his head down, unaware of the inner turmoil clearly expressed on Aria's face.

Her mouth hung open, and her eyes stared widely at him as he passed, and then she said, "We don't have a phone? How long? How am

I supposed to talk to Mom about Katelyn? And what if we have an emergency and need to call 911? What do we do then? We need a phone, Dad!"

As much as I wanted to calm her down by saying we'd be fine without one, I couldn't. Aria was right.

Dad had stopped midstride, and turned slowly to look at Aria. His head jutted slightly forward as he gave her a hard stare, and his lips stayed curled down as he said, "Aria, I don't have a choice, okay? If there's an emergency, you can borrow a neighbor's phone, and if you need to talk to your mom, I guess you'll need to wait for her to come home like most moms do. That's what we really need—your mom, not a darn phone."

He turned back around and swung the garage door open wide as he exited and slammed the door behind him. His words, *what we really need—your mom*, echoed in my head. Why would he say that? Did he think we didn't know that? Did he think saying that was helpful in some way? It wasn't. It only made things worse. I suddenly felt horribly isolated and vulnerable, like all the possible bad things might happen and we wouldn't be able to make a call for help or talk to Mom if we needed her.

Aria marched over to the phone, picked up the receiver, and yelled into it, "Ahhhhh! Stupid phone!" She dropped the receiver to the ground. It hung limp from its cord, grazing the floor, clearly showing its brokenness along with ours. We both stared at it, and then looked at each other. Without speaking a word out loud, I knew she was thinking the same thing as me—that poor phone wasn't the problem.

"It is a stupid phone," I said. "But life right now is even stupider."

"Stupider isn't a word," Aria said.

I didn't want a grammar lesson at that moment. "Well, it should be. I like it. I think I'm going to start using it more often. Stupider, stupider,

stupider!" I yelled. It felt good. I was sick of trying to be patient and nice, shoving down all my frustration to keep everyone else calm while it all boiled up inside me.

Aria joined me, "Stupider, stupider, stupider!"

I went to pick up the phone, held it in front of both of us as we yelled, "Stupider!"

I hung the phone back up, looked at Aria, a smile forming on her face as she began to chuckle, and then I started laughing too. The thought of letting out all our frustration on a phone seemed pretty ridiculous, but it had also managed to help us feel a little better.

"How about we go visit Matthew?" I said. "I need to talk to him about our plan to walk to school tomorrow, and I'll bet we can use his phone to call Mom."

Her eyes lit up and she smiled bright. "That sounds great. I always like visiting with Matthew. I've missed him and Ronnie."

"Me too," I said. I felt a flutter in my stomach at the thought of Matthew, remembering he hadn't seen my new look. I knew he'd be my friend no matter what, but I was nervous about whether he'd like it, a new feeling I hadn't had before.

I was too frustrated to talk to Dad, so I left him a note saying where we were going. Then I slipped on my rubber flip flops with the colorful striped soles that made me feel like summer wasn't ending, and we headed over to Matthew's. Even though it was only seven-thirty in the morning, it was already hot. The birds were fully awake, chirping and flitting from tree to tree, eating seeds from the lawns we passed. I wasn't obsessed with birds like Aria, but I could see why she liked them. Their playful, busy activity made me feel like I should be that way too.

Aria stepped in front of me as we reached Matthew's door and knocked enthusiastically. Luckily his mom was always up early for work or this would have been kind of rude. Moments later, Matthew appeared, looking taller and handsomer than ever.

Aria greeted him with a loud, "Hi, Matthew! There's a big bright blue jay in your tree! Come see!" She grabbed his arm before he could respond.

He stopped for a second as Aria tugged on his arm and looked at me with a wide smile. "Woah! You look totally different! Nice hair!" he said.

"Come on, Matthew! You can look at her all day. The bird might fly away." Aria tugged him away and I stood back, resisting the urge to grab him back in my direction to give him a big hug. I now realized how much I'd missed seeing him.

Aria held Matthew captive under the giant sycamore tree on his lawn, rambling on about blue jays for about five minutes before I said, "Hey, Aria, do you want to see if you can use Matthew's phone to call Mom?"

"Oh, Yeah! Is that okay, Matthew? Our dad can't pay the bill so our phone isn't working."

So much for keeping our family finances private.

"Oh, sure," he said, like it was no big deal.

Aria walked ahead of us, not afraid to enter Matthew's home as if it were her own. I felt Matthew's eyes on me, and looked over to see him smiling while he stared and nodded his head. "I really like the look," he said. "Very cool."

My face felt instantly warm. "Thanks," I said.

"Yeah, it's crazy that summer is already over, right? I'm not happy to start school, but I'm glad to be home. If long distance calls weren't so expensive we could have talked more, you know? So, tell me what's up. What inspired the new look? Were you just bored without me around?" He smiled and nudged me with his elbow.

"Ha! Yes, life is definitely less exciting without you." I thought of telling him it was pretty miserable without him, but instead said, "I changed my look because I'm tired of how people view me, the girl who's lame and weird, afraid to sing. I don't want to be that girl anymore. I figured a new look could help me be different."

He nodded his head, smiled slightly, and said, "I get it, even though you're not weird and lame." He leaned back against the sycamore tree, and I realized as I stared back at him how much I really missed being with him. No matter how I acted or who I tried to be, he always made me feel like I was going to be okay.

"Well, thanks, I know you don't think I am, but most everyone else seems to. And I didn't tell you when I talked to you on the phone, but I'm taking on a new name too."

"A new name?" He glanced at me sideways, clearly confused.

"Yeah, Carol. No one makes fun of it, plus it's the same name as my favorite singer, which you know."

"Ah, right, Carole King. So you are now Carol Simon?

"Yep, Carol Simon. No more North or North Carolina jokes for me."

He squinted his eyes like he was trying to figure me out. "Well, that's going to take some getting used to, but if that's what you really want, I'll do my best to call you Carol."

"Thanks, Matthew. I knew I could count on you, and I think Ronnie will be cool with it. The hard part will be getting everyone else who knew me before high school to go along with it and not make an even bigger deal out of my name."

"Who cares what they say and think, North, I mean, Carol. Just be confident and don't act bothered. They'll give up hassling you if you don't act like you care."

"Well, most will, but you know there are some people who won't, like Dahlia."

"Oh, well Dahlia is the worst. She will definitely give you a hard time, but that's only because she's jealous of you. You should take it as a compliment that she hates you so much."

I definitely didn't think Dahlia was jealous of me, but the thought made me feel a little better about the situation. If I could fake being cool, maybe I could fake that too. Thinking of Dahlia made me also think of Ricky, and how he treated Matthew. "You never seem to be that bothered when people are mean to you, like Ricky. How do you do that?" I asked him.

He crossed his arms and shook his head, "I think it's pretty clear from the past two encounters with Ricky that he bothers me. Shoving someone to the ground usually means you've had it."

"True," I said, "but after, you seemed fine, confident."

"I have to be that way. I can't let him get me down. My family has taught me that. Remember that shootout at my aunt's house?"

I nodded.

"I was so worried about her, and I was mad too, that she and my cousins were in danger, told her I wished she still lived by us where it seems safer. She told me to stop. She said this world can be a bad place, but God is stronger. She told me to keep my head up, that God has a plan that we don't always understand, but we have to trust him."

"Wow, that's brave," I said. "Sounds a little like something Aria might say."

"Yep, it does. That's probably why I like that girl. She doesn't have it easy, but she's got a pretty good attitude most of the time."

As if to prove this point true, Aria burst back outside through Matthew's front door. "Hey, guess what? I talked to Katelyn! "Mom put her on the phone and we decided to meet in front of the library in the morning before we get our schedules and again at lunch time. Now you can sit wherever you want, North. I don't need you to sit with me."

"Oh, that's great, Aria. I knew she'd like to hang out with you."

"Yeah, some people like me, North." She plopped down on the front step and looked up. "Did the blue jay fly away? I don't see him anymore."

Matthew looked at me and whispered, "Did you tell her you wouldn't sit with her at lunch?"

"I told her I thought we should sit with other people during lunch since we're together all the time."

He gave me a suspicious glance, then looked over at Aria. "I like you, Aria."

She smiled big. "I like you too, Matthew."

The blue jay swooped down and landed on the lawn. It turned its head from side to side, then pecked at the grass. Two sparrows flitted down, then another and another. They hopped along the walkway, chirping like they were talking to each other. When the blue jay saw them, she lifted up and flew away while we all watched her, a brilliant, soaring beauty, alone in the sky.

# Chapter 16

Even with my best efforts to prepare for the first day of high school, I still felt terrified. I woke up at 4:45, long before my alarm was set to go off, and couldn't get back to sleep. I laid in bed and thought of the day ahead, the former classmates I might see who knew me before I decided to be cool Carol instead of nerdy, nobody North. I pictured the look on Dahlia's face when she saw me, and imagined it the same as always, one of disgust. But then I pictured it turning to one of surprise. Maybe she would look me up and down and walk away knowing she'd better not say anything mean because I was clearly on the path to becoming popular. I also pictured seeing that boy who told me I had a nice voice on the last day of eighth grade. Maybe I'd finally find out his name, and maybe we'd become friends.

I got out of bed, took a long shower, dressed, styled my hair three times, applied my makeup using all the best tips from *Seventeen* magazine, and finished half a piece of toast. I was way ahead of schedule. It was still only six-fifteen.

I stepped into Aria's room. She was sound asleep on top of her covers, still in the clothes she picked out yesterday, mouth wide open, breathing deep. Those late nights with little sleep had caught up to her on the worst day possible. I nudged her and told her it was time to get up. She opened her eyes part way and mumbled, "You must be kidding. It's barely even light out yet. I'm staying in bed." She rolled over and pulled her comforter over her head.

"Uh, no, Aria. You can't go back to sleep. Maybe you can take a shower to wake up, and I'll get you breakfast. We need to leave early today, remember? We're walking to school, and we need to pick up our class schedule. Matthew will be here in 45 minutes to walk with us."

"I don't need a shower. I need sleep. Mom or Dad can take me to school later," she mumbled.

"Aria, Dad's asleep, and you know Mom isn't here, so you have to walk with me. You can't go later." I tried to pull the comforter off her head, but she held it tight. "Come on, Aria," I said, nudging her again.

"Ugghhh! I need to sleep, North! Leave me alone!" She yelled as she popped out from the covers.

I was not prepared for this. This was not my job. I missed Mom for a lot of reasons, and this was now at the top.

"Fine, Aria, if you want to lay in bed and stay home all day by yourself that's your problem. I'm not responsible for you. I'll either see you soon or see you after school."

I walked out of her room, slammed the door behind me and then let out a loud shout. "Ahhhhhh! I hate my life right now! Can't I just live the life of a normal teen?" So much for remembering how hard things were for Aria. They seemed too hard for me.

I returned to the kitchen, determined to keep moving so I wouldn't sit and stew about Aria and everything else that made me angry. I pulled the lunches from the fridge, set out my notebook, checked that all my folders were labeled for each subject, and that I had enough pencils and pens. Then I paced back and forth a few times while thinking of what needed to be done next. Once Aria was up, she'd need to eat. I set out a box of Hostess mini donuts and a glass of orange juice. Donuts weren't the healthiest choice, but they were too good to pass up, something I knew Aria would eat, and we had ten boxes of them. I popped one in my mouth and was surprised next by Aria's voice behind me.

"I'm here. Don't leave without me."

I turned around to see a slightly more awake Aria, hair a mess, clothes wrinkled, but her birdwatching bag, shoes and socks in hand.

"I'll take one of those donuts if there's time," she said. "Sorry I got you so mad."

As usual, I couldn't stay mad at her. "It's okay. I get it. I don't want to go to school either, but let's try and make the best of it. These donuts definitely help. I grabbed another one and handed Aria the box. "You have time to sit down and eat, and I poured you some juice."

Aria nodded, her cheeks bulging with a mouthful of donut. She set the box down, grabbed her juice, and guzzled it down. "I'm ready now. I'll wait outside for Matthew and watch for birds. I'm thinking that woodpecker I've been wanting to see again might be up now." She headed to the front door.

"You might want to put your shoes on while you wait," I said.

"Okay!" she yelled, already halfway out the door. It was amazing how she could go from completely grumpy to excited, all because she looked forward to seeing a bird. I should have told her the birds were awake when she argued with me earlier. I tucked that away in my mind for later.

After clearing Aria's glass and returning the box of remaining donuts in the stack with the others, I was relieved to see it was 6:45. In fifteen minutes, Matthew would arrive and we could start this day. I went to my room to get my jacket, slipped it on, and checked in the mirror one last time. I definitely didn't feel like the prettiest girl on earth, but I thought I at least looked more like everyone else who mattered. I was glad I had found the jacket in Dad's closet. It was a soft brown suede with fringed tassels that hung on the front chest and along the sleeves. It was a little big on me, but I liked it. I remembered Dad wearing it when I was little, when he used to still play his guitar. It used to remind me of something a cowboy might wear, but now I thought it looked like something rock stars and hippies wore, and with the feathered earrings from Mom, I felt pretty cool.

Outside, the air was still cool, but I knew that wouldn't last. Aria had settled onto the lawn with her bird book open in front of her as she peered through her binoculars. She made a small chirping sound that was followed by the same sound in the tree seconds later. I wished I could let her be there all day. This was truly her happy place.

I stood next to her and put her lunch in her bag. She turned her head and peered at me through her binoculars. "Woah, those earrings look great on you!" she said. "You remind me of Mom with those and the funky clothes."

I wasn't sure that was a compliment. "I'm not really trying to look like Mom, but I'm glad you think I look good." I grasped one of the feathers between my fingertips. I loved the way it felt, smooth and soft. It would be a good distraction at school whenever I felt uptight, sort of like the way petting a dog or cat magically calmed nerves. If it were easier to pet birds, they'd probably get a lot more attention.

A boisterous chatter chimed from the tree as several birds darted to a new branch. Aria instantly followed their movement and giggled as they continued to play a game of chase from branch to branch. I hoped she'd keep that cheery mood once I told her we needed to leave for school.

Gazing past the tree, I saw Matthew making his way down the sidewalk in front of our house. His slow amble let me know he wasn't exactly excited about this first day of school. He had his hands in the pockets of black denim jeans and wore a blue and white striped polo shirt. Both pieces looked new and I wondered if he or his mom had picked them out. They were both fashionable all the time. One morning his mom apologized to me for looking sloppy when she was still in her pajamas, but I thought she looked perfectly put together in her matching pink flannel set.

"Hey, you look thrilled to be up and about," I said.

He smiled his handsome grin back. "Oh yeah, I'm really happy about this day. You look amazing. I like the earrings," he said, making me feel both thrilled that he thought that and bad that I hadn't said anything nice about his obvious good looks.

"They're my mom's," I said. "She made a bunch of them to sell at craft fairs." Touching one of them as I said this didn't instantly calm me like I'd hoped, but it did give me something to do with my hands rather than fidget with them awkwardly. I usually felt so relaxed around Matthew, but I wasn't used to him noticing my looks so much. I didn't know what to do with that.

"Cool," he said. He glanced over at Aria. "Hey Aria, you ready for today?"

She kept her binoculars to her face and aimed them at him. "Wow! Your eyelashes are really long! I never noticed that before," she said. "They're like Dahlia's, but hers are only like that because they're smothered in fifteen coats of mascara. You both have brown eyes too, but yours are so much nicer."

Matthew and I burst out in laughter.

"Wow, you actually remember Dahlia's eye color?" Matthew asked.

"Yeah, she was totally in my face that day I offered her leaves and she told me she didn't want any of my junk. Her eyes felt like they were stabbing me with meanness."

As much as Matthew and I could laugh about Dahlia, we both knew how horrible she made people feel when she didn't like them. She really was one of the people I was dreading today and the person I most wished wasn't in any of my classes.

"Well, we should get going. Come on, Aria. I'll bet you'll see some cool birds on our walk." I hoped that would work, and fortunately, it did.

"Oh, I bet you're right! I usually don't get to see the birds on the way to school when we're driving. This actually might be kind of fun!" She slammed her book shut and grabbed her bag. Then she was off in front of us, eyes to the sky, reminding me of what she'd said over the summer about being more like the birds. They didn't worry, and God took care of them. When Aria wasn't anxious, she could do all kinds of things, like dash down the street with her head up, not watching where she was going, and miraculously not trip or bump into anything.

Aria's speed walk soon slowed as she stopped to observe any bird that caught her attention. In spite of having to stop several times to wait for her to catch up with us, we managed to make it even earlier than I'd planned. Matthew and I stood at the corner of Elm Road and Birch Avenue, with Aria still trailing behind us. While we waited to cross over to the high school, I felt that first day panic rise in me. There were so many kids coming from every possible direction. At least twenty headed toward us from the corner to the right, and on the opposite corner from them, the same size crowd crossed over to the school. When the light turned for us to cross, our small crowd now spilling part way onto the street, I heard Aria behind me. "Hey! Wait! I dropped my binoculars! Don't step on them! Wait!"

I turned around to look for her, but she was hidden by my fellow schoolmates pushing their way forward, some glancing back at Aria's yell, but none stopping. Matthew looked at me and turned back to help her.

"Hey, it's you, the girl with the pretty voice." And there he was, walking next to me with his bright blue eyes and blond hair, the boy who noticed my voice, and there was me, walking right alongside him, too lost in his attention to stop for anything, even my sister.

# Chapter 17

"Hey," I said, "It's the boy with the bike, but, obviously without the bike today." As soon as those words came out, I felt like my old awkward self. Couldn't I have come up with anything better than that to say?

"Yep, that's me," he said, smiling and still staring at me with those gorgeous eyes. Maybe he hadn't noticed how dumb I sounded. "You think whoever was shouting back there is okay?" He glanced backward for a second.

"Oh, yeah, I'm sure everything's fine. Maybe just some first day nerves. Seems like they're fine now." I picked up my pace a little, hoping there was plenty of distance between us and Aria. I didn't want this opportunity to get to know this boy to be ruined. The dream I'd had for so long, of being noticed for me, and even better than that, for my voice, had finally come true.

We'd reached the opposite side of the street and continued walking with the pack of students to the front gate. Once we entered, I felt like the smallest creature on the planet, a tiny little ant in a jungle of bigger and better creatures. A cluster of chatty, laughing girls in colorful shirts, shiny long hair, and long tanned legs stood by the cafeteria. A pod of boys with shaggy hair and faded jeans huddled near them, shouting loudly and glancing at the girls, clearly begging for their attention. All across the grassy quad were clusters of people, sprinkled with the obvious loners who stood and stared at everyone else, probably wondering, like me, how to look cool and play a part in this circus. The one person who stood alone and didn't seem to care about what anyone thought, tossing a ball up into the air and catching it in her baseball glove, was Ronnie. She was where we'd decided to meet, in front of a large wire statue of a tornado, the school mascot. I couldn't figure out who decided a tornado was a good image for the school. First of all, tornadoes never happened in California, and second, it made for the weirdest mascot ever. At football games, the big black and yellow cylinder costume looked like a cross between a rocket ship and a pineapple, sort of embarrassing. As I watched Ronnie, I realized our meeting spot was as bad of an idea as the statue itself. No one else waited there, front and center for all to see.

A tall boy in a black and yellow football jersey smiled and raised a hand as he approached us, "Yo, Brandon, my man! Good to see you!" He reached for a high five from Brandon, and then this boy who had no idea who I was, nodded at me with a smile.

"Hey, Brandon," three girls said in unison as they walked by. One of them with long, dark hair kept her eye on Brandon and gave him a wide smile as she lifted her hand in a dainty little wave and giggled. The one next to her looked at me and said, "Hi!" like she knew me or something.

Amazing how I had become someone to acknowledge simply by being next to Brandon.

I kept glancing at the statue, knowing I was supposed to go there, but relishing every second of standing next to the popular guy.

To our left were tables labeled with alphabetized signs for the first letter of last names. A counselor sat behind each one, crossing off students' names on long lists as they handed them the paper that determined their life for the next nine months.

"Which line do you go to? I'm S for Stone. Oh, and I haven't even told you my first name. I guess you just heard it, but I'm Brandon." He reached his hand out to shake mine. I grabbed it, and he held it there while I got caught up in the pull of his smile.

"I'm Carol," I said, thrilled to introduce myself with my new name. "Carol Simon, so I guess I'm in the same line as you." I felt my heart race and my face grow warm as he kept his hand on mine.

"Carol Simon, nice to meet you," he said. "That's a cool name for a girl with a good voice. It's like Carly Simon."

A familiar Carly Simon tune, *Anticipation*, popped into my head. It was a perfect song for this day, one that seemed to have taken forever to arrive, when a popular, cute boy actually chose to hang with me. "Oh, yeah, I guess my name is a lot like hers, or like Carole King. She's my favorite."

He stared at me blankly, like maybe he wasn't sure who that was. "She's pretty cool too," he said, unenthusiastically.

He grabbed me by the elbow and pulled me with him to the S line. I continued to bask in the glory of people turning their eyes to see me with him.

And then it all changed.

"Brandon! Hey, handsome!" Dahlia appeared before us, flaunting a tiny pink tank top and tight jeans, perfectly bouncy hair, and long thick eyelashes that were the ideal advertisement for Maybelline mascara. She ruffled Brandon's hair, and continued, "Did you get your schedule yet? I hope we have some classes together."

She had so far remained fixed on Brandon, but when her eyes

lowered and saw Brandon's hand on my elbow, she quickly looked up to see me. She stared at me for a moment, squinting like she couldn't tell who I was, then said, "Oh, North! Wow, you look, uh, different?"

Brandon gave the confused look now. He cocked his head to the side and said, "North? Is that your nickname or something?"

Dahlia chuckled. "Nickname? No, that's her name. What did she tell you it was? South? East? West? How about my favorite, Pole, as in North Pole? I also like bean pole, but I'm not sure that works anymore." She gave an intentional glance down at my stomach, which I now realized was exposed from my cutoff shirt. "You used to be so skinny, North, but now, I don't know."

I knew I should have trusted my instinct to wear something else. I watched Brandon's eyes move from my face to my belly, and I quickly lowered my notebook to cover it.

"I'm pretty sure her name is Carol, right?" He looked at me.

"Yes, it is," I said. I dug my fingernails into my palm and blinked back the stinging tears in my eyes over Dahlia's comments. "I used to go by North, but not anymore."

Dahlia rolled her eyes and snickered. "Okay, so you're Carol now. Is that because you're a different person now with the cool feather earrings and new hair? Good luck with that."

"Hey, I don't know why you're being so rude, Dahlia, but I like her look, and who cares what her name is?" Brandon said.

I felt the glory of another first—a boy Dahlia clearly liked telling her I looked good.

But then I heard the familiar voice I'd been trying to avoid.

"North! Where'd you go? Matthew and I have been looking for you!" Aria, out of breath, her face red and sweaty, pushed her way between me and Brandon.

"Woah! Don't let me get in your way!" Brandon said, his hands up and his eyes wide with shock.

Aria looked at him for a second and then turned to me, not concerned at all by her rudeness. "I can't find Katelyn! She's not in front of the library like she said she would be."

I knew my moment of bliss in the cool people zone had instantly vanished. As Brandon slowly moved away, caught up in a group of Dahlia's friends, I felt my anger build. "Aria, she's probably just a little late, or she's stuck in a line to get her schedule first. You don't need to be upset. Why don't you get your schedule and then go back?"

Aria looked in the direction of the library, where at least thirty other people had decided to hang out. It would be easy for Katelyn to be lost among them. A frown came across Aria's face and she jiggled her hands, turned to look at me, then back to the library, her hands moving quicker as she did this. "Oh no, look at all those people over there. She might be there now. I can't get my schedule first. I need to hurry and go back! Will you come with me, North? There's too many people. I hate all these people!"

It seemed like the entire school quieted and turned to see who had said that, even though I knew it was probably only the people near us. I knew she didn't actually hate everyone. She hated the noise, the commotion, but they didn't know that.

I looked around, embarrassed at the faces staring. "She doesn't hate you. She just doesn't like crowds," I said, instinctively defending and protecting her like always.

"Why doesn't she say that? What are you, her mommy or something?" I recognized the voice before I looked up. It was Ricky. He stood next to Dahlia like he had that day at the park, a smug smirk on his face.

How had this day of great new firsts turned into a day of familiar failures? I turned away, unable to voice any sort of comeback that wouldn't make me sound even more like an idiot. I looked at Aria, who looked more terrified than I felt, and did the thing I had hoped to avoid.

"Come on, let's go find Katelyn," I said, and we walked through the crowd that Aria hated, her hand on my elbow now instead of Brandon's, and the faces that admired me when I was with him, now looking at me like I was crazy.

# Chapter 18

By the time Aria met up with Katelyn and then returned with me to get our schedules, there were only two minutes before class started, so while Aria chatted to Katelyn about the crows devouring someone's Pop Tart that fell on the ground, I headed toward the direction of Building A. I was still seven big buildings away at building H when the bell rang. There was no way I was going to make it on time.

To make matters worse, it was math, my least favorite subject, and the teacher, Mr. Fowler, was not at all friendly about my tardiness. He sat at his desk, his pen poised above an attendance pad as I entered a room full of eyes staring at me. With his glasses on the tip of his nose, he looked over the rims and said, "Unexcused Tardy. What is your name?"

It was so quiet I thought everyone probably could hear my heart pounding, my breath growing rapid. "Carol Simon?" My voice squeaked so meekly even I barely heard it.

Mr. Fowler stared at me, obviously annoyed, and said, "Did you say something or did you simply peep like a timid little bird?" He waited for my response, and all I could think of was what Aria might say to that.

She would fearlessly say yes, proud to sound like a bird, but not me. Nothing came out of my mouth. I suddenly felt boiling hot, my face getting warmer, and I knew it was embarrassingly bright red.

"Her name is Carol. Carol Simon."

I turned to see the person who had saved Aria earlier that morning, here to save me as well. Unfortunately, Mr. Fowler didn't appreciate Matthew's help.

"Excuse me, young man. What did you say your name was?"

"Matthew, sir," he said, and then added, "Matthew Jones."

Mr. Fowler stared at him, then began to write something on a yellow slip on his desk. "You may come and get this yellow warning slip, Mr. Jones. It needs to be signed by a parent and returned to the office tomorrow morning. If you forget it, or if you're lucky enough to get one more, you'll spend some time in the principal's office, and if you receive one after that, you will be sent home on suspension. I would suggest that you not speak without being spoken to by me first. Is that clear, Mr. Jones?"

"Yes, sir," Matthew said, his head down.

How did I possibly get Matthew in trouble on the first day of high school? I stared down at the cold, white tile floor smudged with footprints and little scratches from the metal chair legs. I heard Matthew's steps across the room as he approached Mr. Fowler's desk to take the yellow slip that should have been saved for someone who deserved it, not for one of the best people on earth.

"Now, back to you, young lady. I have spoken to you, so you need to speak back in a way that I can hear. Do you understand?"

I took a deep breath, like I would if I were about to sing a solo, and let it out slowly as I said, "My name is Carol Simon. I apologize for being late." I tried to match Matthew's politeness, even though that hadn't really helped him.

He looked at his attendance sheet. "I have a North Simon listed here. Is that you?"

I should have known this would be a problem.

"Uh, yes, that's a mistake. My name is Carol," I said, glad that I could simply call it a mistake, which is what it felt like to me all these years anyway.

"Okay, well, I will probably call you Miss Simon anyway, but I will make note that your first name is Carol. If you get two more tardies, you'll get one of these yellow slips too, like your friend, Mr. Jones got for talking out of turn. I wouldn't make that mistake. Be on time, Miss Simon, and have a seat." He motioned to the seat in the front row, directly in front of his desk, the only open seat left. Lucky me.

Still feeling every eye on me, I made the uncomfortable trek to my desk. I held my binder close, knowing if I didn't that my belly would be on display. The boy in the desk behind me pulled his long legs back, looking a little annoyed that I'd just taken some of his precious foot space under my seat. Compared to the totally humiliating first minutes of class, sitting in the front row actually felt like a relief, and the motivation to get up early in order to be in this seat on time every day was definitely not going away.

When the hour of terror with Mr. Fowler ended, Matthew and I compared schedules outside. I was excited to see that after my next two classes, French and art, I had English with Matthew.

"Ronnie's in that English class too," Matthew said. I still hadn't talked to Ronnie yet, and wished I would have gone over to her when I first saw her at center stage under the tornado statue. That would have been much less embarrassing than my encounter with Dahlia. "I told her your new name too, thinking you'd be okay with that."

"Oh, I'm totally good with that, thanks." I was curious what she thought, but didn't want to be late for another class, so I didn't ask.

When I entered the English classroom, the teacher sat at her desk, chatting with a couple students, and didn't appear at all concerned about where anyone sat or what they were doing. A few boys sat on top of desks, laughing with the girls nearby. Another boy with a football jersey, even bigger than Brandon's friend from the morning, tossed a football over their heads to another boy across the room. Finally, a class I could relax in, or so I thought for that brief moment before I heard the loud, cackling laugh of Dahlia. She sat in the back row next to Ricky, and next to him was Brandon. I glanced around for Ronnie and Matthew, but they were nowhere in sight. I started back toward the door to wait for them outside, but stopped short when I heard my name.

"Hey, Carol!" I turned back around to see Brandon. "Are you in this class?"

He was either being nice in spite of all the mean things Dahlia had said about me, or he was tricking me. Prepared for a rude comeback, I took a breath and answered. "Uh, yeah, I am."

Dahlia stared at me for a second, looked me up and down, rolled her eyes and whispered something to Ricky. He chuckled quietly. Brandon shook his head at both of them, like he was tired of their behavior, and said, "There's a seat over here if you want it."

I still expected a trick from Dahlia or Ricky. Maybe there was something gross stuck to the seat, or maybe they'd simply taunt me the entire time and eventually get Brandon to follow. Lucky for me, Matthew and Ronnie entered before I did anything regrettable.

"Carol! Finally!" Ronnie shouted as she ran over to me and embraced me in a big hug. "I can't believe how long it's been since I've seen you! And man, I love the look. I always thought short hair would work on you. I'm getting used to the new name thing, but glad you at least chose to name yourself after a cool singer."

That answered my question about what Ronnie thought, even though I figured she'd be chill about it. I'd told her I hated my name so many times. She was probably relieved I wasn't going to rant about it anymore.

I looked over at Brandon, who had moved to a seat in front of Dahlia and talked to another girl with long dark hair that was curled into spirals and pulled back from her face with a bright yellow headband that matched the yellow trim on her cheerleading outfit. How many cute girls did he know? He was like a magnet for them.

"Ronnie, don't stare and make it obvious, but that boy in front of Dahlia is the boy I told you about," I whispered.

"Let's hurry up and pick our seats," Ronnie said as the bell rang. "Then I'll sneak a look."

Ronnie pulled Matthew and me with her to a set of empty seats at the center of the room, next to a small boy wearing glasses who looked terrified. He sat up perfectly straight, his hands folded on the desk in front of him. His notebook was already opened, showing a zipper pouch filled with pencils and a large stack of notebook paper. If this teacher gave points for being prepared, he'd definitely be in the lead, but if the popular kids were keeping score on coolness, he'd place even lower than I did. He looked up as we approached, then scooted in his seat and pulled his shoulders back like he was trying to sit up even more, which failed because he was apparently already as tall and straight as possible.

I considered walking right by him, giving him no notice. He definitely didn't match the crowd I was trying to impress and befriend, but instead I smiled and quietly said hi, hoping no one really heard me but him. He stared wide-eyed at me for a second, then looked down, grabbed his pencil, and started to write what was probably his name at the top corner of his paper. I understood him more than he knew, the feeling of simply trying to get through the day. He was a glaring reminder of how much I hoped this year would be different.

I wondered if his mom had helped him organize his binder and pick out his clothes, a striped button down shirt and khaki pants that looked similar to what my dad wore to work, back when he was working. I put my books in the basket under my chair and saw his lunch pail on the floor. It was navy blue, shaped like my mailbox, with a black plastic handle. Someone had taken the time to make a name label for it with one of those new handheld label makers. Jonathon James Price was the name typed in little raised white letters on the red shiny strip. For his own sake, I hoped he lost the lunch box or forgot it somewhere. Even I knew a big lunch box like that stopped being cool at about sixth grade. But it was possible he didn't care. It was possible he needed that lunchbox with him, like Aria needed her bird bag and her big comfy shorts and T-shirts. In that moment my heart dropped with the thought that she was feeling scared in her class too.

"Well, looks like this teacher doesn't care about starting class on time." Ronnie turned back to glance at Brandon, then leaned closer to me. "He's really cute," she said as she raised her brows and grinned at me.

I took a deep breath and hoped I wasn't totally blushing as I said, "Yes, I know."

The teacher finally stood up and got our attention with a handheld bell that magically quieted us down and then got straight to work rather than wasting time telling us all the same classroom rules every other teacher had already explained. She handed out a page of directions titled "How-to Presentation."

"This will be due in three weeks, on Wednesday, October 2. You will be explaining how to do something you think you're good at or want to be good at. I want you to get used to working with each other, so it's to be done with a partner or a group of no more than four people."

As my dread of presenting welled up in me, I grasped one of my feather earrings and glanced over at Jonathon James Price. In the brief moment we made eye contact, I knew that my new image and his lunchbox had a lot in common. Hopefully they'd get us both through the year.

# Chapter 19

"I'll give you the rest of class to get into groups, chat with anyone who you think you might want to work with, or write down some ideas to talk about tomorrow. If you don't have a partner or group by tomorrow, don't worry. I will place you with someone."

So there it was, everyone's fate was their own. Those who didn't find someone they wanted to work with would be stuck in an awkward and potentially terrible fate for the next few weeks. The class immediately became frenzied with people standing to find their friends, moving desks into groups, and yelling across the room to each other. Jonathon James Price looked panicked, not moving as he watched others match up. Matthew quickly stood and began to pull my desk to face his, and Ronnie scooted her desk over closer to ours. While Matthew and Ronnie shared how glad they were that we got to choose our own groups, I couldn't stop glancing at Jonathon. I hoped someone would walk over to him, or that he'd get up and find someone to work with, but he stayed put, unmoving except for his head, which turned side to side, then behind him, looking for someone to be his friend now that nearly everyone had moved away from him.

"Hey, do you think we should invite him to be in our group?" I whispered to Matthew and Ronnie as I glanced at Jonathon.

Ronnie looked at him, then to Matthew, who also eyed Jonathon and then Ronnie, as if he expected her to make the decision. I felt horribly conflicted, knowing that if he did join us, we'd be our typical oddball group.

"He looks kind of scared," Ronnie said as she stared at us, then looked at Jonathon again. "And sad." She paused, then stood and walked over to his desk. "Hey, you wanna be in our group?" she asked.

He jumped in his seat, startled, and looked up at Ronnie. He looked so small, a little island by himself in front of her. I watched his mouth move, but couldn't hear what he said. Ronnie talked loud enough to hear though. "Oh, yeah, no problem," she said. "You just let us know. We don't even know what we're doing it on yet. I'm hoping for baseball, so if you know anything about that, this might be the group for you." She returned to her seat. "He said he'd think about it. He knows some girl he might work with, but she's not here today."

That wasn't the answer I expected, but it was nice to hear he might actually have a friend. I looked over at him again, and wondered if it was true. He still moved his head side to side, and behind, looking for the girl who wasn't here.

"Okay, well, I don't think I want to stand up and give a presentation about how to play baseball, Ronnie." Matthew said. "You know the only sport I can do, which I'm not doing, is track." He looked at me and asked, "What do you want to talk about?"

I felt my heart beat faster as I imagined standing up in front of everyone, the image so strong in my mind of not simply talking to everyone, but singing.

"We could talk about birds," Ronnie said before I had a chance to answer. "We know a lot about them from Aria."

Matthew's face lit up. "Oh, that's a good idea. We definitely know more about birds than anyone else here."

As much as I agreed, I didn't think that was a great idea either. "Ronnie, we're supposed to explain how to do something. That's why it's called a How-to Presentation. So what would we do, explain how to be a bird? How to fly like a bird? I don't think we know either of those things," I said.

Ronnie gave me an offended look, and turned to Matthew, who opened his eyes wide and said, "Woah, someone's sassy."

"No kidding," Ronnie said as she rolled her eyes. "I obviously don't mean we'd explain how to be birds. Are you upset about something?"

"No," I replied, even though that wasn't true.

"Okay, well, what I meant was we could explain how to look for birds, or how to care for birds. I don't know. I'm thinking it would be easy. We do it all the time. Now when we get together and walk to the woods we can say we're doing homework."

She made a good point, but when I thought about standing up in front of the class to explain how to be a birdwatcher, I didn't picture a good end result. These presentations, three weeks away, could determine our social status for the rest of the year, or even for the rest of high school. In my experience, once people had an image in their mind of who you were, they didn't forget it easily. Those who were already popular could get away with almost anything. Those of us who still clamored for a higher place in the social food chain had to be more strategic.

"I really don't want to get up and talk about birdwatching. Everyone will think we're weird."

They each gave me the blank stares again, then looked at each other and shook their heads, confused.

"We've never exactly been the coolest kids on the block," Ronnie said. "I know you've got this whole cool look going on now," she said as she waved her hands at me, "but does that mean birdwatching is off limits too? It's not really a weird thing to do."

The way she said that made me wonder if she actually disliked my new look. "I'm not saying I don't like birdwatching. I'm saying I don't think everyone needs to know that's something we do, like that's the thing that defines us, you know?"

Ronnie leaned back in her chair with a big sigh of frustration, Matthew tapped his pencil on his desk. I sat with my arms crossed in front of me and tried not to feel guilty for shooting down their idea.

"Is this what it's going to be like all the time being friends with Carol?" Ronnie peered at me and emphasized Carol like it was a bad word. "We aren't allowed to tell people about all those supposedly uncool things we do? 'Cause I don't feel a need to hide any of it."

"No, Ronnie, you can do what you want, but so can I."

"Oh, okay, then maybe we shouldn't be in a group together." She glared at me, a look I wasn't used to getting from her. It felt terrible.

"Maybe we could do something about music," I suggested. They both responded with dumbfounded stares.

"Carol, you want to work together?" I looked up to see Brandon standing by my desk. "I'm thinking about presenting on how to start a band. What do you think?"

Ronnie looked at me with a smirk, eyes wide with surprise. I was just as shocked. Some girls dream of being asked to prom. This was way better.

# Chapter 20

The bell to end English class rang shortly after I agreed to do the project with Brandon, and while everyone scurried to get to lunch, Brandon and I exchanged phone numbers. I clutched the scrap of paper with his number on it, feeling like the luckiest girl on earth until I exited the classroom and faced Dahlia. She stood on the patch of lawn outside the classroom with Ricky, facing us, chomping gum, arms crossed, and I knew she was gearing up to hurl her large supply of insults my way. I looked to see if Matthew and Ronnie had waited for me, but they were nowhere in sight.

"You two just can't seem to stay away from each other today," Dahlia said.

"Nope, we cannot," Brandon said. "Is that a problem?"

Dahlia looked surprised by his response. She uncrossed her arms, flipped her hair and laughed, "What? No, why would I care? You can hang with North, I mean Carol, if you want. I'm just surprised you two have much in common. Are you eating with us, North?" She looked repulsed at the idea.

A blonde girl approaching with a pack of other girls thwarted my response. "Dahlia! Hey, girl, finally! How have I not seen you all day?"

"Chrissy? Oh my gosh, I haven't seen you all summer!" Dahlia darted over to her while the girls around Chrissy all stood like adoring fans waiting for Dahlia's attention as well.

"So, lunch?" Brandon asked.

I looked around again, but still didn't see Matthew and Ronnie anywhere in the swarm of people that filled the quad. I could spend the entire lunch alone, looking for them, or I could stay with Brandon. The answer seemed pretty obvious.

"Well, I was supposed to meet up with my friends, but I have no idea where they went."

"Cool," Brandon said, "I guess you're stuck with me, then."

I was back on the wings of bliss again and hoped it would last. After Brandon bought his lunch at the cafeteria, we found a table outside and sat down, and soon we were swarmed with a crowd of Brandon followers who obviously thought he was one of the best people on earth. I sat and watched, occasionally saying hello to someone who he introduced me to, or who chose to nod at me like maybe they knew me but were too embarrassed to admit they didn't remember my name. I was starving, but didn't want to pull out my paper bag lunch while he ate cafeteria food that made my sticky peanut butter sandwich and mushy apple even more disgusting.

"You want some of my food? Looks like you forgot yours," he said as he held out half of his turkey sandwich.

"Oh, no, I'm okay. I can eat when I get home. I'm not that hungry." That was a lie. The sandwich looked amazing, and the warm chocolate chip cookies next to it made my mouth water. The fact that school cafeteria food looked so enticing said a lot about the type of food I'd been eating. Mom was the cook, and managed to make some decent meals even when we didn't have much money. Without her around, meals had been pretty awful.

"Really? Okay, but please take some if you want. I'm definitely hungry, but I always have plenty of food. My mom will probably have leftover food from one of her meetings or something when I get home."

"Oh, what kind of meetings?"

"She does a bunch of volunteer work, so there's always some group at our house, talking about stuff. I don't pay too much attention to what they're saying, but I usually get a nice stack of fancy little sandwiches and treats after they leave."

His world sounded so different from mine. He probably had a perfectly clean house with neatly organized cupboards of food, bowls of fresh fruit on the kitchen counter, cookbooks that opened each night as his mom prepared some homemade meal. He probably had a nice couch and matching chairs that held people, not stacks of stuff, and there was likely a clear path to each bedroom. I noticed his shoes—white and blue Adidas, perfectly clean, definitely brand new. I wondered if he had several new pairs for the school year, in addition to more jeans and perfectly ironed T-shirts like the one he wore today. It was a crisp dark blue, the perfect match with the shoes and faded jeans.

While the group of people that had filled the table stopped talking to Brandon, he turned to me and said, "So, the project," he said as he smiled.

"Yeah, the project," I said back, not sure if he was expecting me to say more or if he was going to continue. When he simply nodded his head, I added, "You said you want to do it on starting a band. That's great. Do you have a band?"

"Yeah, sort of, I play the guitar, and I have a drummer and a bassist, but I'm having a really hard time finding a singer. None of us do that real well, and everyone who's tried out has been terrible. We've had Dahlia sing when we practice, but I gotta be honest, she's not that good. If her parents and mine weren't such close friends, I wouldn't even have her at practice. She's like the daughter my mom never had, I guess, or the sister who constantly annoys me and I have to tolerate. A couple of the other guys like her there because she's flirty and pretty, but there's no way they think we'll get anywhere with her at the lead."

This was the best thing I'd heard someone say ever. It took everything in me to keep from jumping up and saying, "Yes! Finally someone speaks the truth!" I smiled and nodded, hoping my expression didn't too obviously express how much I agreed with him.

"Have you heard her?" he said as he looked around to make sure no one could hear him.

"Yes," I said. "She sang in pretty much all our school musicals. She sounded okay, but she always had backup singers, so she sort of got drowned out by their voices."

"That makes sense. I can't imagine a teacher selecting her over other voices like yours. Why didn't you try out for the musicals?"

I really didn't want to explain all my middle school drama with him. "I was too shy. The teachers would ask me to sing, but I always turned them down." I didn't bother to explain how mean Dahlia was about it, how she managed to get nearly everyone to hate me during the days the teacher waited for me to accept or refuse the part.

"Wow, that's too bad. You have a really good voice," he said. "You could totally save our band, help us get somewhere. You should come over tomorrow after school and practice with us. I live about a half a mile from here, on the other side of Elm Road."

"Thanks," I said, "but what about Dahlia?" As excited as I was to sing, I wasn't up for fighting her. She could completely ruin my dreams of making high school new and different from middle school.

"I'll handle Dahlia. She already knew I was asking you to do the project together."

Every image in my mind of singing in front of others, especially Dahlia, and failing flashed through my mind. What if I did the same thing in front of him and the rest of the band? I'd be back in the same place I was in middle school. This was my shot. I couldn't blow it. In spite of the sheer terror in my heart, I said, "Okay, yes. I can come over tomorrow." As soon as I said this, I realized I had some things to figure out in order to get there, mainly, whether Dad would let me go. If so, would he be fine with handling Aria, or maybe it was the other way around—would she be fine with him? I had an entire afternoon and evening to figure all this out, so rather than panic and tell him I couldn't make it, I soaked in the fact that at this very moment, I was actually sitting with one of the most popular boys in my grade, and he had just given me an opportunity to sing.

Dahlia reappeared and bounced over to a girl who had recently sat down with a group of girls next to me. "Excuse me, can you scoot over a bit?" The blonde, bright-eyed girl looked up, squinting into the sun to see who it was and said, "Oh, sure Dahlia. How are you? Tell me about your summer."

"I'm fine, thanks, but I actually need to chat with Carol here," Dahlia said as she squeezed herself into the small space on the bench. At least she'd finally said my name right.

The girl's initial excitement to be graced with Queen Dahlia's presence shattered into an expression of disappointment. "Oh, no problem," she said and smiled at me like I must be someone super important to get Dahlia's attention.

"So, are you doing the project with us?" Dahlia said to me.

What was she talking about? I'd agreed to do the project with Brandon. I didn't know she was involved. I looked at Brandon, expecting some explanation.

"Carol's doing the project with me. I thought you were working with Ricky." Brandon was clearly as confused as me.

Dahlia laughed and said, "Brandon, you're so funny. I told Ricky I'd work with him, but obviously I'm working with you too if we're presenting about the band. Ricky might be our biggest fan because he comes to watch us practice all the time, but he doesn't know anything about music." She flashed a sly smile. "Plus, this assignment gives us a great excuse to practice and call it homework. We're going to need all the practice we can get. I just talked to Chad, and he said his dad is willing to record us."

Brandon's eyes popped open wide and he almost choked on his sandwich. He swallowed and said, "Really? What changed?"

She twisted her finger through her hair, and said, "Well, I talked to my dad, and he offered to give Chad's dad recording space at one of his properties for nearly nothing. So now that the money and space issue is gone, he's ready to go. The only thing is, my dad won't do it if I'm not in the band, so I know you want a new singer, but I think you need to keep me around." She glared at me.

Brandon closed his eyes, took a breath, and said, "Dahlia, we've talked about this. Your voice is good, but it's not the sound we're going for. If I'm gonna make this band work, I need to have the right people. Chad knows that."

"Well, that's not what he told me. Ask him. He thinks I have a perfect voice."

Brandon groaned and put his sandwich down hard enough to cause it to fall apart all over his plate. He chewed quickly and swallowed, then pushed the plate away.

"Look, I don't have to sing all the songs on my own," Dahlia continued. "I'm sure I can harmonize with Carol occasionally." She nudged me with her elbow and grinned. "I'm also really good at playing that tambourine and being a back-up dancer. You'll be glad to have me on the stage for someone to look at when you perform." She tapped her long purple-painted fingernails on the table and continued to chomp her gum. It was pink and smelled like cherries, or maybe that was her perfume. Either way, it was a sticky sweet smell that made me a bit nauseous.

"Wow, okay, well, I guess we can do the project together. Are you okay with that, Carol?" Brandon asked. He looked at me like he was afraid I might turn him down, his eyes wide, brows raised.

I stared into those eyes and there was no way I could turn him down even though I hated the whole idea of doing anything with Dahlia and Ricky. Matthew and Ronnie were going to freak out when I told them this. "Yeah, I'm okay with that," I said, and as I looked past the group of people in front of us, I saw Aria talking with Matthew and Ronnie under a tree. She was enthusiastically talking and pointing up to the branches while they listened. Ronnie caught my glance and smiled while pointing at Brandon and giving a thumbs up. I suddenly wished I were sitting with them, where I could breathe easy. Instead, I sat with a pit in my stomach, wondering how I could escape from Dahlia's stifling grip on my dreams.

# Chapter 21

After lunch and two more long hours of P.E. and Science, I entered the hot September air and hustled through the crowd of people, ignoring the shoulder-to-shoulder bumps, a step on my toe, and a stack of books that slid out of someone's locker onto the ground. When I neared the gate, Aria was already there, and she didn't look happy. She clutched her bag close to her chest and stared with wide eyes at people walking by like they were dangerous. She rose up on her toes and down, in little bounces. I hoped the whole walk home wouldn't need to be focused on calming her down. I really needed to talk to Matthew and Ronnie.

When she saw me, she stopped bouncing and ran over to me. "North! Hi! I'm so glad you're here. Let's go home!"

"Aria, we have to wait for Matthew and Ronnie, and then we'll go, okay?"

"Uhhhh!" She yelled, and then started bouncing again.

I thought about asking how her day was, but decided that would make things worse. She was already agitated, and repeating the events of her day would only make it worse. Distraction was usually a better strategy.

"There's some birds over there on the grass. What type are they?" I asked even though I knew they were sparrows.

She turned around and said, "Those are sparrows. You should know that. I've told you all about them so many times."

"Oh, right, they are. I sometimes forget. I'm not as good at remembering birds as you are, Aria."

"Yeah, that's true," she said. Her bouncing stopped and she continued to watch the birds.

While she watched the birds, I kept a lookout for Matthew and Ronnie. A couple minutes later I saw them. Matthew's height made him stand out in a crowd, and normally so did his smile when he saw me. There was no smile this time. Ronnie was next to him, chatting away as usual.

"Hey, I thought maybe you would have gone ahead and walked with Brandon or something." Then she put her head close to me and said quietly, "He totally likes you. It's so obvious."

"Ronnie, what are you talking about?" I said, glancing around to make sure no one could hear. Matthew was the only one close. "He does not. We're just doing a project together."

She shook her head and laughed, "Right, is that why he ate lunch with you? So you could talk about a class project? I don't think so. He likes you."

Matthew stood with his arms crossed and still wouldn't look at me. "I gotta get home, so I think I'll go now," he said and started walking.

Ronnie raised her eyebrows and looked at me like she didn't understand his problem. "Okay, well, let's go then," she said. "Hey Aria, you coming with us?" She yelled over to Aria who had moved over to sit on the lawn where the birds hopped nearby.

"Yes! I'm coming!" Aria ran over to us, back to her happy self, and asked Ronnie how her day was, if she liked her first day of high school, if she met any baseball players. Then somehow she got on the topic of why a fly ball is called a fly ball. "I understand it's called that because it's soaring high, but it's not flying. It doesn't have wings. I think it should be called a high ball."

I knew that whole conversation was going to be a long one, so I let them lag behind and talk while I caught up to Matthew, even though I felt a little afraid of what he might say, or more truthfully, what he wouldn't say. He was clearly upset about me doing the project with Brandon.

He walked way too fast. He was already at the corner crossing the street. As I picked up my pace to catch him, the "Don't Walk" warning light flashed. There was no way I would catch him, and what happened next made that fact even worse.

I stood at the corner as Matthew reached the opposite end of the street, and behind him a group of boys yelled to him.

"Hey! Why you walking so fast, boy? Going fast ain't gonna keep you from being noticed around here with that dark skin." A skinny boy with shaggy chestnut brown hair yelled as he tried to catch up with Matthew. He pulled his faded jeans up over his hips so they wouldn't fall down as he jogged. Once he let go, they drooped anyway. The three other boys laughed and kept a bit of distance behind Droopy Pants.

Matthew turned around, but didn't respond, and didn't slow down.

"Yo! I'm talking to you! You gonna ignore me like that? You might want to give us white folks a bit more respect!" he yelled to Matthew and this time added a hard shove to his back. Matthew lurched forward as his books flew into the air and landed on the sidewalk. He bent down to grab them, and as he rose back up, the kid pushed him again, knocking him off balance and onto the ground with the rest of his books. He looked up at the boy for a second, and then reached for one of his books as another boy kicked it farther away.

I was so enraged. This was the most abusive and sad thing I'd ever seen. It wasn't like Matthew to not stick up for himself, but he was clearly outnumbered, and worse than that was the fact that no one bothered to help. The small crowd that had gathered stood a few feet behind and laughed. One person began a chant of "Fight! Fight! Fight! Fight!" Others joined in, and I stood completely helpless on the other side of the street. Cars sped by while I begged that light to change so I could cross. I looked to see if Aria and Ronnie were close behind, but all I saw were a bunch of unfamiliar faces gawking at the commotion across the street.

"Hey! Leave him alone!" I yelled desperately, but the only people who seemed to hear were the few kids next to me who couldn't help, and probably wouldn't anyway.

Matthew stayed on the ground, his head between his knees, and finally, a car pulled over to the sidewalk. A tall bearded man got out, slammed his door shut, and yelled, "What's going on? You guys picking on him? You want to fight? I'll fight you! Come on, show me what you've got!"

The boys looked at the twenty-something-year-old and then another man who got out of the passenger side of the car. This guy wasn't tall, but that didn't make him any less threatening. His tattooed arms, approximately the size of my thighs, bulged from a short-sleeved T-shirt. He walked over to Matthew, leaned down, and helped him up. With the Walk signal finally flashing, I raced across the street and tried to push my way through the gawkers. I could barely see Droopy Pants between the gap in the crowd.

"Hey, we were just joking. We don't wanna fight anyone." Droopy Pants said while continuing to walk backwards. The other three boys, seeing their chance to flee, turned around and ran to the other side of the street.

"Yeah? Really?" Bulging Arms said as he stepped forward, "Because it sure looked to me like you wanted to start something. This boy wasn't sitting on the ground to rest. You guys were threatening him." He continued to inch closer until Droopy Pants finally decided to run in my direction. He shoved a few people out of the way and knocked into two girls who screamed and nearly fell to the ground. As he turned back around to see if Bulging Arms was still after him, he ran smack into me. I felt the impact of his body hit me and grabbed the sleeve of his red flannel shirt to keep from falling. "Woah! Sorry!" he yelled as he grasped my upper arms to balance me. He stared at me with stunned brown eyes, no longer looking like the tough guy he tried to be when he yelled at Matthew. In spite of this tiny effort to apologize and hold me up, I felt nothing but rage for this boy. I was close enough to his face to notice all the little freckles along the bridge and side of his nose, the bushy eyebrows, and the leather rope necklace with a spiral silver pendant around his neck. I opened my mouth to shout at him, but before any words came out I was jolted back from his grasp.

"Get your hands off her!" Bulging Arms yelled as Droopy Pants shot across the street. I looked up at this scary looking man who had saved Matthew from being beaten down anymore, and wanted to hug him. Instead, I simply uttered, "Thank you."

"Yeah, no problem, that guy's a loser. I hope he's not your friend."

"Oh, no, definitely not. He is," I said as I pointed to Matthew. He was now standing as the bearded man and another kid I didn't recognize handed him his books. The crowd had moved on, clearly uninterested in helping.

"Good, he seems nicer, and probably more in need of a friend,"

Bulging Arms said as he eyed Matthew.

I headed over to Matthew who looked at me with a mix of relief and sadness. I hadn't shoved him on the ground, but I knew I'd upset him with my attention to Brandon earlier.

"Hey, you okay?" I asked.

He nodded and looked up at the sky like he didn't want to face me at the moment. He held his books in one arm and had his opposite hand in his pocket.

I reached for his hand and grabbed it. "Let's go home and forget about this stupid first day of high school," I said.

He finally looked at me. "Yeah, okay," he said.

We headed toward our street, but I felt no rush to get to my front door because this was where I felt at home, hand in hand with my best friend.

# Chapter 22

In spite of how much I wanted to talk to Matthew about his apparent disapproval of my friendship with Brandon, I knew the time to bring it up wasn't after he had been shoved down on the sidewalk and humiliated. I also was a little speechless by the fact that we were still holding hands. It definitely put to rest the thought that I'd only imagined something between us. I wasn't sure what to think about it. Matthew had always been my friend. If it became more than that, and then we broke up, would we stop being friends? That thought scared me, but not enough to make me let go of his hand.

"Are you okay? Really?" I asked. "You don't have to pretend around me, you know." I watched his face closely. If he said he was fine and he wasn't, he'd likely turn his eyes away from me, maybe look up or away so I couldn't see tears.

But he looked me in the eye and said, "No, not really. I mean, physically I'm fine. Maybe a bruise will pop up from hitting the cement, but I can handle that. What bothers me is I don't even know them, have never done anything to them, but I'm different from them. I'm Black.

That's the only reason it happened."

I didn't want to believe that was the truth. This was the '70s, where love was supposed to rule the day. People protested about equality, wrote songs and poems about it, but still someone like Matthew was picked out of the crowd for no good reason. I knew he was right, but I really didn't want him to be. "They're idiots," I said. "Be glad you're nothing like them."

He looked back at me but didn't say anything. I knew my words weren't very helpful. They didn't change the fact that these jerks got away with knocking Matthew to the ground and humiliating him in front of a crowd of even more idiots who thought it was cheap entertainment.

"You could have definitely kicked his butt, you know," I said. "But they had an unfair advantage with four against one."

He nodded. "Yeah, I'm glad those two guys showed up when they did 'cause I didn't know what to do."

"If Ronnie, Aria and I would have been with you, we could have helped you take them," I said. "Ronnie wouldn't have hesitated to fight, Aria would have squawked and distracted them, and as for me, well, I don't know. I could entertain them with a song?"

He laughed, finally. It was nice to see some of the happy Matthew again. "But seriously," I said, "Maybe you shouldn't walk home on your own for a while."

"That's probably true, but it seems pretty lame that a six-foot-two guy should depend on three girls to keep him safe. It ticks me off." His hand squeezed mine tighter and his other hand clenched in a tight fist.

"I know, it makes me mad too, and even though we really couldn't do much, there is safety in numbers." I imagined that boy's face again and it made me feel sick to my stomach. "That guy shouldn't get away with what he did. I'm determined to figure out who he is."

"And then what?" Matthew asked. It was a good question.

"I don't know," I admitted, "but there's gotta be something we could do to stop him. I'm sure you're not the only one he's chosen to pick on."

"No, probably not, but that doesn't make me think he's going to quit anytime soon."

I knew Matthew was right, again, but I still wasn't giving up. I wondered if Brandon knew him. He seemed to know nearly everyone, and being so popular, he might be the one with the power to help us out, get him to leave Matthew alone.

We stopped in front of my house and waited for Ronnie and Aria, who probably had no clue about Matthew's horrible encounter. I gently pulled my fingers from him, and gazed up at him for a moment. I felt like I should say something, like thanks for holding my hand, or explain that I was only pulling away to set my things down, but that seemed awkward. I'd never heard of anyone discussing their hand holding. It just seemed to happen. Luckily, he smiled back and said, "Thanks for walking with me and listening to me. I feel better than I did,"

"Of course." I didn't feel like I deserved a thank you.

Even though I couldn't see her, I heard Aria's voice from the other side of the hill about five houses away. Seconds later, she was in view at the top, heading down the street with her arms swinging in rhythm to her big strides as she talked enthusiastically and gazed up at the trees, then at the sky, pointing to a bird that flew away. Her voice boomed louder as she approached. Ronnie looked up, mouth sealed in a slight smile, not a peep coming from her to interrupt Aria's flow. Though I couldn't make out what Aria said, I knew Ronnie was receiving more bird trivia than anyone would ever want.

"Hmm, wonder what they're talking about," Matthew joked.

"Right," I laughed, "Probably discussing how much fun school was or something like that." I was so thankful for a friend like Ronnie at that moment. She was exactly what Aria needed after a day that was probably not as rough as Matthew's, but still a struggle. People weren't normally kind to her for being different from them either.

Aria turned her walk into a soar, one arm holding her bag and the other out wide. "Come on, Ronnie!" she yelled. "It's fun to fly down this hill!" She zigzagged back and forth while she ran down the hill. While hoping no one would see her and make fun of her, I mostly hoped the release of all her pent up energy would make the evening go better than normal.

Ronnie looked around for a minute and then decided to join Aria in the crazy flight down the hill, zipping back and forth, swirling around and then leaping.

As soon as Aria turned around and saw Ronnie, she started laughing harder than I'd heard in a very long time. "See? Isn't it great?" she shouted.

Panting, out of breath, and laughing, Ronnie stopped when she reached Matthew and me. "Man that girl's got energy," she said as she bent over with her hands on her knees, gasping for air.

Aria kept going, weaving her way down the street and then back before plopping onto the front lawn, still laughing. "Oh my gosh that was fun!" she said through her laughter. "I wish more people would do stuff like that with me."

"They'd be a lot happier if they did," Ronnie said, still out of breath, but smiling big and bright anyway."

Ronnie was right. I felt a pang of regret for my refusal to copy Aria because of the way people looked at me when I did. That never seemed to bother Ronnie.

As hot as it was standing in the sun on the driveway, I wasn't too thrilled about heading inside. It would feel like a drastic jolt from the freedom outside into essentially a large box full of stuff and stress. It would be nothing like the feeling expressed by the girl who sat in front of me during science class. She'd said, "Ugh, I just want to go home and lay on my couch with some television and a bag of chips." I wished I could do that. Aside from the fact that I'd have to clear the couch of piles of junk if I wanted to lay on it, there was always something to be done. I consistently felt like things might fall apart at any second if I wasn't on top of it all.

We entered the dark house, curtains drawn, windows closed. It was stuffy and needed air. The warm outside air wouldn't cool it down much, but I hoped opening a window might diffuse the musty smell a little. I stepped over a box of assorted tools Dad apparently had been rummaging through, stacks of torn towels he must have thought would make good rags, and finally leaned over the couch to open the window behind it. Matthew and Ronnie were polite, said nothing, but I knew they were hoping for some relief. For years they'd come over to my house after school on days I needed to be available for Aria because Mom had to work another hour or two. They never seemed to care about the chaos that reigned in every room as we walked to the safe harbor of my bedroom. Sometimes I jokingly told them to hold their breath, or to watch out for secret traps on the floor that we'd set to catch bad guys who might steal all our valuables. It was my way of trying to lighten the fact that my home was actually terrible.

I wiped the sweat that had already formed on my forehead as I led Matthew and Ronnie through the familiar obstacle course to my room. It was a little cooler, with the help of a fan I'd kept running. Unfortunately, the bliss didn't last for long.

While filling Ronnie in on what happened to Matthew, Aria entered my room about every five minutes to ask one of us a question about her homework, or to tell us some random fact, usually about birds of course, or to ask me to help her find something. When my door opened for the eleventh time in less than an hour, I was surprised to see Dad instead of Aria. He held a hammer in his hand and his white shirt appeared to be covered in sawdust.

"Hey, you think you could help out a bit? Your sister is driving me nuts. Maybe it's time for your friends to go home so you can handle her instead of me," he said as he wiped his sleeve on his sweaty forehead.

Seriously? My friends being over wasn't the problem. Ronnie had helped Aria through three confusing math problems, and Matthew patiently sat and listened to her explain why the doves cooed outside our window every morning.

"You know I'm trying to finish building that add-on so we can have more space around here. It's never going to get done if she keeps interrupting me," he added when I didn't jump up immediately. Instead I stared at him, contemplating how to tell him what I thought. Most likely, he'd spent the morning sleeping, the afternoon organizing, rearranging, and scouring through his stuff, and finally started hammering away on the add-on right when I came home. If he would spend all that time finding a job, maybe we could at least stop worrying about money. Before I said anything, Matthew chimed in, polite as ever.

"Yeah, well, I need to get home and help out a bit too, so I'll be seeing you two tomorrow," he said as he gathered his books. "Nice to see you, Mr. Simon," he added with a smile.

Ronnie followed Matthew's example, "Yep, I need to get going too."

"I'll walk out with you guys," I said, annoyed with my dad. I really wanted to talk to each of them about Brandon.

"Make it quick, young lady," Dad said.

I took a deep breath, knowing that I needed to keep my cool or else he wouldn't let me go outside with them. "I will," I said.

"I'll say goodbye outside too!" Aria shouted from the hallway. I really wanted to be alone with Ronnie and Matthew, without any distractions.

"Aria, why don't you say goodbye inside and then go see what you want me to make for dinner? I'll be back in a minute." I hoped that would work.

"Yeah, go find something really fun to make. We'll see you tomorrow," Matthew said.

"High five, Aria!" Ronnie said as she followed Matthew past Aria in the hallway.

Aria gave Ronnie's hand a loud smack, then laughed at the sting of it and headed to the kitchen. "Okay! I'm gonna find something good!" she yelled as we headed out the front door.

The air was finally cooler. A mild breeze had kicked in, and the sun no longer blazed hot above us. I wanted to sit down and chat for a while under the shade of the tree, but Dad's order to make it quick echoed in my head.

"So, can I ask you guys a question before you leave?" I asked.

They both stopped and Matthew said, "Yeah, what's up?"

The thought of our walk home, hand in hand, flashed through my mind. I hoped my question wasn't going to upset him.

"Are you guys disappointed that I'm doing the English project with Brandon?" I looked at them and waited for a response.

They looked at each other, and then Ronnie said, "No, we get it. He's like your dream guy. He likes music and he's cute. Why wouldn't you work with him? Plus, he stuck up for you in front of Dahlia before he even knew you. That gets him points."

Matthew didn't join in Ronnie's encouragement. He stared at the ground and kicked the dirt with his toe.

"He's not my dream guy, Ronnie." I kept my eyes on Matthew as I said this, wishing he'd look at me to see I meant it. "I'd rather work with you guys, but this could really be an opportunity for my singing to finally get noticed. His band needs a singer, and I guess this guy Chad, who's in the band, has a dad in the music industry and plans to record them once the band is complete and ready. Can you imagine how awesome that would be?"

Matthew still said nothing. Apparently my question had set us back.

"What? Really? That would be so cool!" Ronnie said.

While I was glad she was supportive, I wished the same from Matthew. "Matthew, you're awfully quiet," I said. "What do you think?"

He finally looked up, but his expression showed none of Ronnie's excitement. "That's great," he said. "Sounds like an opportunity you need to take."

I wasn't going to pretend anymore that he wasn't mad. "Okay, Matthew, you obviously aren't happy with the idea of me working with Brandon. Why don't you tell me the truth?"

"The truth?" he asked like that was a dumb question. "Don't you feel even the slightest bit uncomfortable with the fact that he's friends with Dahlia and Ricky? Do you actually trust him if that's who he hangs with?"

"Yes, I do because he doesn't even like Dahlia. He's only nice to her for the sake of the band. Apparently Chad's dad rents space for his recording studio in one of Dahlia's dad's buildings for almost nothing. Dahlia's dad has pretty much told Chad's dad that Dahlia gets a spot in the band if he wants to keep the cheap recording studio."

"Woah, that's terrible," Ronnie said. "That means you have to work with Dahlia?"

"Unfortunately, yes," I said. "And Ricky too. He's not in the band, but he's in the group for the project."

Matthew kicked the dirt hard this time. "Okay, well, good luck with that crowd. I need to get going." He turned to leave.

"Matthew, don't be mad. Come on. It's just for a while, so I can be in a band. You know that's been my dream forever," I said.

He kept walking but lifted his hand in the air and said, "See you guys tomorrow."

Ronnie gave me a sympathetic look. "Don't worry about him being mad. You know what a jerk Ricky has always been to him, and Dahlia to you. He's being protective. He'll get over it."

I hoped she was right. I didn't like the idea of living my dream without Matthew. I said goodbye to her and went back into my house where my dad said, "Well, the phone bill is paid, and guess who called? Some boy, asking for you. I told him you'd talk to him tomorrow at school."

"What? Was it Brandon?" I asked, my heart beating a little faster at the thought of him calling me.

"Uh, yeah, I think," he said, "Only one day at high school and you've already got strange boys calling you? You don't have time for that, North."

"Dad, he's calling about a school assignment."

Dad laughed. "Really? Is that his excuse? That's an old line."

"Dad, he . . ."

"Don't even want to hear it," he interrupted. "Go help your sister with dinner. Let me know when it's ready."

I wanted to tell him to make his own dinner, but knew I couldn't talk to him like that. I'd try to explain more to him later. Hopefully he'd give me more of a chance than Matthew did. I heard Aria in the kitchen, humming "Nightingale," and I knew that no matter what my dad and Matthew thought, I had to pursue my dream.

# Chapter 23

Aria's exciting meal of choice turned out to be frozen dinners. While I was glad it was easy to make, I wasn't too thrilled about eating it. I swirled my fork in the compartment containing mashed potatoes and gravy, wondering why it seemed so runny, and then wondered what the dark brown compartment next to it was supposed to be. It looked nothing like the chocolate cake promised on the box. The chicken drumsticks were my only shot at anything remotely edible. With no one talking, I decided to bring up the band. Dad's reaction was about as pleasing as my dinner.

"I understand the excitement of being in a band," he said in between bites of chicken. "Been there, and trust me, it's not what you think. Don't waste your life on that dream. Not worth it," he said.

"Dad, I understand it didn't work out for you, but you would have never known that unless you gave it a try. Plus, you had a kid kind of young. That probably didn't help," I said, hoping Aria didn't take offense. She was twirling her fork around a very large glob of spaghetti noodles, completely unaffected by my comment.

I probably should have been more worried about Dad being offended. He got up from his seat, picked up his frozen dinner tray and said, "Don't try to lecture me, North. Give up the dream, okay?"

He turned to set his tray in the sink, and headed back into the garage. I wanted to remind him to call me Carol, and that I deserved to give my dream a chance. Even though it didn't work out for him, he still tried for a while, and Mom still painted pictures and made jewelry. I reached for my ear and rubbed my fingers along the feathered earring she'd made.

"Your doctor appointment is tomorrow," I said to Aria. "Mom's coming after school to take you."

Her face lit up with a grin. "She is? Yay!" She bounced up and down in her seat. "Are we going to do something after? Maybe get hamburgers?"

"I don't know, but I'll bet we could talk her into it," I said. Mom had made a point to make doctor days something to look forward to rather than something to dread, as Aria hated going. Take a normal person's angst about doctor visits and multiply that about a thousand times and that's probably close to how Aria felt.

"You think Dad will go to dinner with us?" she asked.

I didn't have a confident answer to that question, but to keep her happy and in hope that this was true, I said, "Maybe, if we can get him away from hammering away out there. He needs to eat anyway."

I imagined us all out together, like old times. Maybe it would help them remember the good times too, and Mom would come back home. I wasn't giving up on that thought.

After rinsing out our dinner trays, I placed them on the three-foot stack of saved trays by the garage door, made lunches, and went to my room to listen to music. With my thoughts still on Mom, I placed the Carole King record on the turntable and placed the needle on the song

Mom used to sing with me, "Child of Mine." As it played, I closed my eyes, sang along, and knew that I couldn't listen to Dad's advice. I could hear Mom's voice, back one day when she actually encouraged me, speaking words similar to Carole King's song.

"Did you hear those words?" Mom had said while we listened. "They're true. Don't let anyone kill your dream. You keep singing, no matter what anyone says, you hear?"

"Yes, Mom," I said out loud as if she were there, and then said, "No one is going to take this dream away." I grabbed my binder off my desk and pulled out the piece of paper with Brandon's phone number. I headed into the hallway and saw Aria reading in her room. When I entered the kitchen, I could hear Dad in the garage. It sounded like he was taking down boxes and shuffling through them. Knowing he might come in soon, I picked up the phone and dialed Brandon's number. Then I stretched the cord as far as it would go away from the garage so Dad wouldn't hear me talking. My heart raced while I listened to the ring.

"Hello?" a male voice said after the second ring.

"Brandon?" I said in a voice a little louder than a whisper.

"Yeah," he said.

"This is Carol." I waited for him to respond, a little worried he wouldn't want to talk.

"Oh, hey, you're so quiet. I can barely hear you."

I spoke a little louder, "I only have a second. I just wanted to tell you I'll be there Friday. Let me know tomorrow how to get to your house."

"Oh, awesome, you can just walk with me after school if you want."

"I might not be able to come right after school, so I'll need directions in case," I said, knowing I'd have to get Aria home until Mom came for the doctor appointment.

"Oh, sure, that's fine," he said.

The sounds from the garage had grown quieter. I knew I had to hang up quickly.

"Okay, well, see you tomorrow, bye," I whispered while I walked back to the phone receiver. I placed it down and three seconds later the garage door opened.

"Were you talking to someone?" Dad asked.

"Oh, just talking to myself," I lied, which felt terrible.

He looked at me suspiciously and said, "Okay, well, I'm all done out there." He went to the sink and turned on the faucet to wash his hands. As I started to walk away, he said, "Hey, I'm sorry to be so down on your singing thing."

I turned around and looked at him, hoping he was about to tell me to go ahead and give singing my all. He dried his hands and leaned on the counter.

"Look, I know you need to do this project for school," he said, "but I can't support you being in a band after that. It's too much time. I need your help around here."

I took a deep breath. I knew I had to keep my emotions in check or risk him saying I wasn't allowed to be in the band at all, even for the project. "I know you need my help, Dad. I won't let my singing get in the way of that." I purposely didn't say I'd stop singing. I simply assured him I'd keep helping out. While he stared at me, I wondered if he could tell I had no intention to quit the band once I got in. Instead, I had plans to be super successful and get him to change his mind.

"Okay, we're good then?" he asked, giving me relief that he didn't suspect anything.

"Yep, we're good," I said. I forced myself to smile as naturally as possible, and decided that I might as well dive into another uncomfortable topic.

"So, Mom's picking Aria up here after school to go to the doctor, in case you forgot about that," I said.

He straightened up and picked up the towel again, refolded it and placed it back on the sink. "Yes, I remembered," he said. Whenever Mom came up in conversation, he tried to change topics or walked away. This time he stayed put and looked painfully sad.

"So, Aria asked if we'd be getting hamburgers together after. You think that's a possibility? It would be really good for her. This back-to-school stuff has been rough on her." It was also something I thought could be good for all of us, but I didn't mention that. Dad picked up the towel again, unfolded it, then folded it, and set it back down.

"I'm willing to go, but I don't think your mom will be," he said. He looked like he might cry. I hadn't seen him that way since the night he'd lost his job. I didn't want to see it again.

"I bet she will, Dad," I said. "Plan on being ready tomorrow, probably around five. If Mom doesn't want us all to go out, I'll bring something home for you anyway and we can watch one of those weird shows you like or something."

They weren't really weird shows. One of them was another music show, *The Captain and Tenille*. I kind of liked that one. When Mom was home we used to watch it together as a family and sing along to the songs we knew.

"Okay, sounds like a plan," Dad said.

I returned to my room and replaced Carole King with my Music Power Original Hits album. I set the needle on Captain and Tenille's "Love Will Keep us Together," and sung along, hoping tomorrow might help bring my family back together again.

# Chapter 24

Normally I wouldn't want to listen to Aria go on about every single bird she saw on our walk to school, but this time I was so thankful for her rambling. Without her, the walk would have been a march of silence with Matthew.

"So, I guess I'll see you in class and hopefully at lunch?" I asked when we reached campus.

"Yeah, see ya in class," he said before walking away.

As soon as the lunch bell rang in English class, where we'd been working in our separate groups for the project, Matthew and Ronnie left the room without me again. While Brandon and Ricky argued about who the greatest guitarist of all time was, and Dahlia continued to stare at herself in her compact mirror and touch up her makeup, I debated whether I should stay or go. Part of me wanted to stay because of Brandon. But I also wanted to run out the door and catch up with Ronnie and Matthew. In my unrealistic dream world, we'd all somehow mesh into one happy crowd. Brandon stood and said, "Hey rock star, you having lunch with me again?" I knew I couldn't turn him down, especially after his question spurred Dahlia to roll her eyes and slam her mirror shut.

Dahlia stood and said, "Well, I guess I'll see you guys later for band practice." She unwrapped a piece of gum and popped it in her mouth. "Can't wait to hear you sing, Carol," she said between loud chomps, "and if you get too nervous, I'm happy to sing for you if needed." She flashed a wide fake smile and turned to leave. I tried to ignore the pit in my stomach that had nothing to do with hunger for lunch. I now had that stupid memory of my failed school performance front and center in my mind, and felt like telling Brandon I couldn't be in his band.

"Hey, you okay? You don't look so good," Brandon said.

I never was good at hiding my feelings, especially the anxious ones. I took a deep breath, let it out slowly, something Aria told me her doctor recommended for stressful moments. It did help a little. "I'm fine," I said. "Probably just hungry." I didn't want to tell him, or admit out loud that I was terrified of singing in front of him and his friends.

"Well, good thing it's lunch then. Let's go eat."

I followed him out and this time, instead of being looked at as some unidentifiable Brandon cling-on, his friends greeted me by name, like I was one of them.

"Hey Carol," the pretty cheerleader from English class said, "Love those earrings, super cool."

"Oh, thanks," I said, touching the feathery accessory.

"Carol, I hear you might be joining Brandon's band," a boy with curly dark hair said as he stood behind the cheerleader whose name I was ashamed to admit I didn't yet know.

"Oh, yes, possibly," I said, not ready to fully commit.

"Awesome, nice to meet you, I'm Dylan, the bass guitarist. You joining us after school?"

"Yeah, I am," I said, ignoring every fiber in my being that kept telling me I was going to fail big time again.

"Cool, Brandon says you've got some nice pipes."

The pressure of meeting these expectations Brandon had set was getting to me. I wished they were much lower. "Well, hope I don't disappoint you all, but I guess you've got Dahlia if I do."

He didn't seem too enthused about that option. "Yeah," was all he said as he nodded. "I think she's just temporary, so . . ." he stopped mid-sentence once he looked to his left and saw Dahlia in the group next to us. I took the hint to move on to a new topic.

"So, how long have you been playing bass?" I asked.

Dylan went on to tell me he'd played for a few years, and then the conversation somehow switched into a discussion of the best way to make a peanut butter and jelly sandwich, inspired by the fact that we both had that for lunch. I thought of how much Aria would have loved this conversation. I hoped she was having lunch with Katelyn, or Matthew and Ronnie, not by herself.

After school, I saw her in the same place as the day before, and unfortunately, she didn't look any more relaxed. As soon as she saw me, she jogged over to me.

"North! I mean, Carol, sorry!" she said when she reached me.

"Hey, Aria, how was your day?" I asked.

She bounced up and down on her toes and kept looking around at everyone walking by. "I don't know. I don't really want to talk about it. Can we go?" She asked. This translated to me as not being the best day.

"Yes, we can go as soon as Matthew gets here," I said.

"He already left," Aria said.

I hoped she was wrong.

"Did you talk to him?" I asked.

"Yeah, he said he had to get home right away, and told me to wait for you."

I wasn't sure whether I should feel angry at him for deserting us or for being dumb enough to walk home alone. Both were bad.

"Was he walking with Ronnie?" I asked, hoping that was the case.

"I didn't see her," Aria said. "Should we wait for her?"

"Yeah, let's wait for a little bit. We can walk with her up until she crosses to go the other direction to her house."

Right after I said that, Ronnie showed up, and seemed as frustrated as me that Matthew didn't wait for us, but not really surprised. "He's sort of upset with you," Ronnie said as we started to walk.

"I know he is, Ronnie, but I wish he'd be a little more understanding. I'm not planning to become best friends with Dahlia and Ricky. I just can't turn down this opportunity."

"You know that expression, birds of a feather flock together?" Ronnie asked.

"Oh! I know that one!" Aria shouted, and then proceeded, as expected, to explain the bird origin of the expression. She was still rambling enthusiastically about it when we reached the corner and Ronnie had to say goodbye to her.

"You can tell me the rest later, Aria," Ronnie said as she crossed with a pack of others going her direction, "See you tomorrow!"

Aria stopped talking for a second as she waved goodbye and then continued on. I wasn't really listening. I was instead trying to see if Matthew was possibly still in sight ahead of us, or whether the jerks from the day before were anywhere nearby. I plotted in my mind what I'd say to them, even though in reality I'd likely be too afraid to do that. We were nearly home, with no sighting of either of them, before Aria realized I wasn't really listening.

"You know it's polite to act interested in someone's conversation even if you're not," she said. "That's what Mrs. Flear told me today when I visited her at lunch."

That answered my earlier question about whether she was alone at lunch. Mrs. Flear was one of Aria's teachers last year too, and was really good to Aria, teaching her more than English and Social Studies. She gave Aria really good advice about real life stuff.

"That's true," I said, "I'm sorry, Aria. So are you excited to see Mom?" I knew that would be a positive way to change the conversation.

"Yes!" she said, "Come on! We should hurry so she's not waiting for us!" She turned her walk into a light jog, and even though I knew Mom wouldn't be picking us up for another half hour, I let her go ahead. I watched her as she trotted toward our house and stopped on the lawn to wait for me.

"She's not here yet!" she yelled.

Even though I knew there was no hurry, I decided to jog the last couple blocks home too. It actually felt kind of good, and I picked up my pace, feeling like little shreds of stress were released from each short breath and each quick step.

When I reached Aria, she gave me a high five like I'd finished a race. "Nice running!" she said. "You were like a roadrunner."

As she continued on about roadrunners, I made it a point to listen to her this time.

"A roadrunner's short quick steps are supposed to remind us that when we want to accomplish something, we should take little steps to get there," she said. "That's what roadrunners do. They take short, fast steps most of the time to get where they want to go, preferring that even over flying."

"That's good advice, Aria. Thanks," I said.

"Sure!" she said with a big proud smile before heading inside.

I stayed outside for a moment, watched several sparrows hop along the sidewalk in front of me, and then take flight. I looked down the street toward Matthew's house and wondered if singing in Brandon's band was the next small step I was meant to take.

# Chapter 25

"Mama!" Aria shouted once she saw Mom's car pull up. She jumped back from the window, flopped over the couch, and ran to the front door. I grabbed her bag which she'd left on the floor by the door, along with my binder and purse. As I exited, I heard the garage door open, and then saw Dad appear from behind the wall of boxes and bins and every saved item that didn't fit in our house.

"Hey, have a good time!" he shouted. He looked over at Mom's car, hesitated for a second, and then walked with me. He usually avoided her when she came over. The last time they spoke, maybe a month ago, they argued about his job search. The time before that became a fight about how he needed to help with getting Aria and me to the dentist, and that we'd better be eating healthy, reading books, getting outside, all the things she normally made sure we did. Of course that ended in him telling her she should come home if she was that worried about us. So, I didn't know why he needed to follow me to the car. It would probably not end well.

"Good afternoon, Belinda," Dad said in an obviously phony and formal tone as he opened the back door for me. I missed hearing him say,

"Hey Bel," and stopping whatever he was doing to give her a kiss.

"Hi, Frank," she said as she turned away like she had no intention of carrying on a conversation with him.

I hated this. I sat down and waited for the bomb to drop.

"Are you coming with us, Dad?" Aria asked from the front seat. "Here, let me get in the back with North." She unbuckled her seatbelt and started to get out.

"No, Aria, I'm not coming with you right now, but I thought maybe we could all have burgers together after your appointment."

Mom shook her head, but before she could say anything, Aria chimed in. "Oh, yes! That would be awesome! You mean all of us, right?" She turned from him to Mom, who immediately stopped shaking her head. I couldn't see Aria's face, but I knew exactly how it looked in that moment—big blue hope-filled eyes above a wide, toothy grin that deflected the word no nearly every time.

"Yes, all of us," Dad said. "Is that good with you?" He gave Mom a pleading look that wasn't as heart-melting as Aria's, but definitely came close, especially since it wasn't a normal look for him.

*Say yes, say it's fine, come on Mom*, I said in my head.

"Okay, yes, we can all go out for burgers later," she said.

Before Mom could have any slight regret, Aria reached over and hugged her. "Thank you, Mom. You're the best!"

I let out the breath I'd been holding and smiled at Dad, who looked happier than I'd seen in a long time.

"Okay, well, I'll see you guys in a bit." He shut the door and before Mom took off, she turned around to me.

"How are you? Good to see you." She reached back to grab my hand.

"I'm good, Mom. Glad to see you too." The one good thing from being apart had been that when we were together, she seemed less distracted and more interested in my life.

She pulled away from the curb slowly. "Looks like you brought homework to do in the doctor's office, or do you want me to drop you at the library?" she asked, knowing that I usually got more done when I wasn't distracted by noisy children at the pediatrician's office.

"Actually, do you think you could take me to a friend's? We planned to work on a group project for English today." I wanted to explain what the project was about, to let her know it might land me a part as the singer in a band, but I didn't want to jinx my luck. If all went well, then I'd tell her.

"Sure, that's fine, but you know Aria's appointment is only about an hour, right? I thought we could go walk in the woods or the park before we go to dinner if you want."

"That works for me," I said, glad that I'd have an excuse to leave Brandon's. That way if my singing was horrible I wouldn't have to hang around shamefully.

At the stop sign, she asked, "Where does your friend live? I'm assuming it's not far. Aria's appointment is in fifteen minutes."

"No, not far at all. It's on the other side of Elm Road." I opened my binder to find the note with Brandon's address. "It's 115 Carlisle Street, in the fancy part of town a few streets over from Ronnie's house," I said, feeling comfort in the fact that her house was a relatively close escape plan if needed.

Mom had just pulled away from the stop, but quickly put on the brakes. Luckily, no one was driving behind us. "115 Carlisle Street?" she asked. "Really?"

"Yeah, really. Don't be so shocked. The homes there aren't that great." That was true. They were newer and bigger than ours, but they weren't Beverly Hills status.

Mom laughed, shook her head, and continued driving. "I'm not impressed with the address, believe me," she said. "I'm amused by it."

This made no sense. "Amused?"

Her tires screeched to an abrupt stop when she nearly missed the red light at Elm and Birch, the same intersection I'd seen Brandon on the first day of school and the same place Matthew was harassed. I was beginning to think I should avoid going this direction if I wanted a quiet, normal sort of day.

"Mom, you're obviously upset. Do you want to pull over and talk about this?" I never enjoyed being in the car with her when she was upset, as it was then that I often saw my life flash before me due to missed stoplights, four-wheeling onto curbs, and damaged rear view mirrors from coming too close to poles.

"Honey, I'm fine," she said as she tapped her fingers on the steering wheel. The light turned green and she lurched forward. "I just know who lives in the house, started cleaning it a few weeks ago, and the mother is, well, something else. That's all I can say about her. I met her son once. He seems nice enough, but he probably has to be if he's able to live with that mother of his."

Wow, that didn't sound good. "Am I safe being there?" I didn't think she'd take me there if it wasn't, but figured I should ask.

"Yes, you're safe," she laughed. "She's not going to hurt you. She'll just try to impress you with her fancy things that need to be cleaned a dozen times before they meet her satisfaction, and she might comment on your clothes. She didn't like mine, said they were too wild and unprofessional, and gave me fifty dollars to buy some white pants and a collared shirt to wear when I cleaned if I wanted to keep the job, which is the dumbest thing I've ever done, but I really need the money, and she pays well."

I looked down at my pink tie-dye shirt that I'd spent hours creating and was surprised to find myself wishing I'd worn one of my boring outfits from last year, or at least something that wasn't so bright and loud. "Maybe I shouldn't go," I said, feeling less confident than ever about singing as Mom pulled up to his house.

"Woah, nice house!" Aria shouted. I looked out the window, wanting to sink farther into the backseat and hide as I looked at the long sweeping driveway, the bright green lawn with rows of yellow and red poppies bordering the walkway, that led to the brick-trimmed house with a gigantic black front door with shiny brass knobs. It looked more like Beverly Hills than I'd thought.

Mom turned around after she stopped the car and said, "North, or sorry, I mean Carol, you can't be afraid of her. She is not better than you. Walk in there with your chin up and flaunt that bright beautiful shirt. Her son seems very nice, and he definitely needs a positive girl in his life. Trust me on that," she said.

"Woah, they have one of those big door knockers! You have to go so you can knock on the door with it," Aria said. "I'll go with you if you want."

I knew she would if I asked her to, but of course I turned her down. "Thanks, Aria. I'll be okay. You need to get to your appointment. I'll see you guys in an hour." I said. As I opened the door, the image of Mom scrubbing and cleaning Brandon's house while his mom made fun of her clothes sunk in. I stopped for a moment and said, "Don't come to the door when you pick me up, Mom. I'll pay attention to the time and wait for you outside, okay?" I hoped she didn't realize that I felt a little embarrassed of her at that moment, something I'd never felt before. Brandon might look down on me if he knew my mom was his housekeeper.

I walked to the door and reached for the brass doorknob, knowing Aria was watching with excitement, wishing she could knock for me if it wouldn't embarrass me for her to do so. Shortly after I knocked, Brandon's mom appeared before me, a beautiful blonde woman with bright pink lipstick, and a clean bob haircut. She wore a light pink collared shirt and black slacks, like someone who worked at an important job in a big tall building in the city. Her eyes, the same bright blue as Brandon's, stared into mine and then moved directly to my shirt. She glanced back up at my face and said, "Hello, you must be Carol, the singer," she said.

At that moment I didn't care at all what she thought about my shirt. I was Carol, the singer. I smiled and said, "Yes, that's me," and entered her home with a secret pride at the glossy, white, perfectly clean floors before me.

# Chapter 26

I made my best efforts to be polite to Mrs. Stone after the way she looked at my shirt, but she didn't seem impressed.

"Your house is beautiful," I said, still proud of the fact that a lot of that beauty came from my mom's cleaning skills.

Mrs. Stone held a glass of iced tea in one hand, took a sip, and with a stern tone said, "Brandon's down the hall in the music room to your left," Then she turned the other way toward the kitchen, which seemed to be the same size as my entire house.

Whenever I entered someone else's home, I noticed how different it was than mine, and Brandon's was definitely a palace in comparison. Aside from the lack of clutter, it smelled nice, a clean mix of pine and lemon. A three-tiered glass chandelier hung from the center of the high ceiling, illuminating a large silver-framed mirror I glanced in as I walked by. Ivory sculptures and jade vases adorned side tables perched next to soft blue velvet chairs. A glimpse into the kitchen gave a view of shiny black marble countertops topped with a large blue bowl filled with oranges and an arrangement of fresh white daisies in a crystal vase. It felt more like a museum than a home.

The hallway walls held large framed art, one a painting of a pond edged with lavender and golden yellow flowers; another a wash of shapes in hues of deep blue, black, and purple. Also unlike my home, I didn't have to step over anything as I walked. I could hear a drum beat followed by the strum of a guitar, talking, and laughter. I dreaded entering the room full of eyes on me, the one with the supposed beautiful voice. I took a deep breath and let it out before stepping through the doorway, and instead of Brandon, my eyes caught sight of the face I'd hoped to never see again, the boy who stared me in the eyes the other day after pushing Matthew to the ground. I stopped in the doorway and felt like I couldn't step any farther. All the elegance of Brandon's home immediately vanished in his presence.

He smiled at me, held up a can of A & W Root Beer like he was cheering me and said, "Hey, you're the girl I ran into the other day after school. Sorry about that, again."

Clueless about my friendship with Matthew, he obviously thought that was the perfect apology. I wanted to tell him he was the most disgusting and unforgivable person on the planet, and ask him how he could arrogantly stand there with that smug smile and look at me with those beady brown eyes that had recently seen my best friend knocked down and humiliated. I couldn't will myself to speak to him.

"I guess I should introduce myself. I'm Chad." He reached his hand out. I wanted to grab it and toss him onto his back like Bruce Lee did with his enemies in the martial arts action movie I watched with my dad one time. But as I looked away from him and saw everyone staring at me, I forced myself to acknowledge him.

"I'm Carol," I said as I grabbed his hand, squeezed as hard as possible, and gave it a firm shake before quickly letting it go.

"Woah, nice grip," he said while shaking out his hand. "Brandon told me you have a great voice, but didn't mention you were so tough."

Brandon stepped in and said, "Yeah, I'm not sure I've seen this side of her before. You okay?" The genuine concern in Brandon's eyes once I looked at him squelched some of my anger and made me realize I wasn't hiding my feelings well.

"Yeah, sorry, I'm fine," I said, unable to come up with a more informative lie. I forced a small smile at Brandon and hoped that would be good enough.

Brandon came closer and stood in front of Chad, then quietly said, "Hey, if you're nervous about singing, don't be. Just sing like you did that day in the parking lot."

I was glad he mistook my anger for nerves, but then Dahlia stood up and said, "So, are we going to play some music or what? I can sing if Carol isn't ready."

It was bad enough to think about singing in front of the jerk who bullied my best friend, let alone the girl who did the same to me only in a more subtle way. The only good thing about it was that now I felt angry enough to finally speak up.

"I never said I wasn't ready, Dahlia, but thanks for the offer," I didn't even try to give her the same phony smile she had flashed at me, and I didn't care if I sounded snarky.

"Okay, well, let's go," Brandon said as he led me to the microphone. He began strumming his guitar and then asked, "What do you want to sing?"

"You know any Carole King?" I asked.

His strumming stopped, and he looked at me like I had six heads or something. "Really?"

"Yeah, really. I told you she was my favorite, didn't I? Do you not know how to play any of her songs?" I asked.

"No, we can play her songs. We just prefer not to," he said.

I tried to not be shocked about anything anymore. Reminding myself that this band was only a start for my future career and not where I had to stay, I forced myself to say, "Okay, well what would you like me to sing?"

"How about the Beatles?" he asked.

Even though I knew I should be polite, I also knew I was likely giving him the same look he'd just given me. The Beatles were awesome, obviously, but I didn't sound remotely close to Paul McCartney, also obvious. I didn't think I could even sing a decent female version of any of their songs. "Twist and Shout" popped into my head. That would be horrible. Then "Help!" also a no, even though help was something I desperately needed at the moment.

Brandon started strumming the familiar tune of "Hey Jude." I closed my eyes, listened to him play, and then began to sing along. Soon I heard the tambourine, which I thought would bother me because it was Dahlia, but now it felt okay. Chad came in with the drums next, then Dylan on the bass, and I sang right along with them, the words coming easy. I didn't open my eyes until the "Na na na nananana" part when I heard Brandon harmonize with me remarkably well, followed by everyone else singing along too. Everyone had huge smiles, and as Dahlia danced her way closer to me, shaking the tambourine, she nodded and smiled as if she actually liked me. Even Chad seemed like a much better person to me at that moment. This was why I sang. This was why I needed to do this. Music made things better.

When we finished, Brandon turned to look at me and said, "That was awesome."

"Yep, I think she's in," Dylan said. "That was the best we've ever sounded. I think you were the missing piece we needed, Carol."

"Totally agree," Chad said before banging out a short drum beat and then adding, "I don't know why you were nervous. If I had that voice, I'd be singing all the time. You're definitely what we need if we want anyone to take us seriously as a band."

I turned to the person who'd made me nervous, the one whose friendly smile during "Hey Jude" was now a straight frown that shouted "Hey jerks, she's stealing my spotlight." For a second I actually felt bad for her, but then she opened her mouth and reminded me why that was dumb.

"I just hope you can do that in front of a crowd of people. That seems to be a problem for you. I'd hate to see you humiliate yourself again, or embarrass us."

I stared back at her and tried to find even a slight trace of the Dahlia who minutes ago acted like we were on the same team.

"Dahlia, really? That's your concern?" Brandon asked, clearly annoyed.

Instead of silencing her, this fueled her anger. "Yes, Brandon, I am concerned about that. I'm the only one here who's seen her perform for a crowd, and it wasn't good."

"Okay, well, we all have bad days. If you're the only one who doesn't want her in the band for such a dumb reason, maybe you should be the one to leave," he said.

"Sure!" was her surprising response. "I can leave." She handed her tambourine to Chad. "I guess you can have this back." Then she grabbed her purse and swung it over her shoulder. "Good luck finding a place to record your music. I'm pretty sure my father won't be interested in offering cheap rent for the recording studio if I'm not in the band." She turned toward the door.

"Woah, Dahlia, hold on," Chad said. "Brandon's not the one who decides everything. We don't want you to leave, right guys?" he looked at Dylan, then me, and briefly at Brandon.

I tried to think of something nice to say, but couldn't bring myself to conjure up a good lie, plus I wasn't officially in the band yet.

Brandon sighed, looked up like he might find an answer there on the ceiling, and finally said, "No, Chad, I don't want Dahlia to leave, but she needs a better reason to question Carol being our singer." He looked at her. "You seemed to enjoy singing with her, so let's give her a try, okay? That's all I'm asking."

Dahlia stood with her arms folded, tapping her foot as she stared back at us. "Okay, I'm fine with giving her a try," she said with a tone that screamed insincerity. "But if it gets embarrassing with her in the lead, I get to take over as singer."

"Fine," Brandon said. "You good with that, Carol?"

"Yeah, I'm fine with that," I said, forcing myself to look Dahlia straight in the eye to show her I wasn't afraid. She smiled back at me, but the friendliness I saw in her while we sang together had definitely vanished. "Maybe you should sing a song now while I play tambourine. You'll need to keep your voice tuned if I can't sing for some reason." I held out the microphone for her, daring her to sing better than I had.

She stepped toward me and instead of taking the microphone, said, "That's okay. I'll get my chance to sing," and grabbed the tambourine from Chad. "Why don't you sing the song you were supposed to sing in middle school? What was it called? Something about a bird? Cawing like your sister?" She started to laugh, softly at first, and then a full on belly laugh. "Oh man, that was so hilarious. You guys should have seen it."

Dylan and Chad looked at each other, then at Brandon, smiling like they wanted to hear more of this hilarious story.

"Caw! Caw!" Dahlia belted out while she waved her arms up and down. "Remember that, Carol?" She laughed even harder now. "Actually, never mind what it was called, and we don't need to sing it. Let's just caw together, for old time's sake, for Aria!" She put her arm around me like we were sharing in some fond memory together.

I would have liked to be the strong one at that moment, to do what I was always told to do when someone is bothering you, ignore it. But my breathing grew heavier, my heart beat faster, and all I wanted to do was scream at her or run. So while she laughed and laughed, I set down the microphone and said, "It was 'Nightingale.'" I looked at Brandon, who stood with a confused look on his face. "It's by Carole King," I said.

I left the room, holding back my desire to yell at Dahlia while a tornado swirled inside my heart. Once outside, I sat on the curb to wait for Mom to pick me up, and tried to quiet the echo of Dahlia's caw sounds in my head. I took deep slow breaths, pictured all of us singing "Hey Jude," and reminded myself of what I'd just done. I sang, afraid, on my own, in front of others, in front of Dahlia, and I was asked to do it again. But did I really want to? I couldn't figure out how Brandon tolerated Dahlia and Chad. Did the fact that he wanted me to be in the band mean I was more like them than I realized? That thought was too horrifying to think about, especially when it might cause me to quit the band. I needed this chance to be seen as a singer.

A bird chirped loudly in the tree behind me, its shrill squawk causing me to turn and look. It was a blue jay. I remembered that Aria told me blue jays are louder in the fall because they're done with their summer nesting and are no longer concerned about predators finding their nests. "They're singing their happy little hearts out!" Aria had said.

"I could learn a thing or two from you, Mr. Blue Jay," I whispered. "It's fall for me too, and I'm tired of the predators."

# Chapter 27

The bluejay took no interest in a conversation with me, blasting one more loud squeal as it took off into the late afternoon sky. A chorus of chirps from numerous finches took the bluejay's place as they flitted among the bright pink blossoms of the bushes that edged the driveway.

"I doubt you all really want to talk to me either," I said to them, remembering a time when I actually tried speaking their language. Up until about second grade, I copied almost everything Aria did, including bird sounds. As soon as other kids looked at me strangely and laughed, I knew to stop, but Aria didn't. Even if I nudged her, told her to quit, she would look at me like she didn't understand and kept chirping.

Even though I didn't follow her lead anymore, I got why she loved talking to birds. They never looked at her weird for trying to talk to them. In fact, with Aria, they almost always stayed close, turning their heads like they were listening and understanding as they sung back to her. One time she came home from elementary school in tears and said, "Everyone tells me I'm dumb, and weird, and to leave them alone." I followed her out to the backyard and sat with her, trying to think of something to say to make her feel better. A robin flew right up to her and landed on her hand. It was an amazing thing to see. Aria held her breath for a second to keep herself from squealing in delight. It looked at her and chirped for maybe ten seconds, and then flew back to its spot on the patio chair across from us. "At least the birds want to be my friend," she said. I never told her to stop talking to them again after that. I only wished that more people would be like the birds.

The finches' song grew louder as more flocked the bushes. Normally I would enjoy sitting and listening to them, but I wasn't enjoying anything at that moment. Unlike these birds, I wanted to get far away from Brandon's before he or anyone from the band came out. Fortunately, the next loud bird sound was one I wanted to hear. It was Aria, who chirped and cooed out the window as Mom pulled up to the curb. I jumped up to get into the car.

"How'd it go?" Mom asked when I closed the door.

"Fine," I said, not wanting to explain about Dahlia. "Can we please drive? I really don't want to sit here and talk."

"Oh, sure." Mom kept her eyes on me for a second, then proceeded to drive. "Aria told me this project is about starting a band, and that you're the lead singer?"

I should have known Aria wouldn't be quiet about that. "Uh, yes," I said. "That's the project, and I actually sang today. I did really well."

Mom's face lit up. "I knew it! I knew you'd show off that voice one day. Next time I clean that house I'll picture you singing in it. Then I might actually enjoy scrubbing things multiple times to meet Mrs. Stone's ridiculous standards."

I was so happy to see Mom smiling, and to make her proud. "Their house was immaculate. You do a good job, Mom."

"Ha, thanks sweetheart. I hope you told Mrs. Stone that."

"Well, I did compliment her home, but she didn't seem to appreciate it."

"Yep, that sounds like her. I think she's like that with everyone except the friends she has over for tea. The first day I worked for her was to help her set up, serve, and then clean up after one of her gatherings. When everyone arrived, she was the sweetest, friendliest person on earth. The minute they left, she was right back to cold, hard Mrs. Stone."

"Maybe that's why her name is Stone," Aria said. "She's hard and cold, like a rock."

Mom smirked and said, "I hadn't thought about that, Aria, but don't repeat that anywhere. It wouldn't be nice."

I hoped Aria remembered Mom's advice. Brandon probably wouldn't appreciate her interpretation of his mom's name.

"Well, we've got a little time to stop at the woods before dinner. How does that sound?"

"Yes!" Aria shouted.

"Fine with me," I said, looking forward to being outside with Mom and Aria, without others around to judge us, where we could be ourselves.

"We might see the owls again!" Aria said. "They can be seen more easily this time of year. Did you know that? It's their early nesting season, and since it gets dark sooner, they're out earlier now."

Mom and I listened as she described where we might find them, and of course the cliffs came up again as one of the options.

"Honey, I don't think we'll have time to get to the cliffs, and you do know those cliffs aren't safe to climb, right?" Mom said.

Even though I could only see the back of her head, I knew Aria rolled her eyes at that. "Mom, I know. North has told me that like a million times, but I still don't think it's a big deal. If I knew the owls were there, I would definitely climb to see them."

"No, Aria, don't do that," Mom said in the tone she used whenever the topic was absolutely not debatable.

Aria opened her mouth and leaned toward Mom like she was going to argue, but as soon as she saw Mom's eyes warning her she'd better listen, she sat back and said nothing more.

The parking lot was nearly empty when we pulled into the park entrance where the woods began. The sun had begun to set and the air was cooler now with a light breeze. Aria led the way to the trailhead, skipping and flapping her arms, free and happy.

Mom put her arm around me and I reached up to hold her hand as it rested on my shoulder. "I've missed you, North. Is it okay if I call you that? I know you want to be called Carol, but you're still my North Star."

How could I say no to that? "Yes, Mom. You can call me North."

"I'm really proud of you," she said, "for singing, not giving up on that dream of yours."

"Thanks, Mom," I said, hoping she really meant it. I still felt hurt about what she'd said to Dad about my dream of singing, but she seemed to say a lot of things she didn't mean when she was angry at him. "How about you? Are you painting? Making jewelry?"

"Uh, no, not really," she said. "But when I scrub floors I sometimes imagine that the water is paint and make little designs on the dirty floors. Does that count?"

I laughed and said, "Well, no, but it sounds like a good way to make your job more fun, especially if you have to clean for ungrateful people like Mrs. Stone."

"Yes, it does make it more tolerable," she said. "How about Aria? Is she doing okay?"

I didn't want to tell her the truth. I wanted this time with her to feel like it used to, when she was living with us, and I didn't have to hang on to each precious minute before she said goodbye. I didn't want to upset her, but I also really wanted her to know how hard it was with her away from home. Pretending that everything was fine all the time was making me feel like I might explode. As Aria spun in a circle, laughing, I wished I could feel that happy. I hadn't really laughed in so long, and once this time with Mom ended, I'd go home to all the responsibilities and feel even worse.

"No, Mom, Aria's really not okay." I could feel her eyes on me and refused to look back because I knew then I'd lose the courage to say what I said next. "None of us are, to be honest. Dad's always working on that stupid spare room, the house is always a disaster. I don't know how I'm going to keep up with doing everything you did for us, plus get good grades, plus join a band, which I'm not willing to give up because then I'm giving up on something that might actually help me break out of this miserable existence one day." I took a deep breath and felt Mom pull away as she moved in front of me, stopped and put her hands on my shoulders so I had to face her.

"North, I'm sorry," she said. "You shouldn't have to do everything I did, which by the way, didn't ever stop the house from being in chaos or keep your dad from doing his own thing most of the time. But you have a right to feel overwhelmed."

I waited for her to tell me more, to tell me she was coming back home because she didn't want me to feel bad anymore.

"I just need a bit more time to figure things out," I looked away from her to Aria, who still skipped and squawked freely ahead of us. I removed Mom's hands from my shoulders, feeling defeated.

"North, I'm sorry," Mom said.

"It's fine," I lied, and before either of us could say anything next, we heard two loud bangs, then another. Even though I'd only heard that sound on television, I knew it was gunshots.

Aria came to a halt, like a bird frozen in midflight, then lowered her arms and turned to us with her eyes wide with terror. I could tell she wanted to say something, but nothing came out. She turned back around, then at us, shaking her head with one hand over her mouth and the other one pointing to the trail ahead of her.

Mom grabbed my arm and pulled me as we ran to her. There on the trail, about fifteen feet ahead, was a large white bird. We looked at each other in shock and then together made our way to the bird. "Oh my gosh, is that a swan? A goose?" I said.

"It's an egret," Aria said. "I don't understand how this happened. Why would anyone hurt such a beautiful, innocent bird?" She knelt down beside it, and eyed its limp, lifeless body. "I want to pick it up, but I know I shouldn't. We need to call animal patrol. They'll know where to take it."

"I think the police need to be called first," Mom said. "No one should be shooting guns in this park. There's a payphone in the parking lot. Let's go call."

I began to follow Mom, but Aria looked up without budging. "I'm not leaving the egret," Aria said. "You go ahead. I'm staying here."

"Aria, there's someone out here with a gun," I said. "We need to stay together."

"I don't think sticking together is going to make a difference. Ducks and deer and doves still get shot when there's a bunch of them together. If you need me to go, you'll need to carry me because I'm NOT leaving this bird, okay? Just hurry up and make the phone call!"

I didn't think Mom was going to give in to this, but to my surprise, she did. "Okay, but don't separate. I'll be quick, and if you hear guns again, or anything else suspicious, you head to that parking lot right away, you understand?"

I nodded and said, "We will, Mom, promise."

A couple minutes after Mom left, Aria's stress about the egret heightened. She waved her hands rapidly and breathed in and out with quick, short breaths, like she couldn't get enough air.

"Aria, it's going to be okay, relax. Take deep slow breaths, okay?"

It was like she heard nothing I said. Her breathing got even faster, along with her waving hands. I knelt next to her, rested one hand on her knee and began to sing "Nightingale," and about three lines in, she was singing along with me, her eyes closed, tuned out to the sadness on the ground before her.

Mom arrived a few minutes later, and let us continue singing. On our third time through the song, my voice feeling raspy and dry, we saw two police officers heading toward us on the trail. I stopped singing and said, "Aria, the police are here. They'll help us get help for the bird."

She stopped singing, grabbed my hand and said, "Okay, but let's pray for the bird first. I should have thought of that before." Before I could respond, she began, "Dear God, please bring this beautiful bird into heaven. Let it be free to fly again. Thank you and Amen."

Short and sweet, and surprisingly, that prayer didn't feel weird to me at all. I hadn't figured out how to talk to God on my own. I usually tossed up prayers without much meaning, brief "God, what do I do?" prayers, like one day when I upset Aria over not having lunch with her and asked God how to fix it. Sometimes I said a quick, "Okay, God. Help me" in my mind right before singing in front of people. But even then, I didn't feel like I was really praying the right way. The fact that Aria, who carried her Bible with her everywhere and told me more about God than anyone else, said a short and simple prayer, was a relief. Maybe my simple prayers were okay.

Aria squeezed my hand tighter as the officers approached us.

"Hello girls, I'm Officer Rinaldi, and that's Officer Krayton." He pointed to the female officer next to Mom. "Do you mind answering a few questions?" One of the officers said. He stood a few feet from us, staring down at the bird. He folded his tanned arms in front of him and shook his head like he also didn't understand why the bird was shot. I let go of Aria's hand and stood to answer him, and felt like a tiny child in front of his tall stature.

"No, we don't mind," I answered.

"It's rare to see an egret. Did you know that?" Aria asked as she stayed kneeling and looked up at Officer Rinaldi.

"I believe that," he said. "I don't remember ever seeing one up close like this."

"Yep, in New Zealand it's really rare. The Maori people there say that a great egret, Kotuku, symbolizes everything rare and beautiful, and is a magical bird seen maybe once in a lifetime," Aria said.

"Oh, interesting," Officer Rinaldi said, looking closer at Aria. "So you know a lot about these birds," Officer Rinaldi said, "Where'd you learn all that?"

His tone made me realize that Aria's bird knowledge might actually make her look suspicious in that moment. "She loves birds," I said. "We come here a lot to watch birds and she likes to identify as many as she can, talk to them, learn about them. This is pretty awful for her to see," I said, hoping he understood that Aria would never harm a bird.

He nodded and said, "I'm sorry you had to see this. So tell me what happened." He sounded less suspicious.

I answered, "We were walking along the trail and we heard three shots. Then we saw the bird on the ground. We didn't want to pick it up, but didn't want to just leave it here."

"You did the right thing," Officer Krayton said. She wasn't as tall as Officer Rinaldi, and a bit older, with streaks of gray in her dark hair that peeked out from under her hat. She seemed more relaxed than Rinaldi, like she'd seen stuff like this a lot. "It's not safe for people to have guns out here. You're lucky you didn't get hurt. We're going to search the area, see if we find anyone who might have done this, and make sure it's safe. We'll call animal control to come and get the bird. You all should head on home."

Aria still hadn't left the egret's side. She stared at us, then down at the bird.

"Come on, Aria, we can go now. They'll take good care of the bird," Mom said.

"I just want to look at him for one more minute," she said.

Mom looked at Officer Krayton, like she was asking for her permission to be a kind parent. "That's fine. We can give you a minute," she said.

Aria willingly stood when the time was up, and made the officers promise to call animal control. Then we walked back to the car, no longer feeling as carefree and happy as we did when we arrived.

Mom tried to cheer Aria up with the promise of a hamburger, and even though Aria smiled at the thought of this, she still seemed upset. We drove in silence to the familiar hamburger spot, PJ's Burgers, where Dad's parked car announced he was already there. Aria didn't waste any time once Mom entered a parking spot. She flung her door open before the engine was even off and said, "Wait until Dad hears what happened at the park!" Then she shut the door before either Mom or I could respond and dashed into the restaurant.

"This ought to be interesting," Mom said as she turned off the engine and grabbed her purse.

"Definitely," I said. I got out without hesitation, not because I was particularly excited about our dinner out, but because I knew Dad might need some clarity on the story Aria was about to share and some help in keeping her calm.

Cars buzzed by on the busy boulevard and a few groups laughed and chatted at the restaurant's outdoor tables. All seemed normal and happy outside, but inside was a different story. As soon as I entered, I could hear Aria's voice.

"It was horrible, Dad! The egret laid there, shot, on the ground, and we couldn't do anything to save it!" Aria was standing over him as he looked up from his seat at a table in the center of the room, and aside from the background music playing, there was complete silence as everyone turned to listen to Aria's shocking story.

Mom and I approached the table, and Mom placed her arms gently on Aria's shoulders. "Let's have a seat, Aria, and we can talk more after we decide what to eat. I'm guessing a chocolate shake will taste great tonight, with whatever else you decide."

Aria turned to Mom, "Mmm, yes, for sure a chocolate shake!"

We sat down, and once Mom got all our requests, she went to the counter to place our order. Dad sat with a stack of napkins, along with piles of straws and ketchup, enough for a group of at least twenty. I'd learned not to tell him it was too much. I knew his answer would be that we would be able to save the extras to use at home or to have in the car if needed. I tried to think of something to talk about, anything other than retelling what happened at the woods, knowing that would only stress out Aria.

"How was your day, Dad?" I asked.

"Oh, okay, finished some more of the spare room." He played with the pile of ketchup packs, stacking them on top of each other, and then said, "I'll be right back, just gonna get some salt packets."

Just what we needed, more salt for the already overly salted fries, and for Dad to take home to maintain our supply of restaurant condiments tightly packed into two small kitchen drawers. While he stood at the counter stuffing salt packets into his pockets, Mom returned to the table with our shakes. So far, we'd made it without further discussing the egret situation, and as long as there was a chocolate shake near, there was hope of keeping it that way.

"Oh, yum!" Aria said as she ripped the paper from the straw she'd been holding in anticipation of this moment. She poked it into the lid of the shake and fell instantly into bliss, her eyes closed as she sucked in big gulps of her favorite frozen treat.

Mom looked at the haul of goods on the table. "Well, looks like you won't be low on all the necessities for a while," she said as Dad plopped down a handful of salt packets.

"Nope, we're good for a while," I said, noticing a small boy at the table next to ours staring at our heap of items. The mom also stared, but not in the cute, innocent way the boy did. She eyed the table and then each of us while she chewed on her fries, her eyes moving from Mom, to Dad, then Aria, and finally on me, where her eyes met mine. She looked away, embarrassed to be caught staring.

Again, I tried to think of something to talk about. It seemed like a waste of time to finally sit here all together, the first time in months, and be silent.

"Well, North has something to brag about tonight, right?" Mom said.

I looked up, wishing she would read my expression and see that I didn't want to talk about the band.

Instead, she said, "Don't look so confused, North. Tell your dad about your singing."

So much for avoiding that topic. "Oh, yeah, I sang with Brandon's band today, and it went really well," I said, trying to act like it was no big deal.

Dad raised his brows and said, "Oh, I didn't know you were doing that today."

I could tell he was annoyed. "Yeah, Mom drove me to Brandon's to work on our project after school while she brought Aria to the doctor. They asked me to sing "Hey Jude," which I thought would be awful, but they told me I sang really well."

Dad took a bite of his hamburger. The rest of us looked at him, waiting for some sort of response. He kept chewing.

"Well, I think that's incredible," Mom said. "It's about time someone sees how talented you are."

"Yeah, it is!" Aria said through a mouthful of food.

Dad still said nothing. If he was doing that to discourage me, it wasn't working. It only made me more determined to prove I wasn't wasting my time. He carefully took a napkin from the tall stack and wiped his mouth, then his hands, and then stood up. He walked to the trash, threw the napkin away, and pulled another, after another, after another napkin from the dispenser until he had another armful to add to our already ridiculous supply. It looked like someone had dumped a trash can onto our table. I took a bite of my burger, followed immediately by another, trying to eat faster now so this meal could be over and we could leave. I felt ketchup drip on my hands, and the tomatoes and lettuce slip away from the bread. With lettuce hanging from my mouth, I looked up and saw Brandon enter the restaurant door, Dahlia at his side. I ducked behind the napkin stack and chewed faster than ever, peeking over the napkins. Within seconds, Brandon's eyes met mine. I felt like a little kid caught in a game of hide and seek. I wanted to run and get to the safe place, but it was too late.

Brandon smiled wide, raised his hand up, and said, "Hey! Carol!" Then he headed toward us, while Dahlia came along with him, smiling in a way that seemed more devious than friendly.

She looked me straight in the eye the whole time, and when she neared our table, she said, "Well, look who's here. What a pleasant surprise, especially after the way you ran off during our practice. We really missed you." Her sarcastic tone was loud and clear.

I finally swallowed my mouth full of food and forced myself to smile and match Dahlia's phony politeness. "Practice seemed pretty much over when I left, so I'm sure you didn't miss me that much."

Dahlia rolled her eyes.

"So, you guys grabbing some burgers tonight?" I asked in the awkward pause, as if that were really a question that needed answering since they were standing in a hamburger restaurant.

"Yeah, we are," Brandon said "I hope you're coming back for our next practice. You sounded really great today. Your family must love listening to you sing at home all the time," He turned and noticed my mom. Oh! Hey! You clean my house, right?"

I felt my face turn hot and wished I could crawl under the table and disappear.

Mom nodded as she finished chewing and wiped her mouth with her napkin. "Yes, I believe I do," she said.

"Woah, and you're Carol's mom?" he asked.

"Yes, I am."

"Woah, I had no idea. I guess I should say sorry for having to clean up my mess."

"No, that's what your parents pay me to do, clean up the messes. No need to apologize," Mom said.

Even though only a few sentences had been spoken, I felt like this was one of the longest moments of my life. I began to tear apart the napkin in my hand, bit by bit. It felt difficult to breathe. I felt so uncomfortable, not only because Brandon now knew my mom was his housekeeper, but also because I saw his eyes move from her to Aria, who was rapidly flapping her arms, and then to Dad, who was stuffing the napkins from the table into his already full North Carolina Tar Heels athletic bag. That bag had collected a lot of stuff over the years, its broken zipper proof of that fact. I tore the last bit of napkin in my hands and wadded it into a tight ball.

I saw Dahlia look at my dad next, and wanted to throw my napkin wad at her when she put her hand over her mouth in a weak attempt to hide her laugh. I couldn't sit there any longer. "Okay, well, I'm going to go get some water," I said as I stood up. "See you guys at school tomorrow," I tried to force a natural smile before I headed over to the order counter.

"Bye!" Dahlia said in an overly friendly tone that told me she was thrilled for Brandon to get a glimpse of my real and messy world.

I ignored her and kept walking to the counter, where I was glad to stand in line and escape the embarrassment of my family. When Brandon and Dahlia came and stood behind me, and Aria began making bird calls, I knew the wait in line wasn't going to help. I looked over at our table, hoping Mom and Dad were doing something to quiet her down. Instead, it looked like they were arguing while Aria chirped and cooed louder and louder, probably trying to tune them out. Unfortunately, I could hear Mom loud and clear.

"Put some of those back, Frank! Surely you don't need that many straws!" Mom wrestled straws out of Dad's hands, and I could see every head in my view turn to stare at them, including Brandon and Dahlia. I waited for the laugh or the rude comment from Dahlia.

"I hate when my parents argue in public," Brandon said, and right then I knew we had more in common than music and an English project.

Dahlia rolled her eyes and said, "Your parents might argue sometimes, but they're not as crazy as that."

Brandon shot her an annoyed look. "Dahlia, stop. It's obvious you have a problem with Carol, but get over it."

"Oh, okay. Sorry," she said in the most sarcastic tone possible. She folded her arms in front of her and glared at him. As much as I loved how he had put her in her place, it was difficult to enjoy the moment with the increasing level of chaos coming from my family's table.

I wanted to leave, but where would I go? While I stood in line for the water I didn't actually want, Aria got up, looked at me, and began walking in brisk, short steps toward me. Soon she stood next to me, grabbed my arm, and said, "Let's go. It's time to go." She tugged on my shirt. "Come on, we need to go!"

Mom had also stood up with her arms full of as many napkins, straws, and ketchup packets she could carry. She stomped to the trash, shoved them in, looked at Aria and me as if she wanted to say something, but instead, turned away and exited the door.

Dad was still at the table, gathering the leftover trash and food. He moved with swift, jerky movements, crumpling the paper bag and wrappers, before shoving them in his bag.

Aria still clung to my shirt sleeve, so I moved out of the line, and said, "Well, enjoy your dinner without us here to entertain you."

A sympathetic smile broke across Brandon's face. "I'll try, but it won't be as much fun without you, Crazy Carol," he said, and for the first time, I thought being a little crazy might actually be okay.

# Chapter 28

It was never easy to leave Mom after a visit, but it was much worse that night because we never actually got to say goodbye. By the time we exited the restaurant doors, she had already left. Dad sat waiting in his car, and we joined him, not saying a word as we drove home. It was another one of those moments where the clutter all over the house made me feel like I couldn't breathe. I went straight to my room, closed the door, and plopped onto my bed where I closed my eyes and imagined what it might be like to come home and actually feel at home, rather than feeling tense, sad, uneasy. With an unsettling sort of quiet in the house, I tried to breathe and relax, to tell myself tomorrow would be better. After one deep breath, Aria's voice distracted my brief moment of calm.

"The reason I love God so much is because he never leaves me," Aria said.

I exited my room and peeked down the hallway. Aria sat on the living room floor with Adagio in her hand. Her Bible was open in front of her, and she said, "Joshua 1, verse 9 says, '*Be strong and courageous. Do not be frightened, and do not be dismayed, for the Lord your God is with you wherever you go.'"* She peered at Adagio and then said, "You see? Mom might leave, and Dad might hide out in the garage, but God doesn't leave us, Adagio. Isn't that cool?" She set Adagio down on her Bible, then folded her hands and bowed her head.

While she prayed, I slipped back into my room and thought about those words she read. I'd never heard that passage before, probably because I hardly ever picked up my Bible. I looked over at my bookshelf, where I'd placed the Bible I received one day when we visited a nearby church. I walked over to it, pulled it from the shelf, and brought it to my desk. It actually looked much more inviting than my math and science textbooks. I opened the soft brown leather cover, flipped through the first few pages, the thin paper reminding me for some reason of butterfly wings, delicate and soft. On the Table of Contents page I found where the book of Joshua was located, and once there, I found the passage Aria had read. I read it once, and then a second time, and a third, and each time I felt less alone. I turned to the back of the Bible, where it listed verses for common topics, and stopped when I saw the word "Peace." One of the recommended verses for Peace was John 14:27. I flipped back through the Bible and found it. *"Peace I leave with you; my peace I give you. I do not give to you as the world gives. Do not let your hearts be troubled and do not be afraid."* That was definitely what I needed—peace, lack of a troubled heart, and no fear.

I grabbed my math homework and kept the Bible open, hoping the words about peace might make math seem more peaceful. An hour later, I was done, and saw that Aria had gone to bed on her own, sound asleep with Adagio sitting on the nightstand beside her. I wondered if she'd wake up anxious and sad because of the night we'd had. I hoped she wouldn't.

"I know I don't pray enough, God, but help us have peace," I whispered, and closed her door quietly behind me.

The first thing Aria said when I saw her the next morning at the table eating cereal was, "We need to check on the egrets today."

"Check on them?" I asked her. "What do you mean?"

"I mean we need to make sure there aren't more egrets getting shot in the woods. What if we hadn't found that one yesterday? The police wouldn't have come to search for the people who shot it."

"Well, yes, that's true, but the woods are safe now because the police have been there and know what happened. They're probably checking regularly to make sure there's no more danger. That's their job."

Aria didn't seem satisfied with that answer. She folded her arms and shook her head like that was one of the dumbest things she'd ever heard. "No, we need to check on them too!" She threw her spoon into her cereal bowl, as milk went flying and Cheerios spilled onto the homework she'd left out. She grabbed the paper and wiped it on her napkin, which only caused the ink to smear and her mood to worsen. "Oh no! Now my homework is ruined! And I don't have time to do it over! And Mrs. Flear is going to be mad and tell me it's not acceptable to turn in messy work!"

My prayer for peace didn't seem to be working at the moment. "Aria, it's okay. You have time to write over that one little part, and you can explain what happened. She's a nice teacher. She'll understand."

Mrs. Flear was the most patient teacher I'd ever seen. I remembered meeting her last year when I went with Mom to pick up work for Aria on a day she'd been sick. She told Mom Aria didn't need to do all the work, that it was more important to rest and get better, and that she'd help Aria get caught up when she was back at school.

"I know she's nice, but she still gets disappointed when we don't do our best work. I hate to disappoint her," Aria said, tears filling her eyes.

I decided to try and handle this in Mrs. Flear fashion, with patience. "Okay, I understand. We can fix it. I'll help you." I guided Aria to rewrite the smeared section, which she did with a shaky, nervous hand. When she looked at the finished product, she was not at all pleased.

"It looks like a big blue blob! It's still a mess!"

Knowing a possible ripped up paper might come next, followed by an even later arrival to school, I made her a promise I wasn't sure I could keep. "Aria, the sooner we stop messing around with this paper, the sooner we'll get to school, and the sooner school will be over, and the sooner we can go to the woods to check on the egrets."

Her expression switched instantly at the sound of those last words. Her eyes went wide, the top of her lips curved upward into a smile. "You'll go to the woods with me?" she asked.

"Yes, I will. Now let's go, okay?"

We cleaned up the kitchen and were out the door in record time, with Aria skipping and waving her blue smudged paper in the air like she was proud to show it off. As I followed her, relieved that her stress over homework hadn't turned into a full on meltdown, I remembered last night's prayer. The peace I'd hoped for didn't come as I expected, but it did finally come.

# Chapter 29

While Aria skipped ahead, I checked behind me several times. I was hoping I'd see Matthew, even though I was quite positive he'd already gone ahead and walked to school without us. I thought back to the day we walked home hand in hand. How had we gone from that to not speaking in only one day?

In math class, Matthew wouldn't even look at me, and then left class talking to the girl who sat behind him. She was tiny, maybe five feet tall, with sleek dark hair that reached to her lower back. She giggled out loud and nudged him as she said, "You're so funny." I disagreed. Rude and mean? Yes. Funny? No.

In English, I decided to confront him once we were all in groups, and Miss Enders was distracted by several students asking questions at her desk. "Hey, missed walking with you yesterday and this morning. Can we walk together after school?" I asked him.

He looked up at me, then to Ronnie, who gave him her best "stop being a jerk" look and said, "Seems like a great day to visit the woods. It's a Friday, so we don't have a bunch of homework, and Aria could totally help us with our project ideas, teach us how to make good bird calls and stuff. I say yes. Say yes, Matthew." She smiled and leaned toward him, daring him to object.

Matthew leaned back and heaved a big sigh, like this was the most torturous decision of his day. "Yeah, okay, if you're both out front after school, we can walk together. If I don't see you there, just stop by my house, Ronnie. We can go to the woods from there."

I knew it wasn't an accident that he only asked Ronnie to go to his house, but I tried not to act offended and said, "I actually promised Aria I'd go to the woods today, so let's plan on going together."

Matthew simply stared at me.

Ronnie broke the silence and said, "Okay, great, good plan."

I returned to my group with Dahlia, Ricky, and Brandon, relieved that even though Matthew was still unhappy with me, we'd have a chance to reconnect after school. Once we were all together in the woods it would feel like old times, and then hopefully we could resolve this uncomfortable tension between us.

"So, today's a big practice day after school for the band," Brandon said as soon as I sat down next to him. "Hopefully you can make it. Chad told me this morning that his dad is coming over tomorrow to listen to us. If he likes what he hears, he'll have us come to the studio and record us. Can you believe that? We could be recording tomorrow, and once we're recorded, he can send it to his record label friends."

If we weren't in class, I'd probably jump up and down at this news, and he looked like he wanted to do the same. He was so excited, a huge smile on his face. Then he leaned closer to me and said, "Your voice makes us, Carol. I really think we've got a shot at making it with you singing."

The walk home with Matthew instantly lost priority, and so did my promise to Aria to go to the woods. Spending time with them would have to wait until after practice. "Wow, that's really exciting. I'm not so sure I'm the one who'll get you the recording, but I definitely want to be a part of it. I'll be there."

"Cool, I'm so excited," He said as he raised his hand to me for a high five.

My hands met his in a smack much louder than I expected. Heads turned, one of them Matthew's. He turned away when he caught my eye and shook his head as if we were completely annoying. I wasn't looking forward to telling him I wouldn't be able to hang with him and Ronnie after school. I hoped he'd understand, but so far he hadn't understood anything I did that involved Brandon.

When the bell rang, I jumped from my seat to catch Ronnie and Matthew before they disappeared out the door.

"Hey, Ronnie, Matthew, wait up," I said.

They turned around and stopped for me to catch up. As we exited the classroom, I said, "So, I have something really amazing to tell you." They both looked at me as I attempted to sound positive while bailing on our plans. "Brandon said Chad's dad wants to hear the band play tomorrow, and if he likes what he hears, he'll record them and send a demo to his record label friends. He wants me to be the singer. Can you believe it? This is my chance!"

Ronnie grabbed my hands and said, "Oh. My. Gosh! This is so exciting!"

I looked at Matthew, and luckily, he was smiling too. "Woah, North, I mean, Carol, that's so cool." He lifted his hand up toward me. I grabbed it and savored the brief moment of contact.

"So, what time tomorrow? We can totally help you prep today if you want. We can listen to you belt that voice of yours in the woods, at your house, whatever you need. We've got you," Ronnie said.

"Well, I'm not sure what time tomorrow, but I guess I'll find out when we practice. Brandon told me they need to practice with me today after school to be ready, so I think I'm going to need to meet you guys later for our walk to the woods. Why don't you guys go ahead, and I can meet you there before it begins to get dark?"

Ronnie's bright eyed expression faded a bit, but she said, "Oh, of course. That makes sense that you guys would practice today. No worries. Just come over to Matthew's if you get home early enough, and we can go then." We looked at Matthew.

"Yeah, that's fine. You've obviously got to practice. Good luck, you'll do great." He smiled slightly. While our eyes locked, I tried to gauge whether he was actually happy. He turned away, which signaled to me that he was keeping something from me, probably disappointment. At least he was being nice. That was a start.

Then behind me came a loud voice, "Carol, hey, I hear you're coming to practice! Right on! We're going to nail it tomorrow for my dad!" It was Chad. He gave me a thumbs up, then noticed Matthew. His look of excitement turned to one of disdain, his lip turning upward on one side into a rude sneer. "I didn't know you two were friends," he said, shaking his head. Then he ran off to a group of guys who were laughing and tossing a book back and forth. Little Jonathon James Price stood by gripping his lunch box, yelling at them to give his book back.

If I'd hoped for any sort of peace with Matthew, it was now gone. He looked at me with a mix of horror and disgust. "That's the guy whose dad is the recording artist? He's in the band?" Matthew asked.

Now I wanted to turn away from his stare, but I couldn't. I didn't know what to say. This was not how I wanted him to find out that the same person who had been so horribly racist and knocked him to the ground was the same one who was possibly going to make me a rock star. I was planning to tell him at some point, but hadn't figured out how. I hadn't even figured out how I was going to manage working with someone so awful.

"Yeah, that's Chad Winslett. I was planning to talk with you about it today, Matthew, when we walked home. I don't plan to be friends with him, but I think this could finally be my shot at getting my voice heard. If I had this opportunity with anyone else, believe me, I'd take it."

The anger in his face was worse than when he shoved Ricky back in middle school. He pursed his lips together, glared at me and shook his head. "I can't talk to you right now. Actually, I can't even be anywhere near you. Good luck, North, and yes, I said North because that's the person I used to know, the one who was a friend. I know she's there somewhere, but until she returns, I'm out." He turned around, ignoring my voice when I called out to him to come back.

Ronnie stared at me and said, "Okay, I'm really confused right now. Why does Matthew hate Chad?"

"That's the guy who pushed him to the ground," I answered.

Her mouth dropped and she stood back from me. "Okay, well, I see why he's so mad." She looked up, like she was trying to find the right words, then looked at me and said, "I get that you think this is the perfect opportunity, but wow, I think you're making a mistake. You really want to be in a band with losers like that? Your voice is amazing. You don't need someone like Chad to help you be a singer. You just need a little bit of courage. And based on who you're choosing to help you find success, I'm not sure you've got that."

She walked away, leaving me with a lump in my throat and a weight on my chest that made me question if she was right.

# Chapter 30

When school ended, I waited out front with Aria as we both kept our eyes peeled for Ronnie or Matthew. She was anxious to leave, as usual, but I told her we had to wait for them since I was going to Brandon's.

"I can walk home by myself," Aria said.

While that was probably true, I knew that if something happened, like she got distracted and went down the wrong street, or someone made fun of her, or she tripped and fell, there would be no one around to help her. So even though I didn't want to ask any favors of Ronnie and Matthew, I also knew they liked Aria and would still walk with her, especially if they were going to Matthew's anyway.

"There's Ronnie!" Aria shouted. She ran towards her, bumping into people as she went. One boy yelled at her, "Hey, watch where you're going!" A girl who was knocked sideways shouted, "Really?" and threw her hands in the air as she turned to glare at her. Aria paid no attention, focused only on getting to Ronnie.

I watched as Aria stopped in front of her, talked and pointed to me, then put her hands on her hips while waiting for Ronnie's response.

Ronnie nodded her head and smiled, then Aria did a small jump, like she often did when excited, and turned to give me a thumbs up.

I waved to her, and then looked at Ronnie. The smile she'd had for Aria faded for me, and as they approached, Ronnie said, "See ya, Carol."

"Bye, hope to see you guys soon."

Ronnie nodded, and said, "Yeah, don't plan on it. I'm sure your practice will take awhile. We'll go to the woods another time."

Aria looked at her and said, "Another time? No, we have to go today." She looked at me and said, "Right? You promised me we'd go."

"You and I will go when I get home, Aria. I'll be home in time."

"Okay," Aria said, in a tone that seemed a little doubtful.

As they walked away, I headed toward the tree at the corner of the school's front lawn, where Brandon said he'd wait for me. I was happy to see him, and excited to sing, but I wasn't thrilled about the rest of the crowd surrounding him, which included Chad, Ricky, and Dahlia. Even though they walked several feet behind Brandon and me, they were still the most annoying people ever.

"Yo, dude, buy some pants that fit!" Chad yelled to a tall boy ahead of us whose pants were about two inches too short. "Or maybe you think that looks good. It doesn't." The boy didn't turn around, which was the advice most people take when dealing with a bully. Unfortunately, Chad didn't quit. "Looks lame!" he yelled as loud as he could with his hands cupped over his mouth.

"Chad, stop. Give the guy a break," Brandon said.

"Why? He doesn't need a break. He needs new pants!" He burst out in his obnoxiously loud laugh. Ricky joined him, and Dahlia snickered as well.

"Why are you guys so mean?" I finally said. "Who cares if his pants are short? You're not exactly a fashion statement yourself."

Chad turned to me with shocked eyes, "Woah! Really? Are you really talking to me like that? Brandon, maybe you chose the wrong singer."

Dahlia flashed her thick mascara laden eyes at me, and smiled.

"Uh, no, I didn't make the wrong choice, and don't get so offended that Carol doesn't like your fashion sense. You can always ask your mom to buy you some Garanimals."

I remembered Mom taking me to Sears Department Store where they sold the Garanimals line of clothing for little kids. She let me pick out an outfit for kindergarten. I loved matching the animal tags, like a lion tagged pant to a lion tagged shirt, in order to find the perfect matching outfit. Looking at Chad's signature baggy jeans, bright orange socks, leather sandals, green and brown flannel shirt over a blue and yellow striped T-shirt, I thought he definitely needed some help from Garanimals.

While everyone laughed, Chad shook his head with a defeated smile. With him quiet, the rest of the walk was a bit more pleasant, but not enough to make me feel like part of the group. I felt like I was one wrong note away from being humiliated and shunned by them forever. What if Chad's dad didn't like me? What if he preferred Dahlia because she had the look he thought would sell more records? I repeated Ronnie's words in my mind. "Your voice is awesome. You just need courage." I wished Ronnie and Matthew would have heard me defend the short pants guy, and the way Brandon had shut Chad down. Instead, they probably imagined us laughing and joking with Chad. That thought made me feel sick, but not as much as the words from Chad a few moments later.

"Should have known someone who hangs out with a Black guy would be obnoxious," Chad said to Ricky in a hushed voice. "I might need to mention that to my dad."

I wanted to say something, let him know I heard him, ask how someone could be obnoxious by hanging out with a Black person, or how he, the most obnoxious person on the planet could actually call anyone else obnoxious. I was fuming inside, but I walked along and stayed silent, afraid to stir up more of his anger and risk my shot at this singing thing. Ronnie and Matthew would have been ashamed of me, rightfully so.

Once we passed the final block of older homes that looked similar to mine, we entered Brandon's neighborhood, marked by a low brick wall on each side of the street with a sign that said, Eagle's Nest of Sage Hills in swirly metal letters. I hadn't noticed the sign when Mom drove me to Brandon's, and clearly Aria hadn't either because if she had, she probably would have begged Mom to drive around until she found the eagle's nest.

I thought of Aria now, figuring she was almost home. I imagined her telling Ronnie she'd see her later and then going inside to gather all the things she wanted to take with her to the woods later. I thought of Matthew and how he'd told me I'd sing great before he found out I was singing in a band with Chad. My stomach felt queasy and my heart started beating quicker the closer we got to Brandon's house. It was that same terrified feeling I always got before performing. I tried taking a deep breath, let it out. The pit in my stomach remained.

When we entered Brandon's, there was clatter and conversation from the dining room. Mrs. Stone appeared in the doorway, wearing a matching pink blazer and slim skirt, a shade darker than her perfectly applied lipstick, a delicate teacup in her hand.

"Oh, hello, darling." She put her hand on Brandon's shoulder. "How was school? I'm finishing up with my guests, so if you and your friends want a snack, you can get one in the kitchen." She smiled at the rest of us.

Mom was right. Mrs. Stone was significantly kinder in front of her friends, but I could tell she was steering us all away toward the kitchen, like she didn't want too much interaction between us and her people.

"Thanks, Mom," Brandon said. "We'll grab something, and then we'll be practicing, so we'll stay out of your way."

"That's fine, dear. We still have a few things to discuss, so remember to close the door, and maybe practice a few of your more mellow songs for a bit?" Mrs. Stone said.

"Yep, no problem," he said. "Led Zeppelin's 'Ramble On' is first on our list."

She smiled, eyed him suspiciously, and said, "Okay, thanks, dear."

We walked to the kitchen, and once there, let out the laughter we'd been holding over Brandon's remark.

"Really, Brandon? Led Zeppelin?" Dahlia said. "Your mom would probably ground you for weeks if you actually started off with that in front of her tea friends."

"Yeah, she'd definitely be mad, but it would be fun to try one day, maybe a few years from now, when I'm about to move out because our band is on a big rock tour around the country."

We all laughed again, but not at the idea of touring the country. That was why we were there. In spite of how we might dislike or annoy each other, we wanted to be a hit band. So, with glasses of lemonade downed and chocolate chip cookies inhaled, we headed down the hall with hopes of making that happen.

After a warm-up and a few runs through "Hey Jude," Chad said it was time to practice the song Brandon wrote and hoped to record. "My dad said we don't have to do your song perfectly to get a shot at recording. He just wants to hear a little bit of it, along with some popular hit songs, so he can get a feel for how we sound."

"Okay then, I think the only one who hasn't heard my song is you, Carol." He handed me some pages with lyrics and music. "I can sing it through once so you hear how it sounds."

"Uh, I can sing too," Dahlia said.

Brandon looked at her. "Yeah, um, I want it to sound the way I intended when I wrote it, and you haven't sung it in a while, so I got it this time."

Dahlia rolled her eyes. "You're such a control freak, Brandon." She tossed her tambourine on the floor and stood with her hands on her hips as she glared at him.

Brandon ignored her, sat on a stool in front of his mic, began strumming his guitar, and then started singing. I was shocked. I kind of expected a hardcore rock tune or a fast-paced beat, but what I heard was a folklike rhythm that matched his low baritone voice perfectly, and words that surprised me even more: "When I saw you standing there, I saw something I'd been missing, a rare bird in flight, singing, soaring," I closed my eyes and listened, and knew this was one I could sing.

"It's really good," I said when he finished, "and your voice is perfect for it. You're going to sing with me, right?" I asked him.

He smiled, shook his head. "Uh, no, I wasn't planning on it."

"Why not?" I asked.

"Because I like your voice better," he said. "Something about the way you sing, I think it'll make my words sound better, like people might stop and listen to them."

I couldn't think of a better compliment to motivate me. That was why I wanted to sing, so people might actually hear my voice and pay attention, like what I said mattered.

"Okay, well, thank you. That means a lot to me. I hope I don't disappoint you," I said.

"Come on you two, can we get on with it? We'll never be ready if we stand around talking. Let's go," Dahlia said. She pulled the microphone from the stand, ready to sing with me.

"I think we need you on the tambourine," Brandon said.

Dahlia picked up the tambourine with one hand, kept the mic in the other. "Okay, let's go," she said.

"The tambourine only," Brandon said, "with Carol singing alone."

I imagined invisible darts shooting from her eyes as she stared him down, but then finally put the mic on the stand and stepped back. "Okay, well, let's see how she sounds. Come on, Carol. Don't be shy." She peered at me, forcing a fake smile.

I turned away and looked at Brandon, who nodded at me and said, "You won't disappoint us."

I took the mic from Dahlia, my heart thumping fast in my chest. I set the words on the stand in front of me, waited as Brandon began the intro guitar, and then I joined in. I knew I didn't sing exactly the way it was written. I sang in a slightly higher range, elongated some of the ending notes, shortened others, but like the day before when we all sang together, everything jelled. In spite of a few off moments, nearly every drumbeat, tambourine shake, guitar stroke, and bass boom meshed with my voice. We were like one perfect machine, each doing the part we were made to do.

When we finished, Dahlia folded her arms across her chest and said, "Well, you kind of changed it a bit. Maybe you should sing it with her, Brandon."

"What? Are you kidding?" Dylan said before letting out a "ba-doom-da-doom" on his bass. "That was amazing. No offense, Brandon, but the changes made it better. She nailed it."

"No offense taken. I agree."

Dahlia rolled her eyes. "Wow, okay, I clearly don't count here."

She looked like she might cry, and knowing how that felt, I actually felt a little sorry for her. "Dahlia, you definitely count. I hear what you're saying. It was different, but it was our first time through with me singing. It'll get better."

"Yeah, you definitely count, Dahl," Chad said. "But we don't have time to make it perfect, and we don't need to, remember? My dad just needs to get a good feel overall. I think we did that here." He got up from his seat at the drums and approached her, then put his arm around her. "Come on, don't be upset. We need that pretty smile while you rock the tambourine, and we need you on backup for "Hey Jude" or whatever other songs we do that need more than one singer, okay?"

As annoying as Chad was, he knew how to handle Dahlia, which was a good thing since the recording studio might lose its home in her father's building if she left the band. She wiped a tear and smiled at him. "Okay, yeah, I'm fine," she said.

We practiced the song one more time, and then Brandon said we needed to decide what other songs we should sing to impress Mr. Winslett. "We could try one of my favorite Led Zeppelin songs, but not sure Mr. Winslett would like that. Do you know the lyrics to 'Day by Day' from the *Godspell* musical?" he asked me.

Again, a much more mellow choice than I expected, but I was fine with that. "Uh, yes, I know that song," I said. "My sister used to sing it all the time, so much that I got pretty sick of it. Besides, you really don't want to hear me sing Led Zeppelin."

Everyone agreed with that, and then the music continued, with Dahlia thrilled to practice a song in which she was expected to harmonize along. When we sang, "Oh dear Lord, three things I pray," I realized for the first time why Aria sang this song over and over. It was really a perfect prayer, asking for God's help to see, love, and follow him more each day. She'd be glad to know I was singing it.

We ended practice with another round of "Hey Jude" and "Rare Bird," the title Brandon gave his original song. As I gathered my books from school, Brandon asked, "Hey, we're all going to hang out here, have some food, watch a movie or T.V. Why don't you stay and my mom or dad can give you a ride home later?"

"Oh, no, that's fine. I need to get home. I have plans," I said. He looked a little offended so I added, "I'd love to hang out another time, though, and I'll see you tomorrow. What time should I be here?"

"Mr. Winslett is coming at noon, so come at eleven. That should give us time to warm up and be ready."

"Okay, bye," I said.

"Bye!" Dahlia said with the most enthusiasm I'd heard from her all day, clearly glad to see me go. She grabbed Brandon's elbow, waved three fingers at me and smiled.

I enjoyed the fact that Brandon pulled away from her and said, "I'll walk you out."

When we reached the door, he opened it and said, "If you change your plans, come on back. We should be up late." He paused, looked down shyly, a look I wasn't used to from him, and said, "It's nice having you around."

"Thanks," I said, wondering why I was walking out the door while my eyes stayed glued to his. "Today was fun," I added, which in my mind translated as *I like having you around too*, a truth I was too afraid to admit out loud. I liked him more each time I was with him, but I also felt more confused as to why he was so nice when nearly everyone he spent time with was not. Plus, there was Matthew. I hadn't figured out those feelings either.

He closed the door, and I headed down the walkway, admiring how the lights along the walkway glistened on the puddles left behind from the sprinklers, until it struck me that lights meant it was dark, and dark meant I was late. I had broken my promise to Aria. A crow squawked in a tall palm tree behind me, like a warning cry. Aria was not going to be happy.

# Chapter 31

As beautiful as the night was, a full moon and bright stars in the clear sky, I couldn't enjoy it. I picked up my pace to a slow jog once I realized I was late, and forced myself to keep running even when I felt so tired I could barely breathe. The cool autumn air no longer felt cool, and I wished I wasn't hauling books that felt like weights or wearing a sweatshirt that felt like a heavy winter coat.

When I finally made it home, I threw my books on the lawn for a second and bent over to catch my breath. The lights were on inside, and I heard voices, but I couldn't make out whose they were. I pulled off my sweatshirt, relieved to feel a breeze brush over my skin, then collected my books and took a deep breath. The "Day by Day" tune had been in my mind the entire way home. I sang it quietly to myself as I approached the front door and then opened it.

The first person I saw was my father, who stood looking down at Aria on the kitchen floor. "We can get a new one, Aria. Your mom loves sculpting. She'll be happy to make you another one."

On the floor in front of Aria were little pieces of shattered clay—

shiny shapes in black, white, and brown, the colors of her favorite bird, Adagio. The door closing behind me caught their attention, and when I saw their faces, Dad's red and desperate, Aria's teary and sad, staring me down, I felt as broken as that bird.

"Where on earth have you been?" Dad said in a tone so forced and controlled that I knew a storm was coming. I had no idea how to stop it.

"I was at Brandon's," I said, knowing that answer would not make things better. "We had practice. I told Aria that."

"At Brandon's, for practice, great," was his response. "And it doesn't really matter that you told Aria where you were, because all she remembers is that you promised you'd be home, before dark, to go to the woods. Do you remember that promise, North? Do you know how difficult you make things when you make a promise and then break it? Do you?"

The explosion had officially been released, the storm was officially breaking, except this time, it wasn't only coming from him. Inside my chest, creeping up to my throat, were all my frustrations, all the promises he had broken.

"Dad, are you really talking to me about promises? How about all your promises to get rid of stuff so Mom wouldn't get so fed up she'd leave us? How about the promise you should have made to be a parent and not ask me to take care of all the things Mom did when she was here?" Tears blurred my vision, but not enough to keep me from seeing more hurt on his face than I meant to cause. Part of me, the respectful, patient, nice side, wanted to apologize. The other part, the angry, resentful, impatient one that was currently in charge, did not.

Aria hadn't moved from the floor, sat there with her hands full of broken clay, tears streaming down her face. I couldn't bear to look at her. I turned away, ditched my notebook and books on the kitchen table, clung to my brown suede purse, and headed back to the front door. I had to get out of there, the crowded, chaotic place where I never quite measured up, where my feelings and desires could never be worth as much as the towering stacks of junk. It seemed dumb to go back to Brandon's after hurrying home, but that was the only place at the moment I wanted to be, where someone thought my voice mattered.

"Where are you going, North?" Dad shouted at me.

"I'm going back to Brandon's, where I can do what I want to do, Dad, where I can sing, and people tell me I'm needed for that reason, where I'm not a constant letdown. I'm going to Brandon's."

"If you leave, you might as well not come back. We don't need you here if singing is more important than your family."

I stopped for a second, stared at the piles and stacks on all sides of me, and kept going. As I grabbed the doorknob, I paused again and said, "Singing isn't more important than my family. I shouldn't have to choose one or the other. I can't stay here and be all the things you want me to be right now. " I opened the door.

"North, no! Stay!" Aria shouted.

I took a breath, kept my eyes on the night sky, and said, "You'll be fine, Aria. Dad is with you. He says you don't need me." I shut the door behind me and ran back in the direction I'd just come from. This time, I didn't feel weighed down, or tired, or filled with dread over where I was going. I was ready to be me, to let go of all my fear, to fight for myself for a change.

# Chapter 32

I stopped at the corner of Brandon's street to catch my breath and try to make myself look a bit less of a mess. I pulled my brush from my purse, ran it through my hair, dabbed beads of sweat off my face with a Kleenex, then let the cool breeze do its work on cooling me down as I continued to Brandon's house. I could hear music from his house, evidence that Mrs. Stone's guests had left, and that she and Mr. Stone were either gone or didn't mind the noise.

For the first time, I was excited to knock on Brandon's door. If Dahlia was still there with her snooty glares, I'd glare back. If Chad was there with his rude comments, I could be equally snarky.

"Look out world, here comes Crazy Carol," I said before I grabbed the door knocker, pounded it with enthusiasm, and then pressed the doorbell too, happy to make my presence loud and clear.

"I'll get it, dear!" a man's voice yelled.

Moments later the door opened to a tall man with silver hair, tanned face, and piercing blue eyes like Brandon's. He wore a crisp white sweatshirt and faded jeans, and with a can of Coca-Cola raised to me, he greeted me with, "Hello, there!" like he knew me, even though we'd never met.

"Hello," I said, surprised by how much he reminded me of an older Brandon. "I'm Carol, one of Brandon's friends. Is he here?"

He opened the door wider and said, "Yes, he is. Come on in! I'm Brandon's father, in case you didn't guess that already. He's out back by the pool. I'll show you the way."

This was no tea party anymore. The dining room table was now surrounded by people laughing and shouting with playing cards in hand. Clusters of people holding iced drinks or soda cans stood chatting above the music throughout the living room, hallway, and kitchen, where the counters displayed bowls of chips and pretzels, plates of cheese, crackers, grapes, and platters of chicken wings and little crescent rolls stuffed with mini hot dogs. The music played through every room and continued outdoors where the pool glowed with a mix of colorful red, blue, and green lights, shining on people splashing in the pool and floating on inflatable rafts.

Mr. Stone looked around, and then said, "Ah, there he is, on the lounge chair over there." He pointed to a chair where Brandon sat surrounded by Dahlia, two of her friends, and Dylan.

"Brandon, you've got another guest!"

Brandon sat up and looked our way. The minute he saw me, he said, "What? Hey, you made it!" He got up from his seat and jogged toward me.

It felt good to be greeted like that, to be welcomed without anyone expecting something from me.

"This is quite the party," I said, wondering whether this might be a normal Friday get together for him.

"Well, it is now that you're here," he said. "Your plans changed?"

That was an understatement. "You could say that," I said, suddenly feeling emotional as I pictured Dad and Aria, their faces a mix of anger, sadness and disappointment when I left the house.

Brandon obviously noticed; he put his hand on my shoulder and said, "Hey, you okay?"

Tears welled up and I turned away, hoping they would stop. I didn't want to cry at this cheery party. I wanted to laugh and shout and have fun like everyone else.

"Come on, let's go get a soda," he said as he placed his hand on my back and guided me back inside.

While we walked, I rubbed the tears away, avoiding eye contact with anyone as we weaved our way through huddles of people on the patio and then in the kitchen, where Brandon reached into the refrigerator and grabbed a can of A & W Root Beer. "Is this okay?" he asked.

"Yes," I answered, as I admired the neatly stocked fridge, lined with more root beer, plus cans of Seven-Up, Pepsi, and Coke, along with stacks of Tupperware labeled with their contents and date packed, a head of lettuce, shiny red apples, and a Jello mold that looked like the green twin of the orange one on the kitchen counter. Brandon's family clearly spent a lot of time providing food and drinks for guests, whereas the excessive amount of canned and boxed goods at my home sat unopened.

"So what's going on?" Brandon asked as he took a Pepsi for himself and closed the fridge.

I stared at him, trying to figure out how much information I really wanted to reveal.

"Come on, let's go where it's a little quieter," he said when I remained speechless. We exited the kitchen and walked down the familiar hallway that led to the practice room. The room felt different without the usual buzz of music. Ceiling lights cast a glow on the instruments and a clock on the wall ticked rhythmically like the intro beat to a new song.

Brandon sat down at one of the two leather chairs where I imagined Mr. Winslett would sit tomorrow when we gave our best shot at impressing him. "Have a seat," he said, motioning to the chair across from him.

"I don't want to bother you with all my problems," I said as I sunk into the plush cushions. "I really am okay, just had a little argument with my dad before I came over."

"You're not bothering me with your problems. If you were, I wouldn't have asked if you were okay." He leaned toward me, his sparkling eyes encouraging me to talk.

I stared at the fluffy white sheepskin rug beneath my feet, unable to look at him while I finally sputtered out little fragments of my broken world. "So, the reason I got in a fight with my dad was because I was supposed to be home earlier, before it got dark, which shouldn't be that big of a crime, but in this case, it kind of was," I said.

"Okay, why's that?"

"Well, you see, my sister, Aria, sometimes needs help." I paused, trying to figure out how to describe Aria to someone who didn't know her. "The doctors told my mom several years ago she has autism. I don't know if you know what that is, but it seems to be the reason why she sometimes acts a little different."

Brandon looked at me with a blank stare, the way most people did when they heard this word, autism. Aria's doctor told Mom that the first diagnosis was made about thirty years ago, and doctors still didn't understand much about it. I wanted to ask him how that was possible, but I was never in the appointment room to ask.

"Yeah, I haven't heard of that," Brandon said. "But it sounds like something I might have. I feel like I act different and need help all the time."

I nodded and said, "Yeah, me too." It was nice to explain this to someone who didn't seem to be judging me or acting like what I said was weird. "I wish more people would see it that way, as something that was similar to themselves. I mean, acting different isn't wrong. Once people get to know her, they see how awesome she is, but unfortunately, a lot of people aren't that patient. They see something that goes against the norm and they judge it, you know?"

"Oh yeah, I know," he said.

"Anyway, my dad sort of expects me to be home a lot to help Aria when she needs it, and today I was supposed to go to the woods with her, one of her favorite things to do, and something I've been promising her for days. By the time I arrived home, it looked like she'd been upset for a while, and my dad was at the end of his ropes trying to calm her down."

I stopped as I remembered the shattered bits of Adagio on the floor, the crushed expression on Aria's face, and I felt the tears coming again. When I felt Brandon's hand on mine, there was no stopping them. That simple gesture, done after sharing a little bit of my unusual family to someone who seemed so cool and popular, made me feel accepted for the first time in a long time. As the tears poured out, I tried to wipe them away with my free hand, but then Brandon scooted forward in his seat, and pulled me into a hug.

"Hey, it's okay," he said. As he held me, I thought of how amazing it was that a simple hug could actually make that statement true. For at least a little bit, it felt like the broken, shattered parts of my day were finally being held together.

# Chapter 33

The quiet peace of the practice room didn't last for long.

"Oh, sorry, didn't mean to interrupt!" Dylan shouted as he ran into the room in his swim trunks with an inflatable flamingo around his waist. He held a twisted towel in his hand and stood ready at the doorway. The sound of bare feet running down the hall were soon met with a loud, "Aha!" from Dylan as he jumped into the hall and whipped the towel at the approaching victim.

A loud squeal came next, followed by laughter and quick feet returning down the hall. Dylan reappeared. "Sorry, but can I hang here?" he said between breaths. "I can't run anymore."

Brandon looked at me and shook his head with a smile. "Uh, yeah, I guess," he said. "What exactly are you running from? It didn't sound too terrifying."

"Oh it was. It was Dahlia," he said.

Brandon laughed. "Oh, okay, you're right, but that pink flamingo and a towel aren't going to keep her away," he said. "If you're her flirtatious prize for the night, your only protection is to go home, and you might not even be safe there. She'll track you down."

Dylan raised his brows and smiled, "Yeah, I know. I don't actually mind that, though."

"Okay then," Brandon said as he returned to his seat.

Several minutes later, Dahlia was back, along with Chad and five others I didn't know. Brandon moved to my chair and squeezed in next to me, then held my hand as everyone talked for the next hour about meaningless things, starting with why Dylan should wear the flamingo inner tube on a regular basis, to who has the nicest feet (thankfully mine were hidden in tennis shoes), to more meaningful things, like why teachers should stop assigning homework on weekends (or on any day) to why the voting age should be lowered, and finally to whether civil rights marches are valuable. Of course, Chad started that topic. My heart beat faster with every annoying word that came out of his mouth.

"Seems like people are starting to figure out there's been enough civil rights marches. You don't hear about many of them anymore," Chad said.

"So you're saying everything is perfect and we'll never need to march for people's rights again?" Brandon said.

Chad looked up, thinking, and said, "Yeah, I think things are pretty good. I think they have been for a long time, I mean, it's not like we're living in the 1800s with slavery still around. Everyone's free in this country. I don't see what anyone has to complain about."

That was a shocking statement, especially from him. I couldn't remain quiet anymore. Time to be courageous for a change.

"Don't you think there's more to being free than banishing slavery? Are people who are treated badly because they look or act different actually living a life of freedom, Chad?" I asked.

"Uh, yes, they are. If they're so different that they're treated badly, they're obviously making that choice," he said.

I was fuming now. How can he say something that dumb? "Really?" I sat forward in my seat and said, "You can't possibly think that someone's skin color is a choice, or that someone's mental state is always their choice, or that even if it was, that it's their fault when someone is mean to them. That is the most messed up thinking I've ever heard."

He shook his head, laughed, and said, "Whatever, Carol. I don't really care what you think. You're only here because Brandon thinks we need you tomorrow, but we don't need you forever. You're not the only person in the world who can sing."

"Woah, hold on. That's enough," Brandon said. "We do need her tomorrow, and if all goes well, we shouldn't have to find anyone else. We don't need to all agree on everything, but we need to get along. So, can we end this now?"

Everyone sat silent. Chad nodded and said, "Yep, I'm done." He walked to the door, and I hoped that meant he was going home, but instead, he said, "I'm getting another soda."

The rest of us sat there, awkwardly glancing around at anything but each other. I watched the clock for a moment, still ticking away, then at the leather chair, Brandon's fingers as they nervously tapped his knee, Dahlia's bare feet with perfectly painted pink toenails, and then at the flamingo, its black plastic eyes staring at me. Several moments later, I heard the clacking of heels running down the hallway.

"Brandon?" Mrs. Stone yelled, sounding a bit frantic before she entered the room. "There's a couple people here asking for Carol. Chad stopped them at the door and doesn't want to let them in, says they're not welcome here? Can you please come handle this? I didn't get their names, but I'm assuming Carol knows them."

I looked at Brandon, who looked nearly as confused and concerned as I felt. "We'll be right there," he said as he stood up.

We left the room, and although no one else was asked to follow, I could hear them creeping and whispering behind us, obviously curious about who was there. When we reached the entryway, I saw Chad with one hand on the doorknob and another on the frame, acting as a human wall to keep Matthew outside.

I ran to the door, pulled Chad's arm off the doorframe, and said, "What's your problem? Why would you keep him from coming in? Isn't it enough that you threw him onto the ground the other day?"

His arrogant smile crept across his face again. "No, it's not enough. He wasn't invited, and he's not part of our group."

"Dude, this is not your house," Brandon interrupted. "He can come in."

I glared into Chad's tiny bloodshot eyes.

"I don't want to come in," Matthew said. I only want to see Carol. It's important." Beads of sweat were on his forehead, his breathing short, like he'd run his fastest to get to me. Ronnie was right behind him, pacing back and forth. She never looked frazzled. She did now. "Aria took off. Your dad's out looking for her. Thought you might want to come help."

# Chapter 34

I had never before felt so much panic rise up in myself. A performance in front of a crowd of thousands, millions even, would have felt better. The only difference was that this kind of panic didn't keep me frozen in fear. It made me want to act quickly, urgently.

"Yes, I'm coming," I said, feeling out of breath simply standing there. I turned to Brandon, "I have to go. I'll see you tomorrow."

"Wait, can I help?" he asked.

As much as I liked being with him, I didn't think this was something we'd enjoy together.

"Thanks, Brandon, but no, that's okay," I said as I stepped outside.

"Okay, but call me if that changes, and let me know when you find her."

I liked that he said "when" and not "if." I had a horrible feeling, and needed all the positive vibes I could get.

"I will, thanks." As Brandon closed the door, I turned to Matthew, who was already heading down the walkway with Ronnie. When I realized there was no car waiting for us, I said, "Wait, did you run all the way here?"

Matthew put his hands on his head and paced back and forth, still catching his breath. Ronnie was bent down, hands on her knees, breathing heavy as well.

"Yep," Matthew said between gasps. "We did."

"How'd you find Brandon's house?"

"Your mom," Matthew said. "She called my house after your dad finally tracked her down. Luckily, the lady she lives with had the phone number where she was working. Your mom was helping to serve food and clean at some big party about thirty minutes away. When she asked for help finding Aria, we told her we'd come get you, so she gave us directions. She was planning to leave right away, so hopefully she'll be here any minute.

"So you ran here even though my mom's coming to get me? Why?"

Matthew looked at me like that was the dumbest question ever. "Because we want to help, North. Neither of us could sit around my house wondering whether Aria was okay. We had to do something."

"I don't know what to say. Thank you. You're both so much nicer to me than you need to be."

Matthew nodded. "Yeah, probably, but I can't help it."

Ronnie chimed in. "Nope, me neither."

I wished I would have simply gone home with them. Then we would have all gone to the woods together and Aria would be safe and happy. As soon as I thought that, I knew where to find Aria.

"She's in the woods," I said.

"The woods?" Ronnie asked. "At night? In the dark?"

I nodded as I remembered hearing our front door unlatch in the middle of the night twice over the summer. I knew it wasn't a burglar because I could hear her talking, saying how much easier it would be to sleep in the woods, and how great it was going to be to find the owls. By the time I caught up with her outside, I saw she was talking to Adagio, a blanket wrapped around her shoulders, her trusty bag on her shoulders, prepared in her mind for the perfect sleepover.

"She's tried going to the woods at night before," I said. "I was around to stop her the past few times. This time I wasn't." A wave of guilt swept over me. Why had I chosen to leave her when she was so upset? What was I thinking? I stood at the edge of the driveway, wishing I was able to magically transport myself to the woods. The longer we stood waiting for my mom, the closer Aria got to danger, to those cliffs she always planned to climb. Ronnie clearly knew that, as she'd already marched partway up the street in her inability to keep still. After what seemed like forever, but was probably only a few minutes, headlights approached us.

"It's your mom! Come on!" Ronnie shouted right before my mom's car came to a screeching halt beside her. Matthew and I sprinted to meet them.

"To the woods," I said when I got in. Mom stepped on the gas and didn't say anything. A messy bun wobbled on her head and loose strands fell around her face, smudged with mascara from tears. On the quiet neighborhood street with a speed limit of twenty-five, she gunned it at fifty-eight, slowing only a little to check both ways at stop signs. Normally I'd be afraid to be in the car with her driving like that, but not this time. As she sped around corners, I hung onto the door handle, kept my eyes open for police cars, and prayed for us to get there faster.

Mom squealed into the familiar woods parking lot, the back tires slipping to and fro in the dirt. I opened the door the second the car stopped, and ran to the path we always took.

"North, hold on! I have a flashlight somewhere in the car!" Mom said, and I stopped in spite of everything in me wanting to move forward.

I felt like I knew these woods so well that a flashlight was unnecessary, but the sound of something scurrying in a nearby bush reminded me that the woods in the dark were a bit different from the woods in daylight.

Mom found the flashlight under her seat, then hustled in my direction with Ronnie and Matthew right behind her. Above the crickets chirping, I heard the owls. The flashlight cast a dim light on the path, but only when I stayed close to Mom. As soon as I was more than about five feet ahead of her, I had to navigate more on hope than sight. The farther we walked, the dimmer the light became until suddenly it went completely dark.

"Oh no, you've got to be kidding me," Mom said.

I turned back and squinted to try and see her. I could hear her tapping the flashlight on her hand. "Come on, don't go out on us now." The tapping turned to more forceful slams, followed by her yell, "Ahhh! Why now?"

"It's okay Mrs. Simon, we know this path, and our eyes will adjust. We'll stay close together and we'll be fine," Matthew said.

He was right. Our eyes did adjust to the dark, the moon and stars giving us enough light to barely see the path directly in front of us. I slowed my pace, afraid to get too far ahead, the plodding of their feet assuring me they were close behind. The trail widened and there was less brush around us. I knew that to the left, off the path, the stretch of open space was grassy, and that would be the direction to get to the tree we always sat under, where Aria would likely have gone.

"Let's go left," I said as I stopped and Mom bumped into me.

"Oh! Sorry," she said. She grabbed my hand. "If it's okay, I'm going to stay close."

"Of course it's okay," I said. It was the only thing good about this moment, being close to her, holding her hand. I only wished that it was for a better reason, like walking through these woods for fun, not in search of a lost Aria.

"We're right behind you guys," Ronnie said. "If anything charges at us, I've got it."

I imagined all the potentially threatening creatures—coyotes, mountain lions, and the one I dreaded most, snakes. It seemed frighteningly easy to accidentally step on one of those, especially now that we were off the trail, in the nice cool grass where one might be traveling like us to get to its own secret hideout. I kept my eyes peeled to the ground even though I could barely see it, and prayed, *God, please keep us safe. Please don't let there be any snakes on our path, or coyotes, or mountain lions, or bears, or anything dangerous. Please be with us, and help us find Aria.* I realized I'd been praying more than ever lately, and wondered if that bothered God, that I only checked in when I felt desperate. I remembered Aria telling me God liked hearing from us about anything at any time, so I hoped that was true.

The tree was easier to see in the dark than I thought it would be, its wide limbs stretching across the sky where the moon lit up its branches. As we got closer, I saw something on the ground beneath it, and hoped it was Aria.

"Is that her?" Mom whispered.

"I hope so," I said, but as we approached what we thought was a sleeping Aria, we were disappointed to see only her blanket, covered with a huge pile of leaves, the ones she'd collected for the very purpose of staying warm in the woods if needed. On the ground next to the blanket were her notebook and pencil. I picked it up and held it in the light of the moon, which helped me to see a sketch of two owls, one big and one small, likely a mother and child, like the pair we'd seen together that day with Mom. Around the edges of the page were some of the feathers she'd collected, reminding me of when she'd said she was making something special with them. I flipped through the previous journal pages and saw more sketches of birds—an egret, a dove, an eagle, and more owls, along with soft feathers and words on each page that I couldn't make out with only the glow of the moon and the stars.

"What does it say?" Mom asked.

"I can only make out the pictures—of birds, and owls—and lots of feathers, but I can't read the writing. It's too dark," I said. "I hate to say this, but I think she went to find the owls."

I could see enough of Mom's face to see the terror on it. The owls hooted in the distance, in the direction of the cliffs. "We have to go there," she said.

I knew she was right. In spite of how crazy that was in the dark, with barely any light and no help if we needed it. There was no way we could simply stay put when we knew that was probably where she'd gone.

"Matthew, Ronnie, you guys stay here, in case she comes back, while we go to the cliffs," I said.

"Okay, wait, what if I go with you, North, and Mrs. Simon, you stay here with Ronnie? I know it's your baby out there, but if Aria is hurt or something, I think I might be better at helping. Plus, if you remember, we've been on that trail before. We know how far to go before we have to turn around."

He was right. He would be able to carry her if she was tired or injured. It made sense for him to go, and I'd told Mom about our cliff scare. She knew we wouldn't do something stupid.

"Okay," Mom said as she grabbed my hands. "But if it's too dark to see on that trail up the cliff, I need to know that you won't go anyway. Can you promise me that? I mean it. I couldn't take it if you put yourself in danger too. If you think you can't make it, you come back here and we'll go back to get help. We probably should have done that before we came out here, but it's too late now. Hopefully you'll find her before the cliffs and this will all be over with."

"I won't do anything crazy, Mom. I promise."

With that, Matthew and I headed toward the cliffs, my heart pounding in my chest. Matthew grabbed my hand, and again, I wished it were for a better reason, but I was so thankful to have him there.

# Chapter 35

"Aria!" I shouted and then waited in hopes of hearing her. The sound of a coyote's howl and the far-off owls was disappointing. Matthew yelled her name too, and then we repeated our calls over and over until we reached the trail leading to the cliffs.

The owls were definitely closer, their hoots and screeches loud and clear. If they were that loud with Aria near, nothing would stop her from seeking them out. I looked up at the jagged rocks and winding path that I knew ended abruptly and hoped with everything in me that she hadn't ventured up there.

"I really don't want to go up there again," Matthew said. He crossed his arms and wrinkled his forehead at the cliffs.

Still gripping Matthew's hand, I stepped one foot onto the trail, touched the rocks that jutted out to my right. "Yeah, I don't think we'd make it in the dark."

"Maybe we should call for her," Matthew said. "She'll respond if she hears us, and then at least we know where she is."

"Yeah, okay, we can try that," I said. I stepped down from the trail edge and shouted out, "Aria! Aria! It's me! Carol, or North! And Matthew!"

Matthew joined in with, "Yo! Aria! Where are you?"

We waited for a return shout, or for any noise at all, then tried again, and again, and again. We heard nothing back. Even the owls had stopped talking. It was eerily quiet.

"I think we need to get help," Matthew said.

I knew he was right, but admitting that meant walking away from where she might be. "I know we do, Matthew, but what if we leave and she's here and needs our help?" I started crying and could feel my whole body shaking. I felt so strongly that she was near, but we couldn't get to her, like the dark depths of the woods had swallowed her up and her cries were from too deep to hear.

Matthew held on to both my hands, gripped them tight, looked me in the eyes and said, "Hey, I know. It's scary, but we can't do this alone. Standing here won't help if she's hurt or lost. A search and rescue team can get out here with a team of people, and lights, and helicopters. They know how to do this."

I nodded and through my sobs said, "Okay, let's go."

We returned the way we'd come, with Matthew holding me close for a while, then holding my hand as I calmed myself down. I knew I couldn't be a wreck when I talked to Mom. That would only make things worse.

When we reached the tree, I could see Mom and Ronnie standing together with Mom hugging Aria's journal close to her chest. She looked at me with a pleading expression, like she was begging for good news.

"We didn't find her, Mom," I said. "We need to get help."

With tears running down her cheeks, she nodded, reached for my hand and said, "Okay, let's go."

We marched back along the trail, moving a little quicker than before, but still not fast enough. I wanted to sprint back, throw change into the parking lot pay phone and scream for help to come quickly. I continued to say silent prayers that were more demanding than ever. *Please God, please let Aria be safe. Please let us find her. Please help us. Please,* I begged. And as we neared the parking lot, I was surprised to see he was already answering me. Headlights from police cars, two massive fire trucks, and an ambulance greeted us. A helicopter vibrated overhead. When I saw my dad outside his car, talking to a police officer, I knew he was the one who had called for help, something he rarely did.

"Dad!" I yelled.

As soon as he saw me, he stopped his conversation with the officer, ran to me and embraced me in a hug. "North, I'm so glad you're here." I could hear his heart beating fast in his chest as he held me tighter than ever.

"I'm sorry I left, Dad," I said, knowing Aria was missing because of me.

"It's okay, North," he said. "This isn't your fault."

I wanted to believe him.

"Mr. Simon?" a deep voice said.

I pulled back from Dad's hug to see the black shirt and badge of a police officer.

"Can we ask your daughter a few questions?" he asked.

"Sure," Dad said.

I was glad Dad stayed beside me. Talking to a police officer made the fact that this was serious really sink in. Across from us I saw Mom, Matthew, and Ronnie talking to a couple firefighters, the back of their yellow coats labeled "Search and Rescue" in dark black lettering.

"When was the last time you saw your sister?" the officer asked. He peered down at me with dark eyes and held a pen to a notepad, ready to record my answer.

"At home, earlier this evening, around six," I said.

He jotted notes onto the paper. "And did you see her leave the house?" he asked.

"No, I didn't. I wasn't home. I left to go to a friend's."

I waited as he scribbled more notes. "Did she tell you she was going out this evening?"

"No," I said. "She didn't tell me anything except not to leave. She was upset because I was supposed to walk with her in these woods earlier, before it got dark, but I got home too late." The wave of guilt struck me again and the tears started coming. I sobbed as I pictured her hands trying to piece the bird together on the kitchen floor. I felt Dad's arm around me and watched the officer's hand scrawl notes across the paper. "I told her she would be fine, and I left anyway." I stared into the officer's face, the frown lines between his brows, the neatly trimmed dark mustache. He stopped writing and looked back at me, waiting for me to continue. "That was the last I saw her." The finality of that statement set more tears loose. This was all my fault. I should have listened to her the way she always listens to me. I should have stayed. Dad pulled me into another hug.

"Okay," the officer said, "thank you. I know this is hard, but we're going to do everything we can to find your sister, okay?"

I pulled away from my dad to look at the officer. I wanted to ask him what we could do, tell him where I thought she could be, but I couldn't bring myself to say anything. When a woman's voice blasted from the officer's walkie-talkie, he slowly walked away and answered her back.

A search and rescue worker walked toward us holding blankets.

Dad took one, thanked him, and put it around me. Matthew, Ronnie, and Mom joined us, blanket-covered as well, and we huddled together, quiet except for occasional sniffles from Mom and myself. We watched the rescue crew, armed with bright flashlights and backpacks, head out in groups of ten for the trail. A black and tan German Shepherd and a Golden Retriever energetically led two more groups, sniffing the dirt, trotting ahead, eager to aid in the search.

When only a handful of police officers and rescue workers remained, Ronnie took the lead in sitting down. Matthew followed and said to me, "Come on, have a seat," as he patted the dirt next to him.

I realized how exhausted I was once I hit the ground. I leaned into Matthew, and rested my head on his shoulder. My eyes felt heavy and blurry from crying. Dad's scuffed up leather work boots inched closer to Mom's dirty white sneakers, and I looked up to see them arm in arm for the first time in at least a year. It seemed strange that in such a terrible moment, something good was happening. I closed my eyes for a moment, holding the image of Mom and Dad in my mind, and hoped it would replace the terrible thoughts I kept having about Aria.

# Chapter 36

When I opened my eyes next, I saw a gray sky tinted pink and orange. I turned to see Matthew and Ronnie asleep next to me, and for a second I felt confused as to where we were. The whir of a nearby helicopter, the crunching of footsteps in the dirt, and more walkie-talkie voices reminded me of the nightmare I was living. I sat up slowly, my neck and back stiff and my mouth dry. Several yards away I could see Mom and Dad talking to a couple of search and rescue crewmembers, which meant the search was still on.

"Woah, it's morning," Matthew said. He sat up, rubbed his eyes, and looked around to orient himself to the reality of where we were. "Any news?" he asked me, his eyes barely open.

"I don't know. I'm about to go ask," I said, glancing over at my parents.

"You want me to come with you?"

"No, that's okay. Stay here with Ronnie so she doesn't wake up alone, even though she probably won't. She can sleep through almost anything."

We both looked at her, cocooned in her blanket, mouth open, breathing deep.

"Okay, I'll stay here. Let me know what they tell you," he said.

"I will," I said as I walked toward my parents and tried to assess their facial expressions and body language. Mom stood with her hands folded under her chin, eyes closed. Her mouth moved slightly, like she was whispering something. Dad was pacing back and forth, away from her, then toward her, head down. When I got closer, I could hear Mom ever so quietly saying, "*Our Father, who art in heaven, hallowed be thy name, thy kingdom come, thy will be done on earth as it is in heaven . . .*" Even though we hadn't been to a church service in years, I recognized this prayer. Mom had taught it to us when we were younger, and I remembered saying it when we used to go to Sunday School once in a while.

She opened her eyes and noticed I was standing in front of her. "Oh, you're awake," she said.

"Yes, but don't stop. I'll pray with you."

She took my hands in hers and then continued. When she said, "*Give us this day our daily bread,*" I remembered seeing Aria pray these words often in the woods. While I tried to be focused on Mom's prayer, the image of Aria took over my thoughts. My eyes closed, I saw Aria as she'd pause in the middle of this prayer, scatter bird seed, ask God for daily bread, and then sit and wait. As soon as the birds came to peck the seed away she'd say, "Thanks, God, for the bread!" before continuing the prayer.

I didn't understand why she always thanked God for the bread when I never saw any bread magically appear. One day she explained, "I learned that asking for our daily bread is asking God for the things we need and trusting him to take care of us. Every time the birds come, I feel like I have what I need. They make me happy, so God is answering my prayer. Even if the birds don't come, I still say thank you."

"Why?" I asked her, not because I didn't think she should be thankful, but because it seemed difficult to say thanks when things don't go the way we hope.

"Because he's God," she said, "and he knows better than I do what I need, so if the birds don't fly my way, he obviously has something better in mind for them and me at that moment."

I came back to reality when I felt Mom squeeze my hand, finished with her prayer. I opened my eyes, and saw that hers were still closed. Even with the commotion going on around us—more fire trucks entering the parking lot, people talking, dad still pacing—and the turmoil in my head over the fact that Aria was still missing, I felt oddly calm. When Mom opened her eyes again, she gave me a tiny little smile, the first one I'd seen on her in quite some time. *Thanks, God*, I said to myself.

"The search and rescue team said it'll be much easier to look for Aria now that it's daylight," Mom said. Her smile faded, and she turned away from me as her hands gripped mine tighter. "They're going to search the ravine now. If she climbed those cliffs and fell, she'll need help as soon as possible."

In other words, if she'd fallen, she would be lucky to be alive, and if she was alive, she could be severely injured. The thought of her laying helpless at the bottom of the ravine was too horrible to bear. I pushed it out of my head, imagined her sleeping somewhere instead, safe and peaceful, unharmed.

A crew of tall yellow coats walked by and I blurted out, "Let me help! I want to go with you!"

They stopped and turned to look at me as Mom said, "Honey, I don't think there's much you can do that isn't already being done."

One of the men stepped forward and said to the other crew members, "You guys go ahead. I'll catch up," then he returned his attention to me.

"I can sing," I said.

He and Mom each gave me a blank stare.

"Are you a family member?" the man asked. He waited for my response with deep blue eyes framed with faint wrinkles that fanned out from the corners like little rays of sunshine. His tanned skin had surely weathered many days like this one, with desperate people like me counting on him to save the day.

"I'm Aria's sister. She needs extra help when she gets scared or hurt. She's going to need someone she knows near her, and when I sing, it always calms her. She left the house because of me. I need to be there for her now."

He looked at me like he was trying to see how serious I was, whether I was truly up to the task. "We might be out there a long time, and someone probably should stay back in case she shows up here."

I looked at Mom. Before I even asked, she said, "Your father and I will stay here. I'm still believing she went somewhere else, and she's going to show up and ask us why we're all at the woods without her. I want to be here if that happens, and I don't think I'd be any help out there. I might actually be more of a burden."

"I think that's a good idea," the man said to Mom. Then he turned to me and said, "You can walk with me to the big oak tree and then hang back with the crew there. I can't let you go past that, okay? I don't want anyone else getting lost."

"Okay," I said, relieved I could finally do something that felt helpful. "Would it be okay if my friends over there came too?" I asked as I pointed to Matthew and Ronnie.

He took a deep breath, sighed, and rubbed his forehead while he glanced over at them. "Okay, yes," he nodded, "I'll meet you over at the trailhead."

"Thanks," I said. I gave Mom a quick hug and then ran over to tell Matthew and Ronnie.

At the trailhead, the man handed us each a small backpack. "There's water, a granola bar, and a first-aid kit in there, enough stuff for a short time out," he said as he adjusted the much larger pack on his back. He introduced himself as Jeff, and while we walked he told us how he first became a firefighter and then decided to stay on the Search and Rescue team after saving a lost six-year-old boy in Yosemite.

"The joy in his parents when I found him was incredible. They cried and laughed at the same time, hugging their boy and me. I'll never forget it. He'd been missing for twelve hours, and fell asleep in a little cave to keep warm. Luckily it was summer, so the temperatures weren't freezing, and his only injury was a scraped knee and elbow. He's ten now, and every year the parents send me a card or a thank you gift on his birthday because they say I'm the reason they can still celebrate his life. So, that's why I do this," he said. "Also, it's pretty cool to be outdoors on days like this."

He was right about that. The sun peeked through puffy white clouds in the silky blue sky and the birds were out in full force. With every one that flew near, I thought of Aria, saw her flapping her arms and skipping ahead of me. With each bird song, I heard her mimicking them.

"Maybe if sports don't work out for my career, I can do this," Ronnie said. "It sounds pretty awesome, but I'll bet it can be pretty tough too, especially when someone can't be helped."

A longer pause than I expected followed that comment. Jeff focused on the path in front of him and said, "Yep, that's the side of this job I don't like to talk about."

We continued marching forward, and I wondered whether Aria would become one of those bad sides.

"I like to think of the good moments, especially while I'm on a search. Those positive vibes help. So, keep the faith, right?" He looked at each of us, waiting for a response.

"Yes," Matthew said. "Keep the faith."

Ronnie and I chimed in with the same response, and then I continued in my head with *keep faith, keep faith, keep faith,* in rhythm to my steps, and pictured Aria, alive and well.

When we reached the big oak tree, it looked a lot different than usual. A bright orange tarp was suspended from one end of the tree to an opposite branch to make a covering for workers. A few of them stood nearby, and waved to Jeff as we approached.

"How's it going?" Jeff asked them.

"We've got a group searching the ravine now," said a man with a red bushy beard. He paused and looked at Matthew, Ronnie, and me. "Looks like we've got a few helpers."

"This is Aria's sister, Carol, and her two friends. They've been told to stay here, and if we find Aria nearby, they can be here to greet her and keep her calm. This one's a singer," he said as he pointed to me, "she might be able to entertain you all while you wait."

I hoped he was joking. Singing didn't feel right until I saw Aria.

"Really?" Red beard said. "Well, I'm Tom, not a singer, but I do love music, so sing whenever you want."

"Thanks," I said.

Jeff continued on his way to the cliffs, and I watched him until I could no longer see him, wishing so much that I could go with him. As scary as the climb seemed, I felt like it was better than standing there doing nothing. I took a deep breath, let it out, and looked at Ronnie and

Matthew. "Thanks for being here, you guys," I said.

"Don't even think about it," Ronnie said. "We want to be here."

"Yeah, you don't need to thank us," Matthew said.

I thought about how upset they'd both been with me only a day ago, remembered the anger and hurt on Matthew's face. "I do need to thank you. You both have a right to be mad at me, but instead you're here."

Ronnie reached her arms wide and said, "Come on, group hug."

As we stood there, embracing each other, I realized that no level of popularity, or coolness, or singing fame could ever be worth more than them.

# Chapter 37

Waiting has never been something I've enjoyed, and the wait for Aria was the worst ever. Whenever a voice would pipe through one of the crew's walkie-talkies, I'd be all ears, hoping to hear those three perfect words, "We found her," followed by the next two even better words, "She's safe." But so far all I'd heard was, "No signs of her yet."

I decided it might be better to move farther away, where I couldn't hear the discouraging updates. Ronnie had struck up a conversation with a couple of the rescue workers, wanting to hear all their advice about outdoor safety and survival. Matthew had been searching every square inch of space for signs of Aria, starting from the tree and working his way out. He'd covered a very small radius, circling the tree in slow, careful steps with his eyes peeled to the ground. I copied his strategy as I walked away from the tree that was now search and rescue central. Each step forward didn't bring me any closer to finding traces of her. Dirt, some acorns, pebbles were all I saw. I stopped at a sunny spot and sat down, the sun warm on my head, the fall morning chill still in the air. I looked back at the tree that had been our safe place for so long. The makeshift hammock Aria had made out of a couple blankets still hung from the tree's branches, and the metal bucket with birdseed, piles of sticks, and leaves she'd gathered sat nearby. I'd stopped trying to convince her the birds didn't need her help with gathering things like that for their nests. Whether the birds needed it or not wasn't important; the gathering made Aria happy. As I thought this, a bird swooped down and sat on the edge of the bucket, peeked in, and pulled out a small leaf. Then it flew up into the tree. I could hear Aria's voice in my head saying *See, I told you they liked my help!*

A few seconds later, I heard the caw of a crow, and then several more. I looked up to see the two noisemakers dart across the sky, and then I heard a third caw. It came from the trail that led to the cliffs. Two tall men in bright yellow coats plodded along, carrying a stretcher between them.

My heart beat fast, and I jumped up when I heard Ronnie shout, "It's Aria! They found her!" I bolted toward them, as did Matthew and Ronnie. Tom sprinted past, his red beard easy to spot amidst the rest of his crew close behind him. I felt a surge of gratitude for all these people, racing to help my sister.

As the rescue workers surrounded Aria, I heard someone say, "We need to move fast!" I wanted to push my way through all of them, get a glimpse of her face, let her see I was there, but the fact that I could no longer hear her mimic the noisy crows made me afraid. Why was she so quiet? Why were the crows so loud? It was like they were screaming for more helpers.

"Is she okay?" I shouted.

Jeff emerged from the huddle and approached me. "She keeps falling in and out of consciousness. We need to hurry. She took a really bad fall into the ravine," he said between breaths of air.

Tom and a woman with curly dark hair had taken over the

stretcher. As they passed, I saw Aria, eyes closed, her milky white face smudged with dirt and scratches, her long hair a matted mess under an ice pack that rested on her head. Her arm was tied in a splint.

"I'm gonna follow them so I can be there when she gets in the ambulance," Jeff said.

I followed him as he started to jog and responded, "I'm coming with you."

"Us too," Ronnie said as she and Matthew joined me.

When we caught up to Aria, I kept watch on her face, hoping for her eyes to open, trying to see the rise and fall of her chest to show she was breathing, wondering how they'd know if she had stopped. As if they heard my thoughts, moments later they stopped to check on her, then picked up the pace again. They did this two more times before we finally arrived at the parking lot, where three paramedics stood next to a gurney at the back of the opened ambulance. Mom and Dad came running over the second they saw us.

"Oh, thank God you found her," Mom said while sobbing. "Thank you all, thank you. Is she okay?"

"She's got a pulse and she's breathing, but we need to get her to the hospital," The curly haired woman said. While she looked so tiny compared to big Tom, she was a mighty force. She led the way, stopping regularly to shout out when they needed to check Aria's vitals. Then as they continued on, she kept repeating, "We got this, we're almost there, come on."

I took Mom's hand as the paramedics transferred Aria from the stretcher to the ambulance gurney. Her eyes flickered open and she began to talk.

"What . . . what are we doing? Where am I?" she said in a squeaky, frightened voice.

"Aria, it's okay," Mom said through quiet sobs. "You're safe. You're going to the hospital where they're going to take really good care of you."

"What? Why?" She tried to lift her head, but quickly put it back down. "Ow, my head," she said.

"That's why we're taking you to the hospital," one of the paramedics said.

"My arm hurts too. Ow," she said as tears began to run down her face. I felt so helpless. She was obviously in a lot of pain.

Mom stepped closer and gently placed her hand on Aria's forehead. The paramedic placed a strap over Aria's legs and then her waist. He paused as he held the strap that was about to go over her arms and said, "I'm going to put this over your arms and chest to make sure you don't slip when we lift you into the ambulance, okay? It will feel like a seatbelt. I won't put it too tight since your arm hurts."

I was glad he was letting her know that. She didn't like being confined, so warning her would help her stay calm. She squinted at him like she was either confused or couldn't see him well, but said nothing. When he placed his hand on her upper arm, her eyes widened and as he placed the strap over her, she yelled, "Ow! Ow!"

Mom looked at me with desperation in her face. Without much thought, I started to sing. "When I saw you standing there, I saw something I'd been missing, a rare bird in flight, singing, soaring."

Aria stopped yelling and closed her eyes. I continued singing Brandon's song, substituting words I couldn't remember with my own. "She's brave and beautiful, smart and kind, her name is Aria, a songbird in flight."

Her eyes remained closed as they put her in the ambulance.

"We're taking her to North Hills Hospital. You know where that is?" the paramedic who had strapped her to the gurney asked from inside the ambulance.

"Yes," Dad said.

"Okay," he looked at me and said, "Thanks for the song. It really calmed her down. Wish I had you with me on every emergency call."

As the doors shut and the siren came on, I looked at Dad. With tears in his eyes, he said, "Sorry, North."

I didn't know why he was apologizing. "Sorry?" I asked.

"For telling you singing is a waste of your time. It's not."

# Chapter 38

On the way to the hospital, I realized I was going to miss my chance to sing with Brandon's band. I might never get another chance to sing in front of a record producer. But it didn't really matter anymore. I sat in the backseat between Ronnie and Matthew, looked at Mom and Dad in the front seat, and remembered when going places together like this was the norm. We only needed Aria to make it complete. As we drove, I noticed the birds and missed the sound of Aria's voice, announcing each one's name, sound, and unique traits. The street was lined with giant Sweetgum trees full of vibrant yellow and orange leaves. I wanted to reach out the window and pluck one, feel it in my hand and pretend that Aria had just pulled it from her bag to share with me. The world needed people like Aria more than it might know, and so did I. I tried to tell myself things she would say to me, about being strong and courageous, about having peace because God is always with us. Hearing her voice in my head was both comforting and troubling at the same time because I didn't want her voice only in my head. I wanted it for real.

The hospital parking lot had as much activity as opening day of a theme park. Cars lined the emergency room curb, every parking space appeared full, and two valet parking attendants hurried to assist people who needed to park and didn't want to circle the lot to find a space.

"I'll drop you guys off first and then look for a spot," Dad said.

"Okay," Mom said as she started to open the door before the car had even stopped. "We'll see you inside."

Dad pulled up beside the cars parked parallel to the curb, and we all hopped out. "See you in there soon," he said.

The emergency waiting area was standing room only, with every age and type of person there. It was as if the entire valley were hit by a meteor or a plague. The sounds of crying babies, coughing, moaning, television news, and a nurse calling out patient names created a clash of noise worse than all those middle school band performances I'd sat through. Matthew, Ronnie, and I found one empty space against a wall while Mom went to talk to a nurse at the front desk who looked about as happy to be there as all the patients. The smell of coffee mixed with disinfectant filled the air and made me slightly nauseous. I covered my nose and breathed into my hand, wishing I could have one of those face masks the doctors always wore.

When Mom returned, she said, "The nurse is checking on Aria. She'll call us when we can see her."

Now that I had a moment to pay attention, I noticed how exhausted Mom looked. Her eyes, puffy and red, her lower lids sunken and smudged with mascara, her hair barely hanging on to the rubber band that had slipped down to the last inch of her hair. She kept her arms crossed close to her body like she was cold and stepped nervously side to side.

"Mrs. Simon," the nurse called out.

"Yes!" Mom replied and darted toward her.

I watched her as she talked to the nurse, and waited for her to wave me over so I could go with her to see Aria. Instead, she turned and walked back to me.

"They're recommending that only I go back to see Aria and speak to the doctor," Mom said. "I'll come back out as soon as I know what's going on." Her tears poured out.

"Okay," I said, disappointed that I had to wait longer to know whether my sister was okay.

Once Mom disappeared through the emergency room doors, I turned my focus to the clock on the wall, which read 10:25. Somehow watching the red second hand as it ticked from line to line around the clock seemed better than staring at all the sick and hurt people. It was oddly entertaining to watch the black minute hand advance every time the second hand made a complete rotation. Each time it moved, I hoped Mom would walk back through those doors with a smile on her face and tell me Aria was okay. At 10:29, Dad arrived. When the minute hand moved to 10:34, he went back to see Aria. At 10:42, Matthew and Ronnie took a seat on the floor. Fifty-three minutes later, 11:18, Mom finally reappeared, head down, tears still flowing.

I ran to her. "Is she okay?" I asked.

She pulled me into a hug and said between sobs, "I hope she will be. She's in a coma."

# Chapter 39

When I finally saw Aria, I kept telling myself she was simply sleeping, taking a long nap, and would wake up refreshed and energized. While I stared at her, willing her eyes to open with every possible power in me, the doctor arrived, wearing the typical white coat accessorized with a stethoscope and a shiny name badge that identified her as Dr. Elia Kadir, M.D., Neurology. Amidst the beeping of heart rate monitors, a crying baby, and the nurse in the room next to us talking louder and louder to an apparently hard-of-hearing patient, Dr. Kadir was a calm and collected presence.

"Okay, Mr. and Mrs. Simon, Aria is going to be moved to the pediatric intensive care unit, which is on the first floor of the main hospital," she said as she pushed her glasses up the bridge of her nose and flipped her long delicate fingers through the pages on her clipboard. "She'll be in good hands there, and I'll be in to check on her regularly." Her voice, calm and confident, made me feel better, but what she said next was a little troubling.

"You should know that return to consciousness with an injury like

Aria's is a slow process," Dr. Kadir said as she paused, looked at Mom and Dad, then me. "She should transition into a minimally conscious state within four weeks. She might start to squeeze your hand, indicate yes or no with a head nod or other gesture, maybe say her name or other simple words. She might cry, smile, laugh, reach for objects. These are all good signs. Once she can correctly answer simple yes and no questions or use at least two objects, like a comb or pencil consistently, she is considered to be conscious, and will either have moderate or severe impairment. The sooner she moves through this minimally conscious phase, the better her outcome will be, but everyone is different."

I looked at Aria, rubbed her arm, hoped she could feel it. I watched her head and fingers for any movement.

"What can we do to help?" Mom asked.

"Be with her as much as you can, talk to her, read to her, sing, play music. These all help patients with head injuries to recover. They can hear a lot more than they can respond to, so your presence is important," she said.

I expected Mom to tell me to start singing again, but she simply nodded and said, "Okay, we'll be here as much as we can."

Dr. Kadir nodded and then moved to stand by Aria. "What you're doing right now is great," she said as she looked at me. "Human touch helps a lot. Are you her sister? You look like her."

"Yes," I said. I hadn't thought about our similarities much. I always felt so different from Aria. As I looked at her, I realized that wasn't true. Aside from apparently looking similar, we both had our peculiarities and quirks. Aria simply didn't try to hide hers like I did. Seeing her motionless, unexpressive, so unlike her normal self made me desperately want every unique part of her back.

Dr. Kadir checked the monitors that showed Aria's heart rate and oxygen levels. "Her vitals look pretty good," she said. She gently touched Aria's forehead and watched her for a moment. "Okay, Aria, see you again tomorrow."

Moments later, a twenty-something year old man in blue scrubs entered. "Hi, I'm Ben. I'm here to take Aria to her new room," he said.

I looked at the clock, which read 12:30, a half-hour into the band performing for Mr. Winslett with Dahlia taking my place. I shoved that thought away as Ben wheeled Aria down the hall. I didn't feel entirely hopeful over what Dr. Kadir had told us. I knew Mom didn't either as she kept wiping away tears that flowed nonstop down her face.

"I should probably go update Matthew and Ronnie about Aria," I said, feeling desperate for my friends.

Mom pulled me into a hug. "Okay, sweetheart, take your time. We'll be with Aria."

Back in the emergency room, Matthew and Ronnie were both asleep on the floor with their backs against the wall where we had originally positioned ourselves. I knelt down in front of them and gently tapped their legs. "Hey guys, wake up," I said.

They each jolted awake, and Ronnie said with eyes wide, "Oh my gosh, what's happening? Is Aria okay?"

"Uh, yes?" I said, not wanting to freak her out by saying no. "Let's go walk outside and I'll explain."

It felt good to be outside. The air was cool but the sun was warm on my face as we exited the hospital doors. At the sound of a bird, all I could think of was Aria in that hospital bed. I might not hear from her again. With tears rolling down, I turned to Matthew and Ronnie and let it all out.

"She's in a coma. She could be like that for weeks, and if and when she comes out of it, we don't know what she'll be like. I'm afraid she won't be herself again." For so long she'd been looked at as different and unusual, as loud and weird when she made bird sounds, or rude when she'd say what was on her mind without filtering it to be more polite. People always thought she should be more like them. Even I'd stopped appreciating her and felt ashamed to act like her. I knew at that moment how wrong that was. I longed for her voice, in all its pure, honest, bold, or bird-calling uniqueness, and I knew right then that I would never encourage her to be anything other than her true self no matter what anyone else thought, and I would never feel embarrassed of her again.

Matthew and Ronnie hugged me close, and I stared up at the clear blue sky, wondering more than ever before if anything beyond the horizon could hear my cries.

# Chapter 40

After two weeks, Aria had been moved out of Intensive Care into a regular hospital room. She'd started to squeeze our hand in response to things we said, and on a few occasions opened her eyes for a bit. Dr. Kadir said these were all good signs, but the wait for her to be her old self was excruciating. Mom spent every moment she could at the hospital, which was usually in the evenings and overnight because she had to clean houses during the day. Dad would visit Aria during the day when Mom wasn't there, and was home when I got out of school, hammering away on his extra room or stacking items somewhere in the house. I'd either get a ride from him to the hospital then, or Mom would pick me up when she was done working. I never felt like I was with Aria enough, but I saw her everywhere.

One day when I walked home from school, I imagined her skipping and belting out bird calls in front of me. Under each tree, I'd look up and try to identify a bird, like she would have done. With each chirp and chatter, I'd hear her voice, and knew I had to keep singing. If I felt insecure, I needed to be bold, like she was when it counted. I needed to be myself, so that no matter what happened to Aria, she would live on.

Her joy, her spirit, her courage, her kindness, could stay alive through me, and if people thought I was crazy, then good. I'd consider that a compliment if it meant I was even a little bit closer to who Aria always encouraged me to be.

I noticed a leaf on the ground in front of me and stopped to pick it up, just like she would have done. I examined it as I walked, noticed every line, how it was yellow at the bottom and turned orange near the top. I picked up another one, and another, and kept gathering them until my hands were so full I had to stuff some in my pockets and even down my shirt.

When I got home, I pulled all the leaves in a pile on the floor. Then I went to grab a bag so I could save them for Aria. In the kitchen, Dad was on the phone, a rare sight to see. "Yep, I can be there," he said with an enthusiasm I hadn't heard in a very long time. "Okay, see you then, thank you." He hung up the phone and then did a fist pump in the air. "Yes!" he said as he spun around and looked surprised to see me.

"Hi!" I said. "What's so exciting?"

I hoped it was news about Aria, that she was awake, talking, laughing, telling everyone in the hospital about birds.

"I have an interview tomorrow morning at Smart Shop, that new discount grocery store."

While that wasn't my first choice of good news, it was definitely second, or maybe third, right behind Aria talking and Mom moving back home.

"That's awesome!" I said and lifted my hand to give him a high five.

"What do you say I treat you to ice cream on the way to the hospital?" he asked. "I sold one of my record collections to a friend I used to work with at the grocery store, got a good chunk of cash, so I think we deserve a little reward."

Dad had managed to sell a few things recently out of desperate need for money, but selling his records must have really been rough. He loved his collection of albums.

"Sure," I said, "I'm sorry you had to sell your records."

He looked away for a second and I knew he was trying to hide the disappointment he felt. He looked back at me and said, "It's okay. Hopefully I'll get that job tomorrow and I can buy those albums again one day. In fact, while you're visiting Aria, I think I'll go buy myself a new tie for luck. I've been with Aria all day. She's probably sick of me."

"I doubt she's sick of you, Dad, but a tie's a good idea."

"I hope so. It'd be a shame to spend money on a tie and then not get the job."

I reached for his hand, the first time I'd done that in years. "I think you're going to get it." While he grasped my hand tight, I added, "What if I help you prepare for the interview?"

"Sure, how do you plan to do that?" he asked.

"Practice," I said. "It's like the way I have to practice singing before I get up in front of people. I'm going to interview you."

He turned his head and raised his brows at me.

"Trust me, it'll be good," I said and pulled him toward the front door. "Let's go get the ice cream."

On the way, I asked him practice interview questions, pretending to be a stodgy old interviewer.

He laughed after a few questions and said, "What makes you think grocery bosses are so stern and serious?"

"Oh, I don't know. I figure this way when you greet a nice person tomorrow it will seem relaxing and easy."

"Okay, that makes sense," he said.

Dad pulled into the Thrifty Drug Store parking lot, and once inside we had no problem choosing our favorite flavors. He picked two scoops of Rocky Road, and I chose one scoop of Mint Chip and one of Vanilla Fudge Swirl. We ate in the car while driving to the hospital with nothing much to say other than, "Mmmm, this is good," and "This is the best" and again, "Mmm." This was one of those moments I didn't mind that Dad grabbed way too many napkins whenever they were available. I let the melting ice cream run down my hands and wrists, licking some of them away and catching the rest with a few of the hundreds of napkins stashed in a bag in the backseat.

Aria was alone when I arrived at the hospital and entered her room. Her eyes were closed, but I'd learned that didn't mean she was in a deep sleep. I approached her and said, "Hi Aria, how are you today?" I placed my hand into hers to see if she might squeeze it in response.

"I gathered some leaves for you today," I said.

Her eyes fluttered open as she squeezed my hand and continued to do so as I told her about how many I'd collected, what they looked like, what type of trees they were from, the birds I'd heard, and how excited I was to walk with her again. Then I heard the most beautiful sound. The one that used to annoy me and embarrass me, the one I used to try to ignore, the one I so often wanted to silence.

"North," Aria said.

"Aria!" I exclaimed as I squeezed her hand tighter and leaned in to kiss her on the forehead. "I never thought I'd love the sound of my name as much as I do now." I hoped she'd say something again, let me know I didn't just imagine her voice.

And then she smiled, the first one since her fall, and said again, "North."

A nurse entered the room. "Everything okay?" she said, a little out of breath, eyes wide.

"Oh, yes, everything is great," I said. "Aria spoke, and she smiled!"

Her expression switched to instant joy. "Well, alleluia to that!" she said. "What did she say?"

"She said North," I said.

The nurse looked confused. "Hmm, that's an interesting first word. Does she like giving people directions?"

"Uh, no," I laughed. "North is my name," I said, feeling proud of that fact for a change.

Aria squeezed my hand and smiled again.

"Well, would you look at that? Such a pretty smile," the nurse said, "and that name, North, is beautiful too. She's lucky to have such a wonderful family around. That makes all the difference."

For the first time I could remember, someone had called Aria pretty, my name beautiful, and our family wonderful. And finally, I thought so too.

# Chapter 41

The next day Mom picked me up after school, done with cleaning for the day. I thought we were going straight to the hospital, but instead, she went in the other direction, towards home.

"Where are we going?" I asked.

"You'll see," she said with a smile.

I wasn't really in the mood to be surprised, but since she seemed happy and calm, I didn't question it. When she passed our house and continued in the direction of the woods, I didn't feel so relaxed. She pulled into the parking lot, parked near the entrance, and turned off the engine.

"Mom, I really don't feel like being here," I said.

She looked at me with understanding eyes, reached for my hand, and said, "I know. I don't really feel like it either, but I think we'll be glad we did. I have something I want to show you while we're here." She reached behind to the backseat and grabbed the canvas bag Aria used to carry with her everywhere. "Come on," she said and opened her door, bringing the bag with her.

We walked arm in arm in silence along the trail. Unlike my normal calm when I entered the woods, this time I felt dread and emptiness. It felt weird to be there without Aria, and although she was getting better, I still worried she might not progress to being the way she used to be, and her mind, with all its facts about birds, would be different, making trips to the woods unbearable. When I looked at Mom, she looked as afraid as I felt.

"Are you sure you want to be here?" I asked. "Can't you show me whatever you need to somewhere else?"

"Yes, I can," she said as she kept her focus and her steps forward on the trail ahead. "But I think this is what Aria would want, and I think it will be something good to tell her about today when we see her. It might even get her talking more. It's wonderful that she said your name, and I think there's a reason why she said that first. That's what I'm hoping to show you today."

When we reached the oak tree, it looked like it had when Mom, Aria, and I first discovered it years before. Aria's makeshift hammock was gone, the leaves she'd set in big piles had been scattered. We sat down and leaned against the tree's sturdy trunk.

Mom let out a deep breath. "It's still peaceful here, even after all that's happened."

I breathed in the earthy sweet smell of the tree bark, listened as a songbird chirped above me, and watched the tall dry grass beyond as it swayed back and forth in the breeze. She was right. The peace hadn't been overshadowed by what happened to Aria.

Mom reached into Aria's bag and pulled out her journal, the one we'd found under the tree that night Aria went missing. She opened it, and in the light I could see how beautiful it really was, and could read what Aria had written in it. Mom flipped to the last page Aria had decorated, and handed it to me. I rubbed my hand along the leaves and feathers Aria had carefully glued around the edge of two pages. On one side was a sketch of a bird, similar to the one that sang above me, and under it, in curly decorative letters was my name, *North*. The opposite page was filled with a verse and a prayer in more swirly letters.

## Psalm 91:4

He will cover you with his feathers,

and under his wings you will find refuge;

his faithfulness will be your shield and rampart.

Dear God,

Please help North I know she's upset. Please protect her. Help her to be brave and to know you are with her. Help her to keep singing because she has such a beautiful voice, and when I hear it I feel your presence. If she decides she always wants to be called Carol, let her still know her true north, which is with you and who you call her to be.

Thank you, God.

Amen

I read it over three times through my blurry, tear-filled eyes before I looked up at Mom. "I don't know what to say," I said. "I thought she struggled with writing. Can you imagine how happy her teachers would be to see this?"

Mom laughed and wiped the tears from her cheeks. "Yes, they would be thrilled!"

We stayed there under the tree for a while with the notebook wide open in my lap. Birds fluttered by, a couple squirrels chased each other and scurried up the tree. Life under the tree carried on as usual, but I planned to live outside of it a little differently, thanks to Aria and that prayer.

# Chapter 42

When we got to the hospital a little before five, Dad was in the room, pacing back and forth. "Oh, good, I thought you'd be here by now. I was worried." He peered down at Mom with the same mixed expression he gave me whenever I was late, his brow furrowed with concern, his face red with annoyance.

"Frank, I told you we were going to the woods to talk," Mom said.

"Yes, Belinda, I know, but I didn't think you'd take this long. I've been here all day alone, hoping to at least hear Aria talk since I haven't been home to hear whether I got the job I interviewed for this morning. She hasn't said a word. It feels like a complete waste of a day for me. You could have been more considerate and gotten here sooner.

This was definitely not the example of a wonderful family the nurse had previously described. This was the real us, the family with the ability to go from cute to catastrophic in seconds. Dad had been really irritable since the job interview, probably because he hadn't heard yet whether he got the job.

"Okay, well you can go now. I'll bring North home later," Mom said as she shooed him off with her hand.

He looked at me and said, "So we're calling you North now?"

"Uh, no, I think that was a slip," I said. "But honestly, it's fine. You can call me North or Carol. I like them both for different reasons now."

Dad shook his head and said, "Okay, well, I'm confused, but I'll see you at home." He leaned over Aria, kissed her forehead, and said, "Bye, Aria, love you." He headed to the door, shoulders slumped, head down.

"Love you!" Aria shouted back, and Dad stopped midstride.

We all turned to Aria, bright-eyed and surprised.

Mom ran over to her, laughing. "Oh my goodness Aria, we love you too!"

The three of us stood around Aria, appearing in the moment to be the picture of a wonderful family again thanks to Aria's perfectly timed response to Dad. She said "Love you" several more times that evening as Mom and I told her all about our time in the woods. Dad stayed and listened too. When I thanked her for the prayer, she put all three of her recent words together and said, "Love you, North."

We all left the hospital together a couple hours later, when Aria had fallen asleep. Once I was home, I faced the reality that the English project I'd been avoiding was due tomorrow, and unlike my normal over-prepared self, I hadn't written a single word. Brandon, Dahlia, and Ricky had each finished their parts, writing their ideas about how to form a successful band. I'd read their papers, which essentially all advised to find the right musicians, practice a lot, and produce a professional recording to send to record labels.

We originally planned to play a sample of our music for the class, but the tape was still being edited. When I couldn't show up at Brandon's to sing in front of Chad's dad, Dahlia took the job of singing as I'd expected. In spite of Brandon trying to convince Mr. Winslett to hear me before going through with the recording, Mr. Winslett said Dahlia's voice was good enough, and that he would edit the songs to sound better anyway. Brandon said it seemed obvious that Dahlia's dad had a talk with Mr. Winslett about keeping her as singer. I'd missed a big opportunity, which made writing about it all the more difficult.

Rather than coming up with anything good to write, I kept hearing Dahlia in my head. At school she talked about her future fame to anyone in earshot, and even though most people had no idea whether she was any good, they treated her like a celebrity, asking her to autograph their notebooks, shirts, random pieces of paper. It was pretty ridiculous. If anyone in the band had a future, it was Brandon, but he never bragged about himself.

I needed to think of something original and important to say in my paper. I didn't want to repeat the words everyone else in the group had written. Something was missing. I collapsed on my bed and shut my eyes, picturing Aria as she smiled and spoke at the hospital. I really wanted to say something in my presentation to honor her. Miss Enders had reminded us almost daily to be sure our presentations were meaningful, focused on things that mattered not only to us, but for the betterment of society. Some people, like Dahlia and Ricky, rolled their eyes when she went on about that, but when I heard people practicing their presentations in class, nearly every one of them found a way to explain how their ideas could help the world. I'd overheard how making a better sandwich would decrease child malnutrition, how making the most of your time at an amusement park curbed depression, and how surfing created a love for the ocean that could inspire laws to protect the environment. The only one in our group who had touched upon the value in creating a successful band was Brandon when he mentioned that music was a powerful way to lift people's moods and occupy their time so they wouldn't do drugs or drop out of school, points I agreed with, but I didn't feel the need to repeat.

I remembered Miss Enders' advice about what to do when stuck on a writing assignment. "Just start writing; put the pen to the paper and write what comes to mind. You can edit it later, but you can't edit a blank paper. So get going." If we were writing to one of her prompts in class, she'd walk around, clap her hands together and say, "Go! Come on! Here's your first sentence: 'I don't have any clue what to write about. I'd rather be . . . .' Now finish that."

So, I started with that and wrote:

*I don't know what to write for my project. I'd rather be with Aria, and Matthew, and Ronnie walking down the street to the woods like we used to. Aria would skip ahead, point out every bird, copy their sounds. In the woods, we'd feel free, no worries about what people might say or think about us. We could be ourselves.*

And then I knew what I needed to say. I went to my typewriter, put in a fresh piece of paper and tapped away at the keys. Two hours later, I was done. I stapled the five pages together and read the title of my section out loud. "*How to Form a Successful Rock Band: First Find Your True North.*" While I never enjoyed speaking in front of people, this time I actually felt kind of excited about it. I put the report in my notebook and fell asleep picturing Aria's smile and hearing her say, "North," like it was the sound of her favorite bird.

# Chapter 43

Dad was up earlier than ever the next morning, dressed in a white collared shirt with a red and navy blue striped tie. He stood in the kitchen with about twenty peanut butter jars on the floor in front of him. He bent down to pick one up, eyed it closely as he turned it around, did the same with another, and set them in separate spots on the floor next to the counter. I'd seen this behavior enough times to know he was arranging them by expiration date again, something he did quite often, but even more frequently when he was uptight. The week Aria went into the hospital, I saw him rearrange the cereal boxes four times, the soup cans twice, and the macaroni and cheese at least once every day.

"Good morning," I said. "You look nice."

He stopped eyeing the peanut butter and turned to me, "Oh, thank you. I have to leave in a few minutes for Smart Shop. They called last night and asked me to come in for a second interview. " He returned to his sorting.

"I hope it goes well," I said.

"Thanks," he said as he focused in on the next jar. "You have a good day too." He patted my shoulder and shot me a quick smile, one that appeared very forced and nervous, then he returned his attention to the peanut butter.

I grabbed my books, binder, Aria's bag, and her notebook. Outside, I saw Matthew, leaning against our tree.

"Good morning," he said. "You look happy."

He was correct about that.

"Since Aria said my name the other day, I've felt different. North was the first word she said."

Matthew grinned wide at me. "Ha, that's awesome," he said. "That girl's smart. She's probably the only one who could get away with calling you North these days."

I laughed and said, "Yeah, she is smart. When she said it, I actually felt proud. I don't care what people call me anymore. I'm guessing Carol will stick with all the people in high school who've always called me that, but for people who really know me, I'm okay with North."

"Okay, that works for me. I'm still not used to calling you Carol. It doesn't feel right."

"I know, it's a little crazy that I've wanted to change my name," I said. As soon as I said the word crazy, I remembered when Brandon called me Crazy Carol at the hamburger restaurant, claiming the place wouldn't be as fun without me there. "Actually, I kind of like Crazy Carol. If people are going to think I'm weird, I might as well embrace it and be proud of it." A bird chirped loud in a tree like it agreed with me.

Matthew laughed and said, "Oh, okay! I can work with that. Crazy Carol makes sense. So, Crazy Carol, are you ready for the English presentation?" he asked as he nudged my shoulder with his.

"Yeah," I said, nudging him back. "How about you?"

"I think so. I'm definitely ready to be done with it," he said.

I wanted to tell him what I'd decided to write about, hear him encourage me and tell me my ideas were great, but I also wanted to surprise him. So instead of seeking his approval, I tried to calm my anxiety differently. I pulled Aria's notebook closer to my chest and repeated the words in my head that I'd read over and over since I first saw them: *He will cover you with his feathers, and under his wings you will find refuge; his faithfulness will be your shield and rampart.*

I kept those words in my head as we walked to school, and through every class that dragged on and on before English. I was glad I didn't have any tests, and that I wasn't called on to answer any questions. I probably would have blurted out something about feathers and wings and refuge and faithfulness, or stared blankly back, completely clueless as to what was asked of me.

When English finally arrived, it was obvious it was a presentation day. Several people were absent, one girl was at Miss Enders' desk pleading her case for why she needed an extra day with no penalties to her grade, and a line of three more people probably hoping to do the same stood behind her.

"Okay, everyone, have a seat!" Miss Enders said as she stood up and waved them all away. She shook her head and rolled her eyes, then waited for everyone to sit down and be quiet before she continued. "Anyone who's not ready to present today or turn a report in will receive a loss of one grade. No excuses, got it?" She peered at all of us with a look that dared us to defy her. Other than a few "Yes, Miss Enders," everyone was quiet. She then went on to remind us of the presentation guidelines, explaining that each person in the group was allowed between one and three minutes to share his or her part of the presentation.

I'd spent so much time writing that I'd forgotten about the time limit. I glanced down at my paper, flipped through the pages, trying to figure out if I could read all of it, and quickly knew that wasn't possible. When the first group presented, I heard nothing but my own voice in my head as I skimmed through my paper to practice what I was going to say. Two groups later, Miss Enders called our group.

We all stood and walked to the front of the room, then looked at each other to see who would take the lead since we hadn't planned how we'd present. Brandon stepped forward first and began.

"So, our group is presenting about how to start a successful rock band," he said.

"Yeah! Let's rock!" a boy with shaggy brown hair from the back of the room shouted.

"Uh, Mr. Calloway, let's keep comments to ourselves during presentations," Miss Enders said. "Or I'll have to deduct points from your grade."

"Oh, sorry Miss Enders," he replied as he tried to contain his smirk.

"Well, thanks for the enthusiasm anyway, Keith," Brandon said with a nod.

Brandon went on to share, focusing mostly on the importance of finding the right people for a band, then stepped back and waited for one of us to go next.

"Well, okay, so finding the right people is definitely important," Dahlia started as she stepped up to speak next. Of course, she focused on her role as critical to the band's success. "I'm the singer, dancer, and percussionist of the band," she said as she shook her tambourine in the air and swung her hips back and forth, "so without me, there's not much of a band," she laughed. Nearly every boy in the class had leaned forward in their seats, eyes wide, jaws dropped, and nearly every girl glared at her like they hated her or stared like they were trying to soak in every detail so they could copy her. I predicted a lot of girls would show up in the next few days with a similar ensemble of platform shoes, tight T-shirt, denim skirt, and sky blue eyeshadow. When she finally finished her self-promotion, Dahlia said, "Okay, Ricky, you're up." This gave me the job of grand finale for our presentation. I would have hated this role in the past, but this time, it felt right.

As confident as Ricky acted outside of class, he was horribly insecure in front of the class. He stood stiff like a robot, stared down at his paper the entire time, and spoke so quietly that Miss Enders had to ask him to speak louder, which he did for about three words and then returned to his previous low decibel. The only benefit to no one hearing him was the fact that he really didn't have anything great to say since he wasn't even in the band. He called himself the band roadie and murmured about how being physically fit was important in his role carrying the instruments and other equipment while on tour, something we'd obviously never done.

I breathed a big sigh of relief when the torture of his part was over, and took my place in front of the class. I held tight to my paper and Aria's journal, and set her bag on the floor.

Dahlia whispered behind me, "What does she have all that stuff for?"

"Shhh," Brandon responded.

I took a deep breath and looked at the "stuff" Dahlia asked about. It wasn't simply "stuff." I was finally getting the opportunity to tell why. So in spite of my fears, I reminded myself of the prayer Aria had written in that journal, and I began to speak.

"My name isn't Carol," was the first sentence out of my mouth. "My parents gave me the name North Carolina, after my father's favorite basketball team, the North Carolina Tar Heels." I paused as the class laughed, some because they knew me and always laughed at my name, most because they thought I was joking. "I've spent a lot of years feeling embarrassed of that name, listening to people make fun of it by calling me the North Pole, asking me if my siblings were East, West, and South, and much more."

More laughter arose.

"So this year I decided to change my name to Carol, after my favorite singer Carole King. I've dreamed about being a singer forever, but every time I've tried to sing in front of others I've felt terrified, and because of that fear, most of the time I've failed. I'd try to sing and I'd sound like a dying animal."

People laughed again, but this time I was trying to be funny, so it felt okay.

"I've been able to sing in front of my closest friends, my parents, and only recently with this band, but not in front of a bunch of people, which is sad because if I can sing for others and make them feel as happy as Carole King's music makes me feel, I'm the luckiest girl on earth, whether I become a famous rock star or not.

"So with that in mind, I'm stating that the most important part of starting a successful band is the same thing for success in anything—you have to find your true north. My mom tells me that means discovering your real self, the things about you that make you unique, and staying true to them no matter what others might say or do to try and change you. She tells me that's why I should be proud of my name, North, even when people make fun of it. Instead of believing her, I've tried to be more like other people. I've changed my hair, my clothes, my name, and pulled away from some of the people who always loved me for who I was, like my two best friends and my sister, Aria. Because of that, I almost lost them all, but I'm not going to let that happen again."

I picked up Aria's journal and opened it to the page filled with feathers, leaves, and Psalm 91. I held it up in one hand and picked up Aria's bag in my other. "This is my sister's notebook. She carries it and this bag with her everywhere she goes. You've probably seen her. She's the girl who makes bird calls that sound exactly like real birds, the one who skips and flaps her arms, the one who will tell you the truth most of the time, even when you don't want to hear it."

A few people snickered.

"Her name, Aria, means "song" or "melody" in Italian. Its literal translation is "air," and in music, it's a term that describes an elaborate vocal solo within a larger piece of music, like in an opera.

"My sister is all of those things. She is a pure, sweet song. She is a breath of fresh air if you take the time to get to know her, and she is the beautiful solo in this large piece of music I call life. She lives her life in her true north, as herself, and reminds me to do the same."

I reached into the bag and grabbed a handful of leaves. "This bag is filled with leaves that I've collected for her because that's one of her favorite things to do, and something she can't do right now because she's in the hospital." I saw two girls in the second row look at each other with eyes wide, and one put her hand over her mouth like she was shocked. Behind them, a boy looked away from my glance, like he was sad or ashamed about laughing about her a moment before.

"She's going to be okay though, and here's how I know it." I held up the notebook. "This page has words from Psalm 91:4, '*He will cover you with his feathers, and under his wings you will find refuge; his faithfulness will be your shield and rampart.*' She believes in this with all her heart, and so far, I've seen it to be true. Whether she ends up perfectly healed or whether she's changed from her injury, I believe in these words now too. They remind me to stop being afraid all the time, to be my true north like Aria does, and I'm going to end this by proving that. I'm going to do something I would have never done in front of you all before. I'm going to sing."

I closed my eyes, pictured Aria in front of me, breathed deep, and sang the first stanza and chorus of Carole King's "Nightingale." Then I stopped, opened my eyes, and saw Matthew and Ronnie stand up, clap, followed by Jonathon James Price, and then two more people I didn't know. Others clapped in their seats, and Keith Calloway yelled, "Yeah! Rock on!"

I finally had my first applause from a crowd. I glanced down at the notebook, rubbed my fingers along the feathers and leaves, and knew God was cheering too, like he had been all along.

# Chapter 44

They say everyone has their moment in the spotlight. I was learning to be at one with the fact that my chance to shine was sort of wasted at the eighth grade talent show. The English presentation made up for it a bit, but a month later, Dahlia still received more attention than I did for her tambourine and hip-shaking talents, and while I was still technically in Brandon's band, I had only practiced with them one time since that day, so the chances of his band being my best route to stardom were quickly fading. I spent most days after school with the school chorus team, which I'd joined and earned a spot singing a solo for the school musical. The teacher also asked me to finish an original song I'd written after she heard me sing part of it. I was planning to sing it for the school's talent festival.

Home life was still stressful, but much better than before. Maybe that's what happens when you lose something. It makes you see things differently. Aria was back home, so Mom had moved back in order to help her, and I was thankful we were all together again. Dad's hoarding hadn't improved, so the tension and fighting between him and Mom was still there, but the way I handled it was different. Aria had allowed me to keep the page in her notebook with the feathers and the Psalm on it, so I'd hung it on the wall across from my bed. In that spot, I could see it before I turned my lights out to sleep, when I woke up in the morning, and when I plopped on my bed in frustration or exhaustion. I'd read the words over and over, usually before I prayed. While this wasn't some crazy magic trick that erased all my problems, it always made me feel better, more hopeful, like I could keep going.

I'd also started listening more carefully when Aria read her Bible. I'd hear her in her room, or on the floor of the living room, or occasionally in my room, reading aloud. She read with a sincerity and expression that always made it sound interesting.

"You should work at a library or bookstore and read aloud to kids," I told her one morning when she read to me while I packed our lunches.

She looked up at me and smiled, then continued. "*They will be like a tree planted by the water that sends out its roots by the stream. It does not fear when heat comes; its leaves are always green. It has no worries in a year of drought and never fails to bear fruit.* Jeremiah 17:8."

She paused and then said, "That's like us, North. We're like that tree. We don't need to be afraid when things get tough. God gives us what we need. He helps us."

A month ago Aria could only say three words. Now she was reading and speaking full paragraphs. She didn't always speak eloquently. She sometimes forgot things and stumbled over her words before getting them out right, but other times she was that tree—green, full of fruit, nearly perfect.

"Thanks, Aria. That was beautiful. It makes me think of our favorite tree in the woods," I said.

Her face lit up. "Ah, yes, it is like that tree. I miss that tree. You think we could go there after school today?"

She still seemed pretty tired on our short walk to school. "I don't think you're ready yet, Aria, but we'll get there one day."

The corners of her mouth turned down, but she didn't argue. "Okay, well, at least we have our tree at school."

She was correct about that. It was actually one of the things I looked forward to each day, the big oak tree we'd begun sitting under at lunch. It looked a lot like the one in the woods. "Speaking of school, we need to get going," I said.

Later that day, when lunch arrived, I headed outside of the English classroom, Ronnie and Matthew at my side.

"Hey, Carol," I heard from behind me. I turned to see Brandon jogging toward us.

I stopped and asked Ronnie and Matthew to wait up for me.

"Just checking to see if you want to hang with me at lunch," Brandon said.

This was the second time he'd asked me in the past few weeks, and about the fifth time I would have to say no to an invitation from him of some sort, having turned him down for band practice, a party, and another group assignment in English. It wasn't because I didn't like him. It was more because I didn't want to hang out with some of his friends, especially Chad, who still picked on Jonathon James Price every chance he got and eyed Matthew with a mean glare.

Before I could respond to Brandon this time, Dahlia shouted, "Brandon, you coming?" She stood with one hand on her hip next to Ricky.

He turned to her and said, "Yeah, go ahead. I'll catch up."

She rolled her eyes and turned away.

Feeling bad, I said, "I actually have plans for lunch with Matthew, Ronnie, and Aria. You're welcome to join us if you want."

He stood silent, stared into my eyes like he was trying to figure me out. Then he looked away and said, "Yeah, that's okay, maybe some other time." He started to walk away, and then stopped. "Actually, you know what? Maybe not another time. I get it. You've turned me down enough to let me know you don't want anything to do with me. I'll stop bugging you, including asking you to practice with the band. You're a good singer, but not that good."

I didn't know what to say to him. It was obvious he was offended.

Matthew stepped next to me. "She actually is that good, Brandon, and you know it." He put his hand on mine, and without any thought, I grabbed it back.

Brandon looked down at our hands, then back at me and then to Matthew, his face filled with anger.

"She said you could join us, so why are you so mad?" Matthew asked, even though he knew the reason as well as I did.

Brandon shook his head and said, "It's not worth explaining," as he turned and walked away.

Matthew and I watched him without moving, our hands together again feeling like the only important thing at the moment. But I also felt bad for Brandon. I needed to find that voice of mine again and be honest with him about how I felt.

"Brandon, wait!" I shouted. Then I looked up at Matthew and said, "I need to be straight with him. I'll be right back."

I jogged over to Brandon, trying not to overthink the fact that what I was about to say was likely not what he wanted to hear. I looked up at him briefly, not wanting to look too long at the sadness in his expression. "I want to thank you," I said.

"Thank me?" He looked confused.

"You've been a good friend," I said. "You saw something in me that a lot of people haven't. You made me feel good about my singing. You made me feel like less of a weirdo. I really appreciate that."

He stared at me and said, "I like you, Carol. You don't need to thank me for that."

He wasn't making it easy on me. "I like you too, Brandon." His face lit up for a second before I added, "as a friend."

He let out a deep sigh. "Okay," he said. "Friends. Not exactly what I was hoping you'd say."

"I'd hate not talking with you anymore, and I'd love to keep singing with you as long as Dahlia and Chad aren't being total jerks to me and my friends."

He nodded, rubbed his hands through his hair, and said, "Yeah, I get it." He looked over at Matthew, who stood with his arms crossed, eyeing Brandon with a look that said he'd better not mess with me.

"I'll see you later," he said, and turned to walk away again.

Matthew met up with me, grabbed my hands. "Everything okay?"

"Yeah, everything's fine," I answered, even though I wasn't so sure whether I'd lost Bandon as a friend.

"Okay you two lovebirds, can we go eat now?" Ronnie said as she came alongside us.

"Yes," I said, "let's go."

We walked together, she and I arm in arm, Matthew and I hand in hand, through the crowded hallway, the quad, past the cafeteria, to a big stretch of grass topped with one big oak tree. Although we called it our spot, we weren't the first or only ones to discover it. Clusters of friends filled nearly every space. Some sat on blankets or towels, a few threw a Frisbee or a football. One boy, Manuel Velasco, sat near the tree and played his ukulele.

"What's up, Crazy Carol?" he said as he nodded to me and strummed a tune that sounded like Fleetwood Mac's "Don't Stop."

"Hey, Man," I said, calling him the shortened version of his name, the nickname I gave every time he called me crazy, which was pretty much every day.

Sitting near Manuel was Shalene, who seemed to have a crush on Manuel, telling him how talented he was all the time and looking at him with dreamy eyes as he played. She cheered "Woohoo! Nice tunes, Manny!" and then turned to her three friends next to her. "Isn't he incredible?"

Matthew and Ronnie took a seat under the tree, and I stayed standing to make sure Aria was on the way. In the distance I saw her, striding purposely in our direction with Katelyn and her two new friends, Dionya and Troy. Once she spotted me, her stride became a skip, and she yelled out, "Hi, North!"

I waved, proud to be her sister.

"Hi, Jonathon James Price!" she said when she saw him sitting on the grass with us, as he often did.

I sat down next to Matthew while Aria, Dionya, and Troy sat near Jonathon. We opened our lunch bags, and bit into sandwiches, chips, apples, and carrot sticks, our munching and crunching fading behind the sounds of the ukulele, laughter from a group in the distance, hollers from the football throwers, and birds in the tree above us. Then I noticed the familiar blond hair and confident swagger of Brandon heading our way. He had one hand in his faded jeans, the other holding his cafeteria lunch tray.

He stood behind Jonathon when he reached us and said, "I decided to join you guys, as long as that's still okay."

Two sparrows landed on the grass near Aria as she placed a pile of seed from her bag onto the grass, and the birds in the tree began to chirp louder.

"Of course it's okay!" Aria shouted. "You can sit right here," she said as she patted the grass next to her.

I waited for his response, expected him to decline her offer and sit near me, or Manuel, or even Ronnie.

"Thanks," he said. He sat down next to her. "You want a cookie? They gave me two."

Aria smiled wide, nodded, looked like she'd just won some amazing prize as she took the cookie from Brandon's hand. "Thanks!" she said.

I watched her bite into the gooey chocolate chip cookie and then make sweet peeping sounds to the birds in front of her.

Brandon chuckled. "You sound just like them," he said.

"I know," she said. "I practice a lot."

As I soaked all this in, I began to sing along to Manuel's music without any care at all about how good I sounded or who could hear me.

And Aria continued to speak and call to the birds.

And Jonathon James Price created some sort of structure with orange peels, pretzels, and carrot sticks.

And Ronnie tossed a bag of Fritos to Brandon in exchange for his potato chips.

Everything wasn't as I'd planned. I wasn't popular or famous or cool. I was called crazy now more than before, but I was going to be okay. No matter what I did next, God would keep me pointed in the right direction, following my true north.

Psalm 139:9-10

*If I ride the wings of the morning,*
*if I dwell by the farthest oceans,*
*even there your hand will guide me,*
*and your strength will support me.*

# Acknowledgments

To my loving husband, my beautiful children and their spouses or significant others, I thank you for always supporting my writing dream and encouraging me every step of the way. If I were to write my greatest story, it would simply be the story of each of you and all of us together, which is where my heart is at its fullest and happiest.

To my truly wonderful friends and family members, I thank you for your encouragement and support, and for asking me about my next book enough times to keep me going back to my computer and typing in more words. If this book gives you even some of the joy you give me, then it is a success. I especially want to acknowledge my dear friend, Gail and my magnificent mother-in-law, Carolyn, for their invaluable time and work with reading my novel in its early draft stages and giving me honest, helpful feedback. Your thoughts and recommendations made my story clearer and better, and I am so very grateful for each of you.

To my former students and current youth group friends, thank you for the energy and joy you bring to my life. You inspire me simply by being your unique and incredible selves, and I hope that if you read this book or see these words of thanks, that you are reminded of who you are and whose you are wherever you go in life.

To my amazing editor, Molly Lewis, and to Debra Kennedy, formatter, my appreciation for your feedback and edits go beyond what these simple words express. With each recommendation, my story became closer to the heart of what I wanted to say. With each change, I looked back and thought, "Oh, yes, that's much better! How did I not see that myself?" You have a true gift with words and with refining a story without completely changing it. Thank you for helping me make this story the best it can be.

To author Kat Clark, thank you for reading my book in its earlier stages to ensure my writing about a character with autism was written authentically. My hope is that readers will find greater understanding of people they meet who are similar to my character Aria, and treat them with the value, acceptance, and respect they deserve.

To the Acorn Publishing Co-Owners, Holly Kammier and Jessica Therrien, you set my writing dream into motion with my first book, *Sticks and Stones,* and you've allowed that dream to continue with this next book. Your support and help have kept me on this writing and publishing path, and I will always be so grateful that I found you. To my publishing coordinator, Jessica Hammett, you've guided me in the steps of publishing this book with patience and encouragement, and I know this book wouldn't be possible without you. Thank you for all your hard work.

Finally, I thank God for putting stories in my heart and being at my side every moment to make my writing dreams come true. I hope and pray that all who read my words see you, the loving, almighty God who is always with us and for us, working out every detail for good in the stories of our lives.

# About the Author

**Dianne Beck** has spent most of her career teaching students ranging from kindergarten through adult and currently works as a high school youth director at her church. In each of these roles, she hopes to encourage students to be their own unique selves, to have confidence in who they are, and to follow their passions.

Dianne's debut young adult novel *Sticks and Stones,* winner of multiple awards, was inspired by her years of teaching, where she saw how an understanding ear and relevant literature could make a significant impact on students' lives. She hopes young people and adults can find faith and strength in her stories.

**Visit her author website at diannebeck.com**